BJB

THE MARK

"Pinter's a wizard at punching out page-turning action, and the voice of his headstrong protagonist is sure to win readers over; his wild ride should thrill any suspense junky."
—*Publishers Weekly*

"From the opening sentence to the exhilarating conclusion, Pinter's debut thriller gets the reader's heart racing."
—*Library Journal* [starred review]

"An excellent debut.
You are going to love Henry Parker, and you're going to hope he survives the story, but you're not going to bet on it."
—Lee Child

"[Pinter] dares to take the traditional thriller in bold new directions."
—Tess Gerritsen

"A harrowing journey—chilling, compelling, disquieting."
—Steve Berry

"A stunning debut by a major new talent!"
—James Rollins

"It's 'Front Page' meets 'The Sopranos' with a little Scorsese thrown in."
—Jeffery Deaver

"A top-notch debut... Fast-paced, gritty and often raw, *The Mark* is a tale you won't soon forget."
—Michael Palmer

"A gripping page-turner you won't be able to stop reading."
—James Patterson

JASON PINTER

THE FURY

MIRA®

MIRA®

Recycling programs
for this product may
not exist in your area.

ISBN-13: 978-0-7783-2627-4

THE FURY

Copyright © 2009 by Jason Pinter.

www.MIRABooks.com

Printed in U.S.A.

To Joe Veltre and Linda McFall

For yesterday, today and tomorrow. Thank you.

Beware the fury of a patient man.
—John Dryden

1

At nine in the morning, the offices of the *New York Gazette* are quiet. Reporters read the morning papers, prepare to call their sources and blink off hangovers over steaming cups of coffee. Today, however, it was a different kind of quiet. The kind of quiet where everyone seems to be waiting for the roof to cave in, or the floor to suddenly give way and fall out from under you.

Every morning I would swipe my ID card, wave hello to the security guards who'd gradually warmed to me over the years and wait for the elevator with lots of other people who also looked like they'd rather still be in bed. I would exit the elevators at the twelfth floor, passing the receptionist, always too busy to acknowledge staffers, and walk to my desk. The offices of the *New York Gazette* towered over Rockefeller Center, giving me a panoramic view of one of the busiest streets in the city. Yet when I navigated the mess of chairs and debris and entered the cubicle farm on this day, I noticed the other journalists who shared my row were nowhere to be seen. There were no faces hunched far too close to computer screens, no whispered chats about the umpteenth death knell sounded for our industry. No reporters haggling over verb usage and tense like it was a matter of life or death. It seemed every day across our industry there were more layoffs, more cutbacks, more reasons to fear the end. And it had been drilled repeatedly into us by our corporate overlords and the media that if the sickle wasn't already lancing the air above our heads, it was in the midst of being lowered into place.

I couldn't worry about that. Still a few years shy of thirty, it had been my lifelong ambition to work at a prestigious, thriving newspaper. And while one could debate whether the *Gazette* was thriving, in my short time here I'd had the chance to work alongside some of the greats, including my idol, Jack O'Donnell.

I'd also been wanted for murder and targeted by a deranged serial killer. Hey, who doesn't complain about their job sometimes?

Externally, you might think I looked the same. Internally, though, I was a different man. A man learns who he is when his life, innocence and freedom are challenged. I was stronger than I ever knew I could be, but deep down I wished I hadn't needed to find that out.

When I navigated the maze of empty desks to arrive at mine, I put my coffee and muffin on the desk, sat down and debated whether to ignore the silence or see what was causing the sound vacuum. I reached for the plastic tab on my coffee, but immediately thought twice. To ignore the strange stillness of the office would have gone against every bone in my body, and probably triggered some sort of spontaneous combustion. Curiosity not only killed the cat, but made my breakfast grow cold. So I stood back up and took a lap around the news floor to see what the hell was going on.

I didn't have to go far.

A group of half a dozen reporters were huddled around the desk of Evelyn Waterstone, the *Gazette*'s Metro editor. They were talking under their breaths, worried looks in their eyes. I wondered if there were going to be layoffs. If some of my colleagues—perhaps even myself—would be out of a job. That Evelyn's desk had seemingly replaced the watercooler as center of office scoop was itself noteworthy. Evelyn stayed as far away from gossip as those who gossiped stayed away from her. Whatever happened had to be big enough to pique her interest. I walked up casually, inserting myself into the conversation through proximity alone.

Evelyn Waterstone was a short, squat woman whose haircut resembled a well-manicured putting green—only this particular green was gray with age—and whose broad shoulders would have been a welcome addition to most offensive lines. She was a disciplinarian in the gentlest sense of the word. It took several years for her to warm up to me, but when my work ethic and the quality of my reporting became clear, Evelyn began to grudgingly show me a modicum of respect. Still, I don't think you'd ever see the two of us tossing back a couple of longnecks after hours. I made an effort never to stop by her desk unless I had a specific question, and Evelyn never stormed by mine unless I'd made some terrible grammatical mistake that, to Evelyn, was only slightly worse of an offense than treason.

"Morning, Parker," Evelyn said. She held a black thermos between her fleshy hands, and took a long, drawn-out sip. "Another beautiful day at your friendly local newspaper." She sniffed the air. "Glad to see you've begun showering regularly again."

"Morning, Evelyn," I said, nodded to the other reporters, who offered the same.

"You hear about Rourke?" she said. I hadn't, and told her so. She raised her arms dramatically as if recounting some heroic tale. "This paper's most controversial sportswriter—who incidentally once told a linebacker he would 'whup his ass like a donkey'—got mugged yesterday on his way home from the office. Well, I shouldn't say mugged, because the guy didn't take any money, but Frank ended up getting the donkey side of the whupping."

"Really?" I said, incredulous. "Rourke?" I had no love lost for Frank Rourke, considering the man had once left a bag of excrement on my desk—but the man's swagger seemed to come from years of always being the one guy who was able to leave the fight on his own two feet.

"Seems some hothead took umbrage to Frank's calling the Yankees 'the most poorly run organization since FEMA.' Some disgruntled asshat from the Bronx. Anyway, this guy waits outside of the office until Frank leaves. Then he yells, 'Yo, Rourke!' Frank turns his head, and gets a sockful of quarters up against the side of his temple."

"That's terrible, is he okay?"

"Concussion, he'll be fine. Police arrested the fan, I'm just hoping he might have damaged the area of

Frank's brain that makes him such an asshole. Maybe he'll have one of those *Regarding Henry* kind of epiphanies and come back a better man."

"That's probably too much to expect."

"We can dream, Parker. We can dream."

As we chatted, I noticed another group of reporters huddled together in the hallway looking like they'd just been told management had decided to restructure by throwing them out the twelfth floor windows. The group shifted nervously, whispering amongst themselves. Never wanting to be the last one in the know, I approached, said, "I thought Frank was going to be fine, what gives?"

Jonas Levinson, the *Gazette*'s science editor, said, "Frank is the least of our concerns. Though, as a matter of fact, something has died this morning. Something to be mourned as long as we're employed by this godforsaken newspaper. As of today, good taste, my friend, has kicked the bucket."

I stared at Jonas, waiting for some kind of an explanation. Levinson was a tall man, balding, who wore a different bow tie to the office every day. He very seldom exaggerated his feelings, so at Jonas's remark a flock of butterflies began to flutter around in my stomach.

"I'm not following you," I said to Jonas. "Good taste? Jonas, care to explain?"

"Just follow the eyes, Parker," Jonas said. "Follow the eyes."

I opened my mouth to ask another question, but then I realized what he was saying. The eyes of every member of our group were focused on two individuals making their way across the *Gazette*'s floor. They were stopping at every desk, popping into each office for a few moments. It looks like some sort of introduction ritual was taking place.

Immediately this struck me as odd. I'd never met another employee during a walkaround, and had not received one myself. The fact that this one person was being given the grand tour made it clear he was someone the brass wanted to coddle.

One of the two men I recognized immediately as Wallace Langston, editor in chief. Wallace was in his midfifties, lean with a neatly trimmed beard. His brown hair was flecked with gray, and he had the slightly bent posture of a man who'd spent the majority of his years hunched over a keyboard. Wallace had been a staunch supporter of mine in the years I'd been employed by the paper, and even though now more than ever he was feeling the crunch of his corporate masters insisting on higher profit margins, he knew what it took to print good news. If not my idol, he was a good, loyal mentor.

"Is he," I said, "introducing someone around the office?"

"That is precisely what it looks like," Jonas replied.

Evelyn walked up and said, "I never met a damn person until my first staff meeting. I got as much of an introduction as my stove has to a cooking pot."

"Me, neither," I said. When I started at the *Gazette*, I didn't know anybody other than Jack O'Donnell. Jack was my boyhood idol, the man most aspiring reporters dreamt of becoming. He and I had grown close over the last few years, but recently he'd lost his battle with the bottle and left the *Gazette*. I hadn't spoken to him in a few months. I'd tried his home, his cell phone, even walked by his Clinton apartment a few times, but never got a hold of the man. It was clear Jack needed some time alone with his demons.

Ironically the first reporter I'd met was a woman named Paulina Cole. We worked next to each other when I first started at the *Gazette.* Soon she left for a job at the rival *Dispatch,* where through a combination of balls, brass and more balls she'd become one of the most talked-about writers in the city. Paulina was cold, calculating, ruthless and, worst of all, damn smart. She knew what people wanted to read—namely, anything where if you squeezed a page, dirt or juice came out— and gave it to them. She was part of the reason Jack had left the *Gazette.* She'd managed to pay off numerous people in order to discover the extent of Jack's drinking habits, and then ran a front-page article (with unflatter-ing pictures) depicting Jack as the second coming of Tara Reid. Saying there was no love lost between us was like saying there was no love lost between east and west coast rappers.

Wallace was still too far away for us to make out just who he was introducing around the office, but I got the feeling he would prefer if he didn't have to do it en masse.

"I'm going back to my desk," I said. "Jonas, if you see good taste anywhere, I'll get the paddles and we'll resuscitate the bastard."

"Thank you for the offer, Henry, but I do believe it's too late."

I walked back to my desk, trying not to think about what this could mean. Since Jack left, the *Gazette* had been on a hiring freeze. We were in a war with the

Dispatch over circulation rates, advertising dollars and stories, and our expenses were taking a toll. If Harvey Hillerman, the president and owner of the *Gazette,* had hired a new reporter, he or she had to be important enough to cause a stir. Not to mention someone who would be approved of by the other reporters whose pay raises had been nixed last holiday season.

I sat down and continued working on a story I'd been following up on for several weeks, about the homeless population of New York. According to the New York City Department of Homeless Services, there were over thirty-five thousand homeless individuals living within the city's borders. Including over nine thousand families. That number had increased by fifteen percent in the last five years.

I was about to pick up the phone, when I heard the sound of footsteps approach and then stop by my desk. I looked up to Wallace Langston. And his mystery hire.

"Henry Parker," Wallace said, hand outstretched, "meet Tony Valentine."

Tony Valentine was six foot three, looked to be a hundred and eighty svelte pounds and had the smile of a cruise-ship director. His hair was bleached blond, and his teeth glistened. His tan was clearly sprayed on, as I noticed when he extended his hand to shake mine that his palms were a much paler shade. He wore a designer suit, and wore it well. A red pocket square was neatly tucked into his suit jacket. The initials T.V. were embroidered in white script on the cloth.

As he offered his hand, I noticed his sleeves were held together by two gold cuff links. Also monogrammed with T.V.

Clearly this man did not want his name to be forgotten.

"Henry Parker," Valentine said, gushing insincere admiration. "It's just a pleasure to finally meet you. I've been following your career ever since that nasty business of your murder accusation. All those guns and bullets, and now here I am, working with you. Sir, it is an *honor.*"

While I pried the goop from my brain, I shook Valentine's hand, then looked at Wallace. The name Tony Valentine did sound familiar, but I couldn't quite place it…

"Tony is our new gossip reporter," Wallace said enthusiastically. "We were able to pluck him from *Us Weekly.* Today is his first day."

"And not a day too soon," Tony said, pressing the back of his hand against his forehead, as though diagnosing a strange malady. "As much as I admire your paper—and Wallace, please don't think otherwise—it was lacking a certain *pizzazz.* A certain *panache,* if you will. A certain sexiness."

"Let me guess," I said. "You're here to bring sexy back."

Tony pursed his lips and smiled. "You're a clever one, Henry. I'm going to have to keep my eye on you. So, guess what my new column is going to be called?"

"Do I have to?"

"You most certainly do." Tony waited a moment, then blurted out, "'Valentine's Day.' Isn't that a riot?"

"Better than the ones in L.A."

"True, true. By the way, Wallace told me you covered the Athena Paradis murder a while back. Is that so?"

"You heard right," I said. Athena Paradis was a professional celebrity/diva who was gunned down outside a nightclub where she was performing tracks off her upcoming album. I investigated the murder, and nearly lost my life in the process.

"Let me tell you, the day that girl died, it was like the day I learned Diana had been killed. Athena was just one more reason for me to get up in the morning. I don't think I slept for a week after that. I can't imagine how you must have felt."

"Sure," I said. "Lost tons of sleep."

"No doubt," Tony said. "Listen, Henry, it's been a pretty pleasure. We'll *have* to go out for a dirty martini one of these nights. I want to hear *all* about what you're working on. Okay?"

"I'll be checking my calendar right away," I said.

"Terrific. Wallace, on with the show?"

As Tony and Wallace walked away, I saw Wallace turn back to me. There was a remorseful look in his eye. Immediately I knew Tony's hire was at the behest of Harvey Hillerman. Gossip was a commodity in this town. I knew it; I'd been the subject of it. For the most part, the *Gazette* had kept its beak clean, relegating society and gossip stories to the weekend Leisure section. Now we would all be fighting tooth and nail to compete for page-one space with Mr. Tony Valentine. I wondered how much an embroidered pocket square cost.

After a long day I left the *Gazette* thoroughly exhausted. I checked my cell phone, found one voice mail waiting. It was from Amanda. We'd been seeing each other steadily over the last few months, trying to start over on a relationship that broke from the gate too fast. I didn't want to screw things up this time, so I was more than happy to take it slow. Dinner and movies, walks through Central Park. I sent flowers to her office, she sent me meatball subs for lunch. It was harmony.

As I put the phone to my ear to listen to the message, I heard a strange voice say, "Henry Parker?"

I turned to see a man approaching me. He was dirty and disheveled, wearing rags that looked about to fall off his deathly skinny frame. A black briefcase was slung over his shoulder. He carried it like it either weighed fifty pounds, or he was just barely strong enough to hold it to begin with. His eyes were bloodshot, fingernails dirty. His eyes glowed wide from sunken-in sockets—a skeleton with a pulse. Despite his haggard appearance he looked to be young, in his early thirties. I'd never seen the man before in my life, yet for some reason he looked oddly familiar.

"The city's gonna burn," he rasped. "I need to talk to you."

"You can send any press inquiries through the switchboard," I said, picking up my pace.

"Are you," he said, the words coming out through yellowed teeth, "Henry Parker?"

I started to walk faster. I had no idea how this man knew my name, but from the looks of him I certainly didn't want to find out. The image of Frank Rourke—a pretty strong and belligerent man to begin with—being beaten by a crazed reader with a homemade weapon crossed my mind. In my few years at the *Gazette* I'd received plenty of mail from readers. Mostly positive from people who enjoyed my stories, but still plenty from people who thought I was either a hack or still remembered all the unwanted attention I'd received a few years ago when I was thought to have killed a police officer.

It amazed me how truth was often suffocated in minutes, but lies were given sufficient air to breathe indefinitely.

"I am," I said, offering my card. He looked at it, just stared at me with those sunken eyes. I turned to walk away, speeding up as I headed through Rockefeller Plaza. I turned back. The man began to walk faster, too. The rubber on his sneakers was falling apart, and the gray overcoat he wore was tattered and soiled.

"Please, Henry, I need to talk to you. Oh God, it's important. You don't know what's going on. You don't know what's going on. Never seen anything like it."

Suddenly he closed his eyes and retched, a cough threading beads of phlegm through his gaunt fingers.

"Call the *Gazette* tomorrow," I said. I gave him the switchboard number. He didn't seem to care. I walked faster, a slow trot, but my heart began to race when I saw that the man was matching my pace.

"Henry," he said, his eyes now terrified. "We need to talk! I'm begging you, man!"

"Sorry, don't have time," I said. I picked up the pace, broke into a run and crossed the street just as the light was turning red. As I reached the other side I looked back. The man was about to race through the oncoming traffic, but then apparently thought better of it.

Our eyes met for one moment. His were pleading, scared, and for a moment I debated crossing back over to see what he wanted. Then I saw him reach into his pocket, put something to his nose and take a quick snort. That was all I needed to see.

I turned around and headed toward the subway. If he really needed to reach me, he could call. I'd been through enough over the last few years to know there were some things you needed to turn your back on.

2

I arrived home half an hour later. I left Amanda a message. We had plans to have dinner and catch a movie tomorrow night, and I wanted to order tickets in advance. New York prices being what they were, between service charges, snacks and tickets themselves, you practically had to win the lottery to afford them. A few months ago Amanda had received a nice year-end bonus, and Wallace Langston had told me to expect a promotion in the near future. Both of our salaries had crept higher over the last few years, and we'd begun to think more about where we wanted to be. This apartment had served its purpose, but I wanted more space.

We weren't living together, but she would spend three or four nights a week here and then crash in her friend Darcy Lapore's guest room the rest of the time. The number of nights spent next to each other had begun to creep up over the last few weeks. It was still early and we were still healing from recent wounds. Regardless, our relationship had grown more serious and I started to think about where *our* future was headed. At some point we'd have to have one of those talks.

Where you each share your hopes and dreams. The "where do you see yourself in five years" part of the job interview, only for a position you wanted the rest of your life. Tonight, Amanda was crashing with Darcy. I figured I'd eat dinner, pop in a movie and veg out. Nights like that were sorely underrated.

I peeled off my clothes, stepped into a hot shower. The day seemed to rinse right off me. I thought about that man who'd confronted me, how there was a look of genuine terror in his eyes. I began to regret turning from him. And hoped he actually did call the next day.

When I got out of the shower, I threw on a pair of shorts and a T-shirt. I was six foot one depending on the shoes, a hundred and ninety pounds of lean, mean, vendor hot dog-eating machine. My brown hair was getting a little longer, and I made a mental note to stop by Quik Cuts tomorrow during lunch. I warmed up a plate of leftover chicken masala Amanda had cooked over the weekend. In my place, leftovers were made to last.

I sat down and began to eat, washing the food down with a glass of iced tea. I splayed a few newspapers in front of me and read while I did. The *Gazette*'s pages looked naked without the familiar byline of Jack O'Donnell. I hoped wherever he was, he was getting the treatment he needed.

Dinner was a long affair. I made the pasta last, and made the newspapers last. I gorged myself on every word, fascinated at just how many stories there were within this small teeming city.

When I finished, I was getting up to put my dishes in the sink when the phone rang. I picked it up. Didn't recognize the caller ID.

I clicked Send and said, "This is Parker." I'd struggled with my greeting for a long time. Since this was my work phone as well as personal, saying hello felt too casual. As did "Henry." I considered, "Parker, Henry Parker," but Amanda threw a dirty sock at me the first time I tried it. "Parker" sounded nice, succinct.

"Is this Henry Parker?" the voice on the other end said.

"Yes, who is this?"

"Henry, I'm Detective Makhoulian with the NYPD. Are you busy right now?"

I looked at my watch. It was nearly ten o'clock. What the hell did the cops want with me at this hour? I wasn't working on any stories that had NYPD involvement, and I didn't speak to any cops on a regular basis with the exception of my friend Curt Sheffield.

"Detective, it's pretty late and I just got home from work. What's this about?"

"I apologize for the hour, but I was hoping you could answer a few questions."

Not wanting to appear defensive, I said, "Question away."

"Does a man fitting this description sound familiar? About six-two, thin as a bone. Brown hair, hazel eyes, the look of a serious drug problem, among other issues, much of which involve hygiene. That ring a bell?"

I felt my pulse quicken. "Actually, a man fitting that description was waiting for me outside my office when I left work tonight. I didn't really speak to him. A colleague of mine was recently assaulted by a disgruntled reader, and from the look of this guy he wasn't much of a conversationalist."

"Interesting," Makhoulian said. And he genuinely sounded interested. "Listen, Mr. Parker, I need you to come down to the county medical examiner's office tonight. You know where it is?"

"Thirtieth and first. I've been there before. I'm a reporter with the *Gazette,* I've spoken with the medical examiner. Leon Binks still works there, right?"

"Yes, he does. And I know who you are, Mr. Parker. This has nothing to do with any previous involvement you may have had with the NYPD." He didn't need to say it, but I could tell Makhoulian was speaking about Joe Mauser and John Fredrickson, the two cops who were involved in my being hunted across the country for a murder I didn't commit. "I'm going to need you to meet me at the M.E.'s office in one hour. Will that be a problem?"

"No, but I would still like to know what all this is about. Like I said, tonight was the first time I ever saw this guy. If my night is being interrupted, please have the decency to tell me why."

"This man I'm speaking of, he was found two hours ago in an apartment in Alphabet City, dead from two gunshot wounds to the head. We have reason to believe you were the last person to see him alive."

"Okay," I said, my stomach beginning to turn. Dead? What exactly had that guy wanted to talk to me about?

While the last thing I wanted was to get tied up in the murder of some junkie, I felt some sense of remorse. "Listen, Detective, no disrespect, but this guy probably saw one of my stories and figured a reporter might be more inclined to listen to him than a cop. Maybe he just wanted attention. And now he's dead, and while it really is a shame, I don't know what I can offer to help the investigation."

There was silence on the other end. Then Makhoulian said, "This man's name was Stephen Gaines. Does sound familiar?"

"No, sir, it doesn't."

"That's very interesting." I was beginning to worry. Why was that interesting? "I'm still going to need you to meet me at the M.E.'s office. One hour," Makhoulian said, "because according to his birth certificate and medical records, Stephen Gaines was your brother."

3

There are times in your life when you walk forward despite knowing that something unexpected, even dangerous, lies just around the corner. This allows you to steel yourself; to prepare for it. You go over the different permutations in your mind, positive and negative, weighing how each might impact you. Then when the blow comes, you're able to soften it a bit. Retaliate if necessary.

When Detective Makhoulian said those five words—*Stephen Gaines was your brother*—they hit me, knocked the wind out of me. I had no time to prepare, no time to soften the blow.

At first I didn't believe it. Or I didn't want to. But I'd heard the name Makhoulian before. I'd spent enough time with cops, mainly my buddy Curt Sheffield, that it rang with a modicum of familiarity. If Curt mentioned him, that was a good sign. The man spoke earnestly, a minimum of sympathy. Like a cop.

Sitting in the back of a taxi, I tried to wrap my head around it. I'd never heard of a Stephen Gaines before. The last name did not sound familiar. *Gaines.*

On the street earlier, Gaines looked older than me by four or five years. Of course, considering how strung out he looked, it could have swayed a few years in either direction. But if he was older, it meant he was gone from my life long before I was aware of his existence. I had too many questions to ask, and unfortunately Leon and Detective Makhoulian wouldn't be able to answer them. At least not all of them.

I stepped out at the corner of Thirtieth and First in Manhattan's Kips Bay. The medical examiner's office had a facade of light blue, the stone dirty, as if the building refused to modernize. It was a block away from Bellevue Hospital, one of the more notorious medical centers in the city. Prisoners from Riker's Island, as well as criminals from New York's central booking requiring medical attention, were among the most frequent guests. And if you happened to be in the emergency room late at night, you'd be in the company of numerous men in orange jumpsuits and chains, armed police at the ready. Just a few blocks away were a coffee shop, a bookstore and a multiplex movie theater. Scary to think that while you were busy munching on popcorn, evil lingered so close by, cloaked in formaldehyde.

I approached the entrance tentatively. Who was I going to ID? I'd never met this man before last night, and now I was expected to point him out, feel some deep-down emotion like I'd known him my whole life? I'd never bonded with this person. Never done things most brothers did. Never played catch. Snuck a drink from Dad's liquor cabinet. Never smuggled dirty magazines under our covers, or smoked cigarettes until our lungs burned. I was identifying a stranger, yet expected to act like he was my blood. Impossible.

Pushing the door open, I went up to the receptionist. He was wearing a white lab coat, and didn't look a day over twenty-five. I figured he was some sort of medical intern, manning the phones while studying for his exams.

"May I help you, sir?" he asked. His name tag read Nelson, Mark. He chewed on a pen while he waited for my answer.

"I'm here to see Binky…er Dr. Binks," I corrected. No sense ruining the illusion that Binks was a sane and respected member of the medical profession.

"And you are…"

"Henry Parker," I said, taking my driver's license from my wallet. "I'm here to identify Stephen Gaines." The name felt foreign on my tongue, yet Nelson's eyes melted with sympathy. He looked down at his desk, pursed his lips.

"Right," he said. "I'm sorry for your loss."

I didn't bother to point out Nelson's faux pas. That it was a little premature to console someone for their loss before they'd actually identified the body. Or that I felt no loss at all. How could I? Nevertheless, I told him I appreciated it. He asked me to have a seat while he paged Dr. Binks.

I took a seat on a light blue couch. It was hard. There was a small table in front of me. No reading material. This wasn't your typical waiting room. If you were here, I supposed not even *Golf Digest* could take your mind off of what lurked below.

After several minutes, I heard the *ding* of an elevator

and out strode Leon Binks. Binks was in his late thirties, graying hair matted against his brow. His eyebrows were as messy as his hair, a collection of short pipe cleaners bent every which way. The medical examiner was perpetually disheveled, as though he cared no more about his appearance than those corpses he worked on would. His hands always seemed to be moving, offering gestures that his dialogue (and lack of social skills) presumably could not. I imagined that if, like Leon Binks, my whole life was spent amongst the dead, I might have some personality idiosyncrasies as well.

"Mr. Parker," Binks said, approaching me with his hand outstretched. I went to meet him, and he shook it vigorously. An awful smell wafted off of Binks, iodine perhaps. I didn't want to ask, but I hoped he showered before attending any dinner parties. "Thanks so much for coming. Detective Makhoulian is downstairs already." Then Binky's eyes lowered, and he said, "I'm sorry for your loss."

I sighed, thanked him. "Can I see the body?"

"Oh, of course," Binks said. "Follow me."

Binks led me into a gray metal elevator. He took a key chain from his pocket, inserted it into a slit next to the sole button. Once turned, he pressed the button, and the doors opened. Once inside, he pressed a button marked M. For Morgue. The doors closed, and we traveled in silence, down several flights. Finally the elevator stopped and the door slid open.

Whatever odor had been stuck to Binks was even stronger down here.

Outside of the elevator, the hallway divided into two separate pathways. A plaque mounted on the wall had arrows pointing in either direction. To the left, the arrow read, Morgue. To the right, the arrow read, Viewing Room.

Binks began walking toward the right.

I followed behind him as he opened a door and led me into a small room. A man was waiting for us inside. He was about five-eight and built stocky and muscular, like one of those NFL linebackers who had trouble seeing over the center but could deliver a hit like nobody's business. His skin was dark, a neat goatee, and he wore a dark gray suit. He looked at me as we entered.

"Detective?" I said.

"Detective Sevag Makhoulian," he said. He approached and shook my hand. "For short, people call me Sevi."

"Makhoulian…what background does that name come from?" I asked stalling for time.

"It's Armenian," he answered patiently.

"Were you born here?"

"I was born in Yerevan, my parents emigrated here when I was very young." His accent was noticeable but not thick, and his suit was as American as they came.

"Gotcha, don't mean to pry."

"I know it's your job to do just that, Mr. Parker. I do appreciate your coming down here on such short notice. And I must say I enjoy your work. Insightful, not to mention how nice it is to see a young man achieving success based on something other than setting fire to hotel rooms. It's a shame we had to meet under these circumstances. Curtis Sheffield speaks very highly of you."

"How's Curt doing?" I asked.

"Aside from the bullet in his leg? He's just peachy." Makhoulian said this with a slight smile. Last year Curt had taken a shot that nicked his femoral artery while looking for a family that we believed had abducted a child. He'd been assigned to desk duty since then, and I was lucky to have remained on his good side. Though he hated being off the streets, I think he secretly liked the attention from the opposite sex. Nothing sexier than a guy who took a bullet for a good cause. "Anyway, I'm sorry for your loss, Henry."

"It's not really *my* loss," I said. "The first and only time I met Stephen Gaines was a few hours ago."

"Well then," Makhoulian said, "if his death isn't your loss, whose is it?"

"Someone else's," I replied. "Just not mine."

"Somebody cared for this guy," Binks interjected. We both stared at him. The M.E. was right. Yet as much I tried to, I still didn't know what to think about everything.

The viewing room resembled a typical examining room, if all the machines and instruments had been removed. The only thing remaining was a long metal table. The table was covered by a sheet. Underneath the sheet was a body, about six feet long. Most likely belonging to a man named Stephen Gaines. A man who was presumably my brother.

"Before we begin," Binks said, "be warned that there's been extensive damage to the cranium."

"Extensive?" I said, looking at Makhoulian.

"That's right," he said. "From the damage, we can gather that the muzzle of the murder weapon was held less than a foot from the back of his head, a 9 mm fired at near point-blank range. The apartment we found him in wasn't a pretty sight."

"From the wounds," I said.

"Not just that," Makhoulian said. "We found…how can I put this simply…*paraphernalia.* Pipes, needles. You name the drug, it looked like Gaines was on it."

I took a deep breath, said, "How old is…was he?"

"Turned thirty a month ago," Makhoulian said. Four years older than me, I thought. Still a young man.

"He's cleaned up the best we could, but…" Binks said, his voice trailing off. He knew from the look on my face that this was best done quickly, with minimal cushioning. "Anyway, here he is."

Binks leaned over the body, took two folds of cloth between his hands and gently pulled the cover back until it stopped just below the corpse's neck. From there I could see the victim's head. Or at least what was left of it.

Stephen Gaines was lying on the table faceup. A half dollar-size hole was blown out of his forehead. I could see the man's skull and brain, both shredded from the bullet's impact. His eyes were closed, thankfully.

When that cover came down, I felt like everything in my body dried up. My insides felt like a black hole, my heart, lungs, my blood, all of it drained away.

"That's him," I said. "The man I saw on the street."

"This is your brother?" Binks said, eyes raised, curious more than sympathetic.

"According to the detective here," I said.

Binks nodded, his mouth still open, as though expecting me to relate just how this felt. The truth was I wasn't sure yet. I'd seen enough corpses, visited enough morgues to have been able to distance myself for the most part from the realities of death. A reporter could go crazy letting each individual horror pile up upon their psyche. Like a doctor, you couldn't think of blood as blood, but more a by-product of your work.

"Where'd you say he was found?" I asked.

"Apartment near Tompkins Square Park," the detective said. "Odd place for someone with your brother's seemingly…limited means to be these days. Twenty years ago, maybe. But now? That's the heart of Stuy Town. All young families and old folks."

I nodded, trying unsuccessfully to process this while staring at the body.

"That's the exit wound we're looking at," Binks said. "The bullet entered just below the back of the right parietal bone and exited through the forehead with a slightly upward trajectory."

Makhoulian took over. "The first entrance wound, combined with what we know about Mr. Gaines, suggests that his killer was right-handed and slightly shorter than him."

I listened to this. "Wait," I said, looking at Makhoulian. "You said 'first' entrance wound."

Makhoulian eyed Binks. Then he turned back to me. Binks said, "There was a second entrance wound. It went right through the occipital bone in the back of Gaines's skull. That bullet was still lodged in his head when Gaines was brought here."

"I thought you said he was shot point-blank," I said. "How can you shoot someone in the head twice from point-blank range?"

"Only the first wound was delivered from close

range," Binks said, his voice growing softer. His fingers traced the path of a bullet as he showed where the first bullet entered Gaines's skull. "The second was delivered from about four feet away. From a downward trajectory."

Binks raised his arm with his forefinger and thumb cocked like a gun. He pointed it at the floor to demonstrate the likely scenario. He continued, "There were no muzzle burn or gases expelled from the second shot. Despite the brain matter, the wound itself is oddly clean."

"What does that mean?" I said.

"Well," Binks said, scratching his nose with a gloved hand. "The impact and the trauma suggest the initial shot was fired from very close range. The brain matter and impact site…"

"Impact what?" I said.

"It's where the bullet impacts after exiting the body," Makhoulian said. "In this case, ballistics found the first bullet in the wall about six feet off the ground. But they didn't find the bullet itself."

"So the killer took it," I said.

Makhoulian nodded.

Binks continued. "The entry wound is nearly devoid of gases or burn marks. Considering the devastation and the impact site, it has all the marks of a point-blank shooting. See, normally when a bullet is fired, especially from close range, the wound will leave burn marks on the flesh, which is literally seared from the heat. In this case, the burn marks were nearly undetectable."

"Why?" I asked.

"My guess?" Binks said. "The killer was using a silenced weapon. Now, very few guns have those kind of professional silencers you see in movies, that screw on like a lightbulb. Usually they're homemade, a length of aluminum tubing filled with steel wool or fiberglass."

"Forensics is checking for both," Makhoulian added.

"It's not just professionals who use them. Some hunters use silencers out of season. Even guys in their backyards shooting beer bottles who don't want their neighbors to hear. Of course, there's a chance the killer simply did it the old-fashioned way," Binks said, "and covered the muzzle with a pillow. The killer didn't need to be an expert in weaponry. In fact, there's a reason you see that in the movies. It's not going to dampen the noise completely, but as a quick fix—"

"Please," I interrupted, pleading to either man. "Explain to me what the hell all this means."

Makhoulian said, "It means whoever killed your brother shot him once in the back of the head with a silenced weapon. Then while he was lying on the ground, dying, the killer shot him one more time to finish the job. Your brother wasn't just killed, Henry. He was executed."

4

I followed Detective Sevi Makhoulian out of the examiner's office. An unmarked Crown Victoria sat outside, and Makhoulian approached it. He leaned up against the door. He took a white handkerchief from his jacket pocket and wiped his forehead. I stood there watching him, unsure of what to do. What the next step was.

"You still haven't told me why you're so convinced Stephen Gaines is my brother. And even if he is, why did you call *me?*" I asked. "I barely spoke two words to Gaines in the entire thirty seconds I knew him. So again, why me?"

"You weren't our first choice, Henry," Makhoulian said, pocketing the cloth. "The first person we called was James Parker, your father. And Stephen's father."

"Wait," I said. "We had the same father?"

The detective nodded with no emotion. "You thought you were related through osmosis?"

I hadn't had much time to really think about everything, to consider what all this meant, but if Makhoulian was right and Gaines was my brother, we had to share a parent. And I could never picture my mother holding on to that kind of secret. There was no way she could keep that from me.

My father was another story.

From the first time I could think clearly, I recognized my father was the kind of man, who, if not your blood, you would go out of your way not to know.

Even as a younger man, he was mean, belittling, nasty, vicious. Violent.

That man was fifty-five now. In the last twenty years he'd never held a steady job. Never made enough money to move out of the house I grew up in, never desired to give my mother anything more than he had when they married. If anything, he took much of it away.

He preferred swinging from branch to branch on the employment tree, always looking for a vocation where the bosses didn't mind if you showed up late, left early to drink, and showed no ambition to rise above foot soldier. Comfort was given highest priority. When I began to write first for my school paper, then took various internships before taking a paid job with the *Bend Bulletin,* James Parker approached it like I was upsetting the gods of apathy. And hence upsetting his life. The harder I worked, the more work came home with me. My editors and sources would call at all hours of the night, and because this was before cell phones were more common than pennies, they would call my family's landline.

I remember sitting at my desk, the phone resting inches from my hand while I wrote, my eye always flickering to the headset, waiting to pick it up the millisecond it rang. The system wasn't foolproof, but it's the best I could come up with. The trick was to simply be the first to answer the phone when it rang. The moment that shrill bell rang, the phone was in my hands. "Henry Parker," I would say, hoping if the call was for me, my father would simply leave it alone. Every now and then I was slow, distracted or in the shower, and he'd pick up. It meant I had to deal with hang-ups from sources who were scared off by unrecognized voices on the other end. And if, heaven forbid, someone called during dinner, I could count on James Parker locking me in the garage. If I was lucky. And if I wasn't—I had a scar or two to motivate me to quicken my reaction times.

My mother, Eve Parker, was withdrawn. I hate to say aloof because that wasn't it, but it seemed as though she'd been shell-shocked by her husband into a perpetual state of submission. She rarely flinched, just went through the motions like an automaton who forgot that at one point she was human. I wondered what she had been like before she'd met James. If she'd been strong or vivacious. If she'd hoped to marry the man of her dreams. Or if somewhere, deep down, she was resigned to a life married to this thing that called himself a man.

If anything, though, I had to credit James Parker with making me stronger. He made me work harder, longer, better, if only to give myself every chance of getting the hell away from that house. When I was growing up, I wasn't strong enough, mentally or physically, to stand up to him. Now, I was twice the man he ever was. And I considered him lucky that his son left before he could stand up to him the way that he deserved.

"Wait," I said to Makhoulian. "If Stephen Gaines and I had the same father…who's Stephen's mother?"

Makhoulian nodded, as though expecting this question to be asked sooner or later.

"According to the birth certificate, her name is Helen Gaines."

"I've never heard that name before," I said. "Where is she?"

"Actually, I was hoping you could tell me," the detective said. "All we know about Helen Gaines is that she was born in Bend, Oregon, in 1960. Her financial records show that she closed out her bank accounts in Oregon in 1980, and moved. Where, we don't know."

"So if she was born in 1960, and Stephen Gaines was thirty, that means he was born in, what, 1979?"

"March twenty-sixth," Makhoulian replied.

"Then Helen Gaines was only nineteen when she gave birth to Stephen."

"That's right."

"And my father was…twenty-six. I know he married my mother when he was twenty-five. Jesus Christ, my father's mistress gave birth to his child while he was married to my mother."

Makhoulian stood there silent. I don't know what he could have said. I rubbed my temples, still trying to process everything. I still hadn't spoken to Amanda all day. I felt like crawling into her arms, just sleeping for a while, hoping this would all have been some dream when my eyes finally opened.

"Have you contacted my father yet?" I asked.

"We've left several messages for him and your mother at home. None of them have been returned."

"Not totally surprising," I said.

"Is your father prone to ignoring calls from the police?" Makhoulian asked.

"He's prone to ignoring any calls that aren't either Ed McMahon with a giant check or someone offering him a free longneck."

Makhoulian let out a small laugh, not wanting to distort the gravity of the situation too much. "What about your mother?"

"I think he purposely bought an answering machine she wouldn't know how to use. Let's just say last I heard, she didn't get many calls, didn't return many calls."

The detective nodded. "Listen, if you do hear from your father, tell him to call me." Makhoulian took a card from his wallet, handed it to me. I looked it over, put it in my pocket.

"I promise you I won't hear from him."

"But if you do…"

"If I do, I'll make sure he calls."

"That's all I ask."

"In return," I said, "will you keep me in the loop? Let me know if you have any suspects, how the investigation is going. If you catch the bastard."

"Far as it doesn't interfere with the investigation, sure. I'll keep you informed. Again, I'm sorry for your loss."

I shook Makhoulian's hand, then watched as he climbed into the Crown Vic and drove off. Once he was gone, I trudged to the subway, took it back uptown to my apartment. When I got out I called Wallace Langston at the *Gazette*. Nobody picked up, so I left a message on his voice mail.

"Wallace, it's Henry. Listen, I don't know how to say this…a man who was apparently my brother was shot and killed last night. His name is Stephen Gaines. I don't know much else, but I had to let you know. I'll give you a call when I know more but…I thought you should know in case anyone calls for comment. Anyway, call me back."

I hung up. Thought about it. I knew the *Gazette* would run a piece on the murder. Even though crime was down in the city, murders still got ink. It wouldn't be a long article. As of right now there was no suspect. There was no conspiracy. Gaines was a junkie, likely killed over whatever drug fiends were killed over. Stolen stashes. Territory beefs. He wasn't famous, wasn't some rich guy's son. Nobody knew him. Not even his family.

It would get a paragraph, two at most. I wouldn't write it. And unless there were future developments, my brother's death would be just another junkie murder in a city where you'd need a landfill for all his brethren.

Stephen Gaines's death was just as short and seemingly unremarkable as his life.

I entered my apartment to find Amanda sitting on the couch. She was reading a sports magazine, but didn't seem that interested in it. Her eyes perked up when I entered, then narrowed when she saw that mine did not. I took a seat on the couch next to her.

Amanda and I had met several years ago. When I was wanted for murder, she was the only person brave enough to help me. She trusted me despite all common sense saying she shouldn't. I fell for her right away. It was easy. I'm a sucker for a beautiful woman with crisp, auburn hair, a smile that will make you stop in your tracks, wit that will keep you laughing all night and a perfectly placed mole by her collarbone that you could trace every night with your finger. Hypothetically.

But despite all that, I nearly lost it all. I had pushed her away, and it wasn't until I spent time without her that I realized just how much I'd lost. She knew that because of the kind of person I was, the kind of job I had, she might be put in harm's way. As long as we faced obstacles together, she'd said, there was nothing we couldn't overcome. Since we'd reconciled, the last few months had been wonderful. We started our relationship going backward, in a way. We went out to dinners. We saw movies. I sent her flowers at work, she gave the best neck massages this side of the Golden Door Spa.

Once we restarted our relationship, I made two promises to her. First, I would tell her everything. Even the hardest things, she would be allowed to judge and decide for herself. And second, every decision would be a joint one. I would never again make a decision about our relationship on my own. That was a hard-learned lesson. One I should have known right away.

So sitting there next to her, I knew she had a right to know about what Detective Makhoulian told me about Stephen Gaines. And she had a right to know about my father.

So I told her. Everything. I told her about seeing Gaines on the street. About the call from Detective Sevi Makhoulian. That Gaines had been murdered, viciously. And that my father had sired Stephen when his mother, Helen, was just nineteen. I still couldn't wrap my mind around the idea that Gaines was my brother. Certain things you can be told and accept as gospel. This was not one of them.

When I finished, we both sat there. Amanda looked stunned, unsure of what to say. Putting myself in her shoes, I'd be lost for words as well. Finally she got up, went into the kitchen. I heard a few clanking noises, turned to see what was going on, but the door frame blocked my view.

Amanda came out carrying two plastic cups, and a bottle of red wine. She sat the bottle down on the coffee table, peeled off the foil and uncorked it. She did so without a problem. She then poured two generous glasses, handed one to me.

"I thought we might need this," she said.

"It's amazing how you can read my mind even if I'm not thinking something."

She took a healthy sip, and I did the same. Then I sat, twirling the cup in my hand.

"What are you going to do?" she asked. I shook my head.

"I don't know what I can do," I replied. "It's a police investigation. As far as the *Gazette,* they'll cover it, but nothing more than standard murder reporting unless something else breaks that gives the story legs."

"Do you feel," she said hesitantly, "I don't know… sad?"

I thought about that. "I don't think *sad*'s the right word."

"So what is?"

"Angry," I replied. "Mad. Pissed off. I want to know why I've lived nearly three decades without knowing any of this. If this is true, how could my father not have told me? I mean I know he's a bastard, but this is a life he chose to ignore. And I want to know why Stephen Gaines, after all this time, came to me for help. He'd lived thirty years without Henry Parker as his brother, and all of a sudden he decides to have a family gathering outside my office one night? I don't buy that for a second."

"You didn't know about him," Amanda said. "Do you think he knew about you?"

"I honestly don't know. He knew about me right before he died. I don't know when he learned. If Helen Gaines told him about his family, or kept him in the dark like my parents did with me. I wish I knew."

"So find out," Amanda said. "At least that much is in your hands."

"What do you mean?"

"You know where your parents live. Where your father lives. Go ask him. Make him tell you the truth."

I stood up, paced the room. "I don't know if I can do that. I haven't seen him in almost ten years. Bend isn't really my home anymore. I don't know if it ever was."

"Your heart might be here, but the truth is there," she said. "Today's Thursday. I can call in sick tomorrow."

"Why would you do that?"

"To go with you," she answered. "We're going to find out how much your father knows."

5

.We woke at five in the morning having purchased plane tickets online the night before. We threw a few days' worth of clothing into a suitcase, then caught a cab to La Guardia. The minute the cab pulled away I realized I forgot my toothbrush.

Living in New York had become increasingly difficult over the last few years. After some time when it looked like Manhattan would be the only city unaffected by the subprime crisis, real-estate prices came tumbling down. Of course, we were renting, and therefore unaffected, and inflation was still rising faster than a hot-air balloon. My salary at the *Gazette* had barely seen a bump in my tenure, and working at the Legal Aid Society, a not-for-profit organization, Amanda wasn't exactly rolling in dough. At some point we would have to make a decision about our future. Where to live, where we could afford to live.

I didn't want to leave the city, but I also wanted to think long-term. Many reporters commuted. Yet the fantasy of living in New York City always captivated me. It was one of the motivating factors that led me to the *Gazette*. And the possibility of working in the big city, seeing things I couldn't see anywhere else in the world, was one of the motivators that kept me going when I could barely stand another day in Bend with my family.

We got to the airport and loaded up on coffee, a fattening muffin nearly crumbling in my hands as I shoveled it into my mouth. We stopped at the magazine stand, where Amanda picked up her fashion and celebrity mags and I bought a selection of newspapers.

"I brought something else to read," she said, "but just in case." Amanda wasn't the kind of girl who waited in line at sample sales and had a separate closet for her shoes, but something about reading about the hottest beach bodies made plane rides go by quicker. Maybe I should give Cosmo a whirl.

Sitting at the gate, I leafed through the *Gazette*. I felt my stomach clench when I turned to page eight and saw the two-paragraph article that started:

Stephen Gaines, 30, found shot to death in Alphabet City apartment
by Neil deVincenzo

I'd met Neil deVincenzo about a year ago. He covered the crime beat, had some good connections on the force. Because of my tenuous relationship with the NYPD, they'd often talk to him rather than me. He was a good guy, around forty-five, and in terrific shape. He'd been a boxer in the navy, even had the tattoo of a pugilist on his upper biceps, though only a few of us were privy to the knowledge, and that only came out after a few rounds of drinks.

The article was brief, perfunctory. There wasn't much to the story to report. Gaines was found murdered, two bullet wounds in his head. There were no suspects, no leads. And no locations or whereabouts for his mother, Helen Gaines. Sevi Makhoulian was quoted, saying, "No comment."

I wondered where Helen Gaines was. If she knew her son was dead. And if so, why Makhoulian couldn't locate her. I wondered if she knew her son was in trouble. And I wondered if she knew about me.

Our flight had one layover in Chicago. We would then go on to Portland, and rent a car for the drive to Bend. The plan was to stay in Bend over the long weekend. I didn't have any desire to spent any more time with my father than was absolutely necessary to get all the details about his relationship with Helen Gaines and her son. After that, I figured it could be good for us to spend an extra day or two in the city of my birth. It had been the better part of a decade since I left for college, I was curious to see how much had changed.

After a half-hour delay we settled into our seats. Amanda took the middle, I got the aisle, and my legs thanked me. I took out a paperback novel, a thriller to help pass the time, and noticed Amanda reach into her knapsack and take out a book.

The cover seemed familiar. It was worn, the spine cracked, color faded. And when I look closer, I understood why.

The book's title was *Through the Darkness.* It's author was Jack O'Donnell. The book was a chronicle of the rise of crack cocaine and the massive crime wave that nearly tore New York apart in the '70s and '80s. The book was nominated for the Pulitzer Prize, though it lost out to a book that, as far as I knew, was no longer in print. *Through the Darkness* was the very book that officially gave Jack O'Donnell the moniker of my living hero.

Amanda noticed me staring. She smiled nervously.

"You talk about this book a lot," she said. "I just want to understand you better. And Jack, too."

"It's a great book," I said. "Holds up like it was written last year. I really appreciate this."

"Hope you don't mind that I took it from your shelf."

"Are you kidding me? You don't know how happy this makes me."

"Don't be silly, I wouldn't let you do this alone."

"Not the trip," I said. "The book. It means a lot that you want to know more about what matters to me."

"Why wouldn't I?" she asked, confused. "I mean, we're together right? What kind of relationship would it be if neither of us cared about what mattered most to the other?"

I felt silly. I'd never read a book because I thought it meant a lot to Amanda, and for the most part she didn't like to talk about her work at home. Working at the Legal Aid Society, she had to deal with some of the most horrific cases of child abuse. She saw things that would stay with you. I didn't blame her for not wanting to bring that kind of work home with her.

"Is there anything I can do?" I asked, feeling somewhat stupid. "You know, to know more about you? What makes you tick? Does Darcy Lapore have a memoir out or something?"

Amanda laughed. Darcy Lapore was her coworker,

a professional socialite-in-training. And considering how much value was inherent in that job title, especially in New York where the title socialite was practically a blank check, it was likely only a matter of time before Darcy's obsession with jewelry, makeup and shoes that cost more than my rent were bound to find the printed word, or more likely, a reality series. It was no doubt that vacuousness and superficiality were the country's drug of choice, and self-promotion was the new black.

"Tell you what, Darcy's husband has enough money that they could pay you to ghostwrite it and you wouldn't have to work at the *Gazette* until your midthirties."

"Hmm…that's an intriguing possibility. Provided I can get past the whole 'crying myself to sleep every night' problem that would come with that."

"Would leaving your job really do that to do?" Amanda asked with a mixture of rhetoric and actual curiosity.

"I think so," I said. "I mean I believe, *really* believe, this is what I was meant to do."

"Must be a great feeling to know what you're meant to do at your age," Amanda said. She reached into her purse, took out a stick of gum and popped it into her mouth. The plane began to back up, then we turned and approached the runway. Amanda began to chew her gum with a fury rarely seen outside of nature videos where a gang of lions rip a poor gazelle limb from limb.

She looked at me, saw I was staring. "My ears pop," she explained. I nodded, smiling. "Come on, we both know you snore like a chain saw. We both have our little *things*."

"I wasn't judging, but thanks for bringing up a sore subject. You know I got tested for apnea a while back. It came back negative."

"Maybe you should get a second opinion before I 'accidentally' smother you one night," she said, settling back into her seat, closing her eyes. "Okay, I'm going to sleep now. If you're going to snore, it'd be sweet if you wouldn't mind sitting in the bathroom."

"It's reassuring to know you always have my safety in mind."

"Oh, come on," Amanda said. She sat up, leaning over and gave me a long kiss on the lips. I tasted her ChapStick. Cherry. Delicious.

When she finished we were both smiling. And the old woman across the aisle was grimacing. "If you two are even thinking about joining that so-called Mile-High Club," she said, "I'll call the flight attendant and have you ejected at 30,000 feet. Don't think I won't be watching you."

We both nodded, embarrassed. Actually, the thought had crossed my mind, but with Mother Teresa sitting there I wouldn't want to be banned from the airline before the trip back.

"Have a good nap, babe," I said, squeezing Amanda's hand. "See you in Bend."

"I hope we find out more about Stephen Gaines," she said through a yawn.

I nodded, watching Amanda drift off to sleep, not knowing just how much there was to learn.

6

We landed in Portland at five o'clock, or eight o'clock New York time. We'd both slept a good portion of the flights. While Amanda was awake, she tore through Jack O'Donnell's book with incredible zeal. It thrilled me to see that she was clearly enjoying the book. It brought back memories of the first time I'd read it, in junior high. I spent the next week plowing through every O'Donnell book I could find at the Deschutes County Library. My teachers were less than impressed, since I'd read the books in lieu of completing my actual schoolwork. Safe to say O'Donnell's tomes taught me more about myself and what I wanted to be than years of school could ever do.

After landing, we rented a car, a nice little compact that probably got twenty-eight miles to the gallon. Given how you practically had to sell a kidney to fill up a tank of gas these days, I would have seriously considered a motorized skateboard if Hertz had one available.

The drive to Bend took just about three hours. Once we merged onto US-20, I began to feel my stomach rumbling and beginning to churn. I wasn't quite sure what to expect. I hadn't set foot in Bend in nearly ten years. The same amount of time had passed since I'd last seen my parents. And while some children might find a hole in their heart, in their soul, due to this absence, mine was finally able to fill up.

I wondered if coming back here was a good idea, whether it was best to let dead dogs lie. Yet that image of Stephen Gaines lying on an examining table, his head nearly blown apart, made this trip a necessity. Anger had driven me away from my home. Now the same was leading me back.

As we approached the city limits, I could immediately tell that the last eight years had changed my hometown a great deal. And all the changes looked to be for the better.

To the west, the spectacular beauty of the Cascade Mountain Range. The lush green foliage was tipped with hints of snow from winter. I could make out the magnificent peak of Mount Bachelor, rising to a snow-capped point. I rolled down the window to breathe in the fresh air. It was warm, dry and clean. For a moment I considered what I'd given up. Part of me missed the air, the scenery. Being able to see for miles, the horizons rising blue and bold above the skyline. For everything I loved about New York—the hustle and bustle, the thriving heart of media and business, the diversity of its inhabitants—I missed the open world.

By seven-thirty, we were approaching Eastview Drive, the street in the northeast section of Bend where James and Eve Parker had lived for nearly thirty years. I still didn't have the timeline sketched out completely, so I wondered if my father had had his affair with Helen

Gaines in the very house I'd grown up in. Perhaps a quickie in the room that later became my bedroom. Every moment spent thinking about it made me more angry. I'd have to restrain myself once I saw him in person.

I turned the car onto Eastview Drive tentatively, slowing the car down as my old house came into view. The first eighteen years of my life forgotten and now remembered. A bad dream interrupting a peaceful sleep.

The dark green paint hadn't been refreshed in years. The two-car garage was still surely filled with old records, antiques my parents had grown weary of and empty photo albums. A black 1994 Chevy C/K 1500 flatbed truck was parked outside the left garage. The paint was scratched and faded, but I had no doubt the old truck still purred like a kitten. The grass was fairly short, so as least they cared about some sense of decorum, and the cobblestone walkway leading up to the front door was still there like the day I left. Much had changed in Bend over the last decade, and it seemed as if my parents had resisted that change as much as possible.

I steered the car into the driveway, parking next to the flatbed, then turned off the engine and sat there in silence. Amanda did as well. Neither of us said a word for a long time. Finally Amanda said, "Henry, do you want to do this? We can go to a hotel, wait until you're ready."

"I'm ready," I said. "Or at least I need to be."

I opened the car door, cautiously stepped out as though expecting the driveway to swallow me whole. Amanda climbed out, and we walked up the cobblestone path to the front door. A faded yellow button popped out like a pimple to the right of the front door. I could see a faint glow from inside one of the windows. Somebody was definitely home.

I looked at Amanda, smiled weakly, tried to gather my strength and rang the doorbell. The bell startled me for some reason, like I wasn't ready to accept that there was actually a person who lived here.

I hadn't phoned ahead because I didn't want him to know I was coming. Didn't want to give him a chance to think, to make up excuses. I wanted him face-to-face. To see how he reacted. If he did at all.

I heard footsteps, someone mumbling under his breath. I shifted my weight from foot to foot, trying to forget the resentment I had toward this man. Knowing the pain he'd put us all through. Knowing there was a young man lying in New York with two bullets in his head, a man who my father could, like me, call his blood.

The front door opened with a creak. A man stood in front of me, rubbing his eyes. He looked older than I remembered, lines creasing his face like small ditches, a thin coat of gray stubble covering the worn skin.

When his eyes came into focus and he saw me, the man's mouth opened slightly, his reflexes working faster than his mind was able to keep up with. He shook his head slightly, unsure.

I took a step forward and said, "Hi, Dad. It's been a while. It's Henry. Your son who's still alive."

7

We sat there in his living room. James in an easy chair, me and Amanda on a faded, stained, uncomfortable brown couch. It was probably uncomfortable because nobody ever sat in it, nobody ever told James the springs bit your legs. My father wasn't exactly someone who entertained. James Parker was wearing a tattered light blue bathrobe, the same one he used to wear years ago. It was worn. Threads hung out, waiting to be yanked free. The robe looked as if it was now worn out of convenience rather than comfort. A skin that couldn't be shed.

Though it had been eight years since I'd seen my father, it felt like longer. He looked as though he'd aged twenty. The brown hair—the same color hair I'd inherited—was streaked with gray. The skin around his neck had begun to sag into full-on jowls, and whatever was left of the muscle tone in his forearms had turned soft. His eyes were lined, as though tired of keeping up the appearance of the rebel he'd long considered himself to be.

Maybe thirty years ago James Parker was a man to be feared and possibly even desired. Now, though, he was just an angry old man with a distant wife and an estranged son. A man whose indifference to any life but his own had driven away everyone who'd ever cared for him, driven him to the point where his very voice brought up anger inside of me.

When I was hidden in a dingy building and needed to hear something, anything, to keep me going, I called my father. I'd spent much of my adult life trying to hard to distance myself from him and what he represented. My anger had, in essence, become a fuel. Recently, the fuel had begun to burn itself out. But sitting there, watching this man in front of me, knowing what he'd done in his past, knowing just how little of the story I knew, it was all I could do not to leap up from my chair and knock him head over heels, that ugly bathrobe flailing like paper in a gust of wind.

Those striking green eyes kept flicking to me, then to Amanda, then back to me. Anytime he had unexpected visitors, James Parker figured it was either a court summons or an IRS audit. Amanda sat leaning forward, eyeing James, as though trying to understand an entire family history through those eyes.

He held a beer in his hand. The bottle was half-empty, and the bottom half was covered by his hand, which was sweating. The air was hot, blowing from some unseen fan that appeared to simply recirculate the warm air over the whole house. He eyed me with a look of confusion and contempt.

"Where's Mom?" I asked.

"Bridge lesson," he said. "Plays with her girlfriends once a week. Whatever keeps her busy and out of my hair."

I bristled at the comment. "When will she be home?" I hated being here, hated that he'd even put us in a situation where we needed to be. But my hatred for this man couldn't get in the way of finding out the truth about Stephen Gaines. About myself.

"Listen, I don't know what you want from us," he said, swigging from the bottle, grimacing because the beer had likely grown warm. Not quite the "you never call" line you'd expect from a parent you hadn't seen in years.

"I just want to know the truth about you and Helen Gaines. And how much you know about Stephen."

"What does it matter anyway?" James said, looking off at the wall. "It was years ago. Before you were even born."

"I know that," I said, anger rising inside me. "Did you ever think to tell me I had a brother somewhere? You never thought that I might be interested to know that? Never occurred to you, huh?"

"He wasn't your real brother," James said slowly. "Helen was not your mother. I never considered myself that boy's father."

"What the hell does that mean?"

"She wasn't supposed to keep the baby," my father said. I heard Amanda gasp under her breath. So far my father had barely looked at her, like Amanda was a referee, a third wheel, something to be ignored. I hadn't bothered introducing her because I knew he wouldn't care.

For a brief moment I glimpsed a flicker of pain behind those eyes. A memory he thought forgotten had come back to him.

"But she did," I said. "And then she left. Tell me what happened."

"I don't need to tell you anything," he snapped suddenly, the beer sloshing liquid onto his bathrobe. "It's thirty years ago. It's over."

"It's not over," I said, my voice quivering. "Your son was found dead in a seedy apartment *this* week. It's not over. You were the boy's father. I know it meant nothing to you, but it damn sure meant something to him, and to Helen Gaines. And it damn sure means something to me."

"What?" he said, lurching out of his chair, knocking the bottle flying. I recognized that look. The look of rage, the look that said he didn't owe anybody anything. "What does it mean to you? You never knew him. I never knew him. He's a fucking stranger. What, just because you share some, like, microscopic strand of DNA in common all of a sudden this matters to you? Please. Spare me, Henry. Go back to New York. Go back to your big city and do whatever you do there." He pointed at Amanda. "And take this...*whatever*...with you."

"This is Amanda," I said. "And she's given me more in just a few years than you have in a lifetime."

"Are you finished?" he asked, sitting back down. "Because I have a league game tonight and I bowl like crap when I'm not prepared."

"Right," I said. "Your bowling league. You cared more about those pins than you did us."

"Pins don't talk back," he said. "Pins don't waste your hard-earned money on books that don't put food on the table. Speaking of that, will you be joining us for dinner?"

"I'd rather break bread with Bin Laden," I said. "How long were you sleeping with Helen Gaines while you were with Mom?"

James sighed, leaned back, searched his memory. He spoke as though this was a mere trifle to him, like I'd asked what he had for lunch yesterday.

"Must have been about a year. Maybe a little more. Who keeps track of these things?" he said. Who keeps track of these things. Like it was a bowling score from a few years ago.

Without warning, my father stood up, cracked his back and went up the rickety stairs. Amanda and I sat there unsure what to do. We heard some rummaging around, and soon after, my father came back down. He held something in his hand I couldn't see. Then he gave it to me.

It was a photograph of a young woman. It was worn, faded, kept somewhere it was not removed from often. The woman in the photo had pale skin, curly brown hair and luminous green eyes. She was sitting on a grassy hill, a blouse covering her knees. Her mouth was open in a smile, the shot taken in the middle of a laugh. Despite her young age she had deep laugh lines. She looked like the kind of woman it would be easy to fall in love with.

"You kept this?" I said. "Why?"

"I'm not keen on throwing things out. Never know when you might need them."

"Didn't you worry Mom would find it?"

"She hasn't yet."

I handed the photo back to him. He hesitated, then took it, slipping it into his pocket.

"You didn't care that you were married?" I asked. His glare told me he didn't.

"When did you first learn about Stephen? That you had a son?"

"When Helen was about four months along. She told me she wouldn't have sex anymore. And that was the reason. I thought she was going to get an abortion. That's what we both wanted, I thought. Then her belly keeps getting bigger and bigger and…" James looked down at his hands. "Then one day he's there. This little kid."

"What then?"

"She wanted to know where we stood. Whether she was going to raise the boy on her own. I told her I already had a wife, and she wanted her own kids. And that I didn't have the time or money for two families."

"And then?"

"And then she left. One day she's living a few streets over, the next Helen's moved out, packed up her stuff, sold her crappy house and disappeared forever."

"Forever," I said. "You were never curious to see how your other son was doing?"

"Didn't much care how the son who lived with us was doing, ungrateful as he was."

Point made.

"When was the last you heard from Helen?" I asked. My father looked down. His eyes twitched for a moment. I tried to look past them, tried to see just what this man was holding on to.

Then he said, "The day before she disappeared. That's all I know. That mother of his never took care of Stephen. Maybe if she'd made some different choices he'd still be alive."

"By different choices, do you mean never shacking up with you?"

"Don't get smart," he said. "I guess that's one of those whaddaya callems, rhetorical statements."

I bristled. "What do you mean, different choices?"

"She was always one of those wild women, doing things to her mind and body. Tough to find a woman who drinks more than you do. And that's all I know. I don't wish the boy died. I'm not some monster. But he's no more my son than I was his father. Blood's only as thick as you make it."

"Don't I know it," I said. Then I stood up. Amanda did as well.

"I'd like to say it's been a good visit, *Dad,* but there's been enough lying in this family. The buck's gotta stop somewhere. Say hi to Mom for me."

"I will," he said, and I actually believed him. As I left to go, all of a sudden Amanda spoke.

"Are you sorry?" she asked. She was staring right into his eyes, not letting him go. In that moment I knew just how strong this woman was.

James sat there, silent, for what must have been several minutes. He looked back at her. She wouldn't turn away.

"No," he finally said. And oddly enough, I didn't believe him.

I reached for the door. Took Amanda's arm. Nodded toward my father.

And just as I was about to turn the knob, there came a loud knock at the door.

At first I thought it was my mother, but she wouldn't have bothered or needed to make that much noise.

"James Parker?" came the male voice from outside.

My father stood up. Approached the door. He looked through the peephole, then stepped back. A look of concern and fear crossed his face.

"What is it?" I said. "Dad?"

"Sir, open up," the voice said.

My father unlocked the bottom latch and opened the door.

Three police officers—two men and one woman—were standing on the front porch. One of them held a piece of paper. The others held their hands at their hips. Specifically by their guns.

Clearly, they were worried they might need to use them.

"James Parker?" the lead officer said.

"Yuh…yes?"

The officer stepped forward through the doorway. He grabbed my father, spun him around until his chest hit the wall with a thud. The other two cops swarmed in, and within seconds my father was in handcuffs. I saw his eyes go wide, this proud, arrogant man. And in those eyes I saw emotion I'd never seen before in nearly thirty years.

My father was afraid.

"What the hell is going on?" I shouted.

"James Parker," the cop said, "You're under arrest for the murder of Stephen Gaines."

8

Amanda and I sat on a small wooden bench in the lobby of the Bend police department. After they'd taken my father away in handcuffs, pressing his head down as he climbed into the backseat of the car like some common thug you'd see on *COPS,* we followed practically bumper to bumper in our rental car.

Upon arriving at the station, I didn't have a chance to talk to my father before they led him into booking. The City of Bend Police Department had two sections: a two-level structure that sat next to a taller tower, both with sloped, tiled roofs. The sign outside read City of Bend Police and underneath that read Public Works.

I parked the car in a lot in back and we ran around to the entrance. Inside we refused to leave, or sit down, until we either spoke with my father or an officer who could tell us just what the hell was going on. My stomach was tied in knots. Though I'd long ago learned to give up loving my father, I knew this man wasn't, couldn't be a killer. Not to mention I couldn't even imagine what kind of evidence they had that would enable a warrant to be issued so quickly.

From everything Makhoulian and Binks told me, it seemed as if Gaines was murdered. Not an impulse killing, but exterminated. How could the cops be so blind? How could they *possibly* connect my father to this when he was in Bend the whole time?

For perhaps the first time in my life, I found myself feeling sorry for the man. He was alone, scared, accused of a crime beyond comprehension. It was all bogus, though. No doubt there was some mistake and he'd be released.

I tried to call my mother, but she didn't have a cell phone. I left a message at home, hoped she would find it.

Finally after an hour of waiting, a cop approached us where we stood. He was about forty, lean, with salt-and-pepper hair, a square jaw and dark, tan skin. His badge read Whalin. We stood up, desperate to hear why they'd taken my father in for such a horrendous crime.

"You must be Henry," the cop said. He offered his hand. I looked at him, then shook it grudgingly. "I'm Captain Ted Whalin of the BPD. I'm in charge of the criminal investigations division."

"Where's my father?" I demanded.

"Your father is in a holding cell. Tomorrow he'll have to go before a judge to be properly processed. There is an outstanding warrant for his arrest in New York City for the murder of Stephen Gaines."

"That's impossible," I said. "First of all, Stephen Gaines is his son. And second, my father's never even been to New York."

Whalin looked confused. "I can't go into specifics,"

Whalin said, "but the warrant states that physical evidence does exist that links James Parker to the crime."

"That's impossible," I said again. "I don't think he's left the state in twenty years."

"That's not up to me to determine," Whalin said.

"If he's wanted for murder in New York," Amanda said, "won't he be extradited?"

"That depends on him," Whalin continued. "When he goes before Judge Rawling tomorrow, he'll have the opportunity to sign what's called a nonjudicial waiver of expedition."

"What does that mean?" I asked.

Whalin said, "It means that he agrees that he is in fact the same James Parker wanted on this murder charge. If he accepts the charge, he'll be brought back to New York City where he'll be entered into their system. Though that might be a problem."

"What do you mean?"

"We believe that your father is the James Parker referred to in this warrant. We know he has a relationship with Stephen Gaines…"

"That's not true," I said. "They didn't actually know each other at all."

"Regardless," Whalin said, "it'd be a mighty coincidence if the NYPD happens to be looking for a completely different James Parker in regards to the murder of Stephen Gaines. Wouldn't you agree?"

I didn't have to. The odds were pretty nonexistent.

"As of right now, your father is refusing to grant the nonjudicial waiver." Whalin said this with frustration evident on his face.

Amanda said, "And what happens if he refuses to sign it?"

"Then it's our job to prove that he is—or is not—the James Parker referred to in this warrant. We'll take fingerprints, blood samples, and confirm with one hundred percent accuracy that he is James Parker. Of course, all that testing takes an awful long time, which means…"

"He stays locked up in your jail until he's extradited."

"Consider it time not served. Not a second of time he spends in prison here will be taken off any eventual sentence. So if your father wants to contest his identity, so be it. Not my ass sleeping every night on a metal bench. And did I mention he refuses to consult with a lawyer?"

"We need to see him," I said. "Right away."

"He's with two detectives right now, but I think he should be available in an hour or two."

"Wait," Amanda said. "Are they questioning him?"

"If they're doing their job."

"But you said he didn't have a lawyer."

"That's right."

"Then we demand to see him. I have a license to practice law in New York State, where any legal hearings pertaining to this case will occur. Right now your police station is acting as nothing more than a glorified holding pen. So I can promise you that anything James Parker says now will be disallowed in a court of law under the assumption that your officers coerced him into making a statement without legal counsel."

"Listen," Whalin said, "right now he isn't even admitting to being the *right* James Parker, so I doubt we'll get much—"

"Now," Amanda yelled.

Whalin looked her over, then said, "Follow me."

He led us into the heart of the BPD station, down a long brick corridor. At the end was a series of three rooms, marked simply 1, 2 and 3. He took us to the right, knocked on the reinforced-metal door.

A small slat opened at about eye level, then the door opened. Inside were two cops, one in uniform and one plainclothes. And sitting in a metal folding chair, his wrists handcuffed to the table, was my father.

His eyes were red. I could tell he'd been crying. He was still wearing the same clothes, but they were soaked through with sweat. He was shaking, as though his body was simply unable to process what was happening. When he saw us, his mouth opened and his face lit up.

"Henry!" he exclaimed.

"His son," Whalin told the cops. "And Parker's lawyer." Whalin nodded at Amanda. She went to say something, but I nudged her. She got the tip. This was the only way we'd get to speak with him.

"You have half an hour," Whalin said as the other cops exited the room.

"We'll take as much time as we damn well please," Amanda said, staring right into the captain's eyes. He frowned, told the cops to take a hike.

"We have to lock the door from the outside. Procedure. If you want to leave, just knock."

Amanda pointed at the camera hung up in the upper corner of the interrogation room. A small red light was blinking on it.

"I want that turned off," she said. Whalin looked at it, then nodded, making a slicing motion across his throat, telling the cops to kill the feed. They walked away, and a moment later the light went off.

"Thank you, Captain," Amanda said. "We'll be in touch soon."

We went in and closed the door. A metal *snick* came from outside. The cops locking us in with the alleged murderer.

We took two chairs and pulled them up to the table. My father reached out to us, but the handcuffs held his wrists firm. He looked dejected, then said, "Henry, thank God you're here. Did they tell you? They think I killed Stephen."

"I know, Dad. The question is *why* do they think that?" My father leaned down, started to bite his nails, his head comically close to the table. "Dad?"

James shrugged, but there was nothing behind it.

"Listen, Mr. Parker," Amanda said. "Your best option right now is to sign the nonjudicial review waiver. Once you do that they'll bring you back to New York and begin actual legal proceedings. I'll help you get a lawyer, or at least weed out the bad ones."

"I don't want to leave here," my father said softly.

"Dad, jail isn't exactly comfortable," I said.

"I mean, I don't want to leave Bend," he said more forcefully. "I didn't do anything. I didn't kill Stephen. They can't just take me wherever they want."

I looked at Amanda. She said, "Mr. Parker, if you don't sign the waiver you'll stay in Bend, but you'll be in prison until they prove your identity. It could be weeks, months. And that's *before* any sort of trial. And trust me, you won't be doing yourself any favors with the judge assigned to the case. They will take you if you make them."

"This can't be right," James said. "*Goddamn* it I shouldn't be here! Henry, you know me, you know this isn't right."

I knew him, but I didn't. I'd seen the depths of his anger, his rage. It was up to me to believe he wasn't capable of reaching another level.

"Dad…" I began. "Why do they suspect you?"

Without hesitating, James said, "They told me there's evidence linking me to the crime. They said they found it in Stephen's apartment."

"In New York?" I said. "How is that possible?"

He looked down at the floor, his whole body seeming to sag into nothing. "They said they found my fingerprints on the gun that killed him."

9

"Wait, step back," I said. It took me a moment to regroup, to process what my father had just said. "How could they possibly have found your fingerprints on the gun that killed Stephen?"

"I don't know," my father said. He said it unconvincingly. There was more to this. Amanda looked at him with incredible frustration. She had a great legal mind, but I could already tell that she was thinking about James Parker's chances during a murder trial. Even if he was innocent—which he had to be—this man would never do himself any favors with his lawyer or a judge. He was already refusing easy extradition, and he was lying—or at least hiding the truth—from the only people here who gave a damn.

Sadly, I knew what it felt like to be accused of a terrible crime you didn't commit. I knew just how lonely it could be, and how much a friendly hand meant. Amanda had been that for me. If not for her, I'd either be dead or in prison. She'd reached out, offered a hand, and I'd smartly accepted. My father, meanwhile, was dangling from the edge of a cliff, slapping our hands away in the misguided belief that he couldn't fall.

"Mr. Parker," Amanda said. "You need to tell us what happened. All of it. You know why they arrested you. Even if you're innocent, you don't seem surprised. Shocked, maybe, but not surprised. I can see it in your eyes. You're thinking about the circumstances that led to this. How events could have been misconstrued. We need to know this so we can understand what happened."

My father looked at Amanda, confused. She'd illuminated a path for him and his reluctance to see it was waning.

"I was in New York," James finally said, the words coming out in a rush like air that had been compressed. "The day Stephen died. I was there."

"You were in the city?" I asked, incredulous. "Why?"

James looked at me, then Amanda. He stayed quiet. I got the picture. He wanted to talk to her. She was impartial. A lawyer. I was his son. And I would judge.

"Mr. Parker," she said. "Why were you in New York?"

"I saw him," James said. His eyes had grown wide, for the first time fully beginning to piece together the circumstances. There was terror in those eyes. They ripped a hole through me because right then I knew he understood why he'd been accused of the crime. "Helen called me."

"Helen Gaines?" Amanda said. "Stephen's mother?"

James nodded. "I hadn't spoken to her in, God, almost thirty years. After she had Stephen, I wanted nothing to do with either of them. I had a family. A wife. I *told* her that," he said, slamming his fist on the table. "From the beginning, I told her this won't go anywhere. It wasn't my fault the crazy bitch lied about being on the pill."

"How did she get your number?" Amanda said.

"It's called the phone book," James said drily. "Last I checked I'm not the president."

"Why did she call you after so long?"

James leaned over again, chewed his thumbnail. He ripped off a ragged piece of white, spat it across the room. I saw a small line of blood well up from where he'd ripped.

"She said she was in trouble. That she needed money. That Stephen was in trouble."

"Did she say what kind of trouble?"

"She said Stephen had a drug problem. She needed to get him help before it was too late. She couldn't afford treatment."

"So why did you come all the way to New York?"

"I hung up on her. She called back. She said if I didn't help them, she would sue me for child support and make sure my name was in every newspaper as one of those deadbeat dads. She said technically I owed her thirty years' of payments, and that if she hadn't wrecked my marriage thirty years ago she'd make it her mission to do it now. I couldn't afford thirty years back payments for the life of me. I told her I could give her some money, a little, but that's it. She said she needed to see me. That maybe meeting his father would snap some sense into Stephen."

"And you agreed to go?"

"Not at first," James said. "I told her I could send it Western Union. She said those two words again, 'child support,' and I was on a plane the next day." He looked at me and grinned. "Sorry I didn't call."

"Where did you tell mom you were going?" I asked.

"I don't know, just said I was going fishing or some shit. She didn't ask many questions."

"They say your fingerprints ended up on the gun that killed Stephen," Amanda said. "That means two things. One, they found the murder weapon. And two, your prints were on it. Can you explain how that happened?"

"Helen," he said, shaking his head slightly. "When I got to their apartment—a real rats' nest. Ugh, just disgusting. Cockroaches everywhere, food left out. Anyway, I hadn't seen Helen in almost thirty years. I had some money with me. Not much, I ain't Ted Turner in case you haven't noticed. Stephen wasn't there. Helen told me he was working. It was late, and I didn't care much. I'd gone that long without seeing the boy."

"The gun, Dad," I said.

"I'm getting to that. So I give her some money, two grand. It's all I can do without biting into my 401k. Of course, Helen tells me it's not enough. Rehab centers cost tens of thousands of dollars. I tell her if she kisses my ass, she can keep whatever money she finds in there."

"And then what?" Amanda said.

"Then…Helen goes to the closet. I have no idea what she's doing. And suddenly out she comes holding this…this *cannon*. Then she pointed that thing at me and told me she needed money. Of course I've handled a gun or two, and I notice the safety's off. But she's holding the thing all awkward, and even though I didn't think she'd shoot me on purpose, the way she was holding it—both hands on the butt, two fingers in the trigger guard—that thing could have gone off by accident and blown my head off."

I looked at Amanda. She was thinking the same thing I was. If Helen Gaines didn't know how to handle a gun, chances are the gun she pointed at my father belonged to Stephen. He was killed with his own gun. But if my father never saw Stephen, how did his prints get on the gun? And who *did* kill him?

"So I go up to her, slowly. And before she can move I grab it out of her hands."

"Slick, Pop," I said.

"How did you take it from her?" Amanda asked.

"Just like this, I guess." My father mimicked grabbing the barrel of a gun and yanking it away, the chains holding his wrists preventing much of a visual demonstration.

"The cops say your fingerprints are on the murder weapon. If your prints were just on the barrel, and not on the trigger, they wouldn't immediately think you killed her." Amanda and my father met gazes. Then he looked down. We both knew he was lying.

"So I might have held it normal," he said.

"Come on, Dad, we're trying to help you. Nobody else will, trust me."

"I might have pointed it at her," he said.

"You might have or you did?" Amanda demanded.

"I fucking did, all right? The bitch wanted to take my hard-earned money for her junkie son, then she points a gun at me? What am I supposed to do? I just wanted to scare her, is all. Just scare her."

"Did you fire that gun?" Amanda said.

"Absolutely not," James replied. "I pointed it at her once."

"Somebody used that gun to kill Stephen Gaines," Amanda said. "If it wasn't you, someone was able to kill Stephen while keeping your prints intact."

"The killer must have used gloves," I said. "Something that didn't disturb fingerprints that were already on the weapon. Human skin has oils, that's what leaves the marks. Dry rubber gloves, if used carefully, would leave whatever marks were already on the weapon. Whoever it was not only knew enough about firearms to keep those fingerprints intact, knew him well enough to shoot him in the back of the head from close range, and was cold-blooded enough to shoot him again after blowing his brains all over the wall."

"They say keep your friends close but your enemies closer," Amanda said. "Stephen's killer must have been somebody he knew."

I noticed my father sitting there, his face looking older than ever, fear gripping his whole body. He was waiting for us to say something, to offer some piece of advice or solace that would prove he was innocent. The story he told us, assuming it was true, would have to be proven in court. But from what Detective Makhoulian had told me, Helen Gaines had disappeared. As of right now she was the only person who could corroborate my father's story. And she was a woman who certainly owed him nothing.

"Sign the waiver, Dad," I said grimly, gritting my

teeth, trying to force him to see that his only option would be to fight nobly. The longer he held out, the more public opinion would tilt away from his favor. "Go to New York. We can do more for you there than we can here."

"I don't want to go to jail," my father said. His words were whispers, and if there was ever a moment my heart might have bled for this man, it was now.

"Mr. Parker," Amanda said. "James. All we can do right now is try to prove your innocence. We can't do that here. Henry's right. We'll find you a lawyer. We'll help you."

He looked at both of us. I could sense gratitude trying to squeeze its way through his hardened veins. Instead, James Parker simply nodded and said, "I'll sign it."

Amanda nodded, smiled. I couldn't show that emotion, that happiness. My father had been lying to me his whole life. Innocent or guilty, I had a hard time mustering pity for him. Many times over the years I'd hoped someone would lock him up for one of his crimes. As a young boy I'd wished I was strong enough to stand up to him. It didn't matter how far I went, how much I distanced myself. His sins followed me wherever I went.

Amanda got up and knocked on the door. A cop opened it, keeping his eyes on James Parker. As we left the room, saw Captain Whalin talking to two uniformed officers. When he saw us, Whalin came over, folding his arms across his chest.

"Well?" he said.

"He'll sign the waiver," I said. "Let's get this over with and get him back to New York."

Whalin let out a pleased sigh. "I'm glad to hear that. Last thing we need is another body taking up a jail cell we can't spare. He still needs to appear before the judge tomorrow morning, but that's a formality. I'll call the NYPD. We'll have the waiver ready for him to sign at tomorrow's hearing, and they'll send officers to escort him back to New York. Then he's all yours. Thanks for talking some sense into him."

Whalin walked away. I was glad to hear he wanted my father out of his hair, it would help the process move faster. I felt Amanda's hand loop through my arm. I put my palm on it. Her skin felt warm.

As we headed toward the exit, I saw a woman sitting in the lobby. Her hair was blond, unnaturally so, as though she kept her hair colorist in good business. She had on a white cotton blouse, simple jewelry. She was teetering, swaying back and forth. Her arms were wrapped around her thin body, one hand covering her mouth. She looked like she was debating between falling over and vomiting. A pair of knitting needles poked out from her handbag. Memories came flooding back. The more he raged, the more she knit. Losing herself in stitches and patterns.

"Mom?" I said, approaching nervously. I hadn't seen her in a long time. That pale, thin body turned around, hand still at her mouth. She cocked her head to one side, trying to determine whether she knew the man standing in front of her.

"Is that…oh my God, is that you, Henry?"

Suddenly she righted herself, ran over as fast as her sensible shoes could carry her. She flung her arms around me and I found myself nearly supporting her entire body weight. She sobbed onto my shoulder as I bit my lip, did everything I could not to break down as well.

"The police...they called me at Spano's house.... What have they done to him?" she wailed. My mother pulled away, looked at me, hoping for some answer, some assurance that this might have been a terrible joke.

"He's going to be okay, Mom," I said, trying to inject belief into that line when deep down there was none. "It's a big misunderstanding."

"When are they going to let him out? I bought chicken breasts for dinner."

"Mom," I said, "I don't think he'll be back in time for dinner."

"Then when will he be back?"

I looked at Amanda. Her eyes said, *What do you want me to do?* My mother looked so lost, confused. It wasn't that I didn't have the heart to tell her the truth about my father and Stephen Gaines, it was that for whatever reason, she'd lost the ability to truly understand just how many wrongs this man had committed toward her. Over the years her defenses had rusted. Nothing allowed in, no anger, hostility or resentment out. I wondered, now, if my attitude toward him, my anger, was compounded by the lack of hers.

"I don't know when," I said. I took her hand. Held it. She held on to mine, but her eyes were far off, distant, trying to process the situation but clearly failing. To her, the notion of my father being arrested was like him being sent into outer space.

"Well, what do I do?" she said. "Should I wait at home for him to be released?"

"Home is a good idea, Mom," I said. "Do you have money?"

She thought about this. "I don't know our checking-account information, but we keep a jar of emergency money in a safe."

"How much is in there?" I asked.

"Five thousand dollars," she said.

"That should be enough for now," I said.

"Mrs. Parker?" Amanda said. My mother turned to her. "My name is Amanda Davies. I'm Henry's...friend. I'm a lawyer, so please don't talk to anybody you don't know. Don't speak to reporters, don't give anybody money, and only talk to the police if you have a lawyer present. If you need one, tell the detective on the case and he'll help you retain one, free of charge. We'll do our best to get your husband out of this as soon as we can. So put that chicken in the freezer."

"Thank you, dear," my mom said, her eyes twinkling as she smiled at Amanda. "You said you're a friend of Henry's...are you two in college together?"

My mouth opened, but I didn't say anything. Amanda responded, "Something like that. You're welcome to come to New York with us if—"

"Oh no, I could never do that." It was definitive. I wondered when my mother last left the state.

"Do you want us to, I don't know, come over for dinner?" I asked.

"Oh no," she said fervently. "The house is a god-awful mess."

I nodded, felt my eyes begin to sting.

"Then I'll call you as soon as we get back," I said. "Be strong. We'll sort this out. Remember what

Amanda said. Don't talk to strangers, and also don't believe anything anyone says about Dad."

"I know your father," she said sweetly. "If anyone says he did something wrong, they just don't know James."

"I love you, Mom. It's good to see you." I approached, wrapped my arms around her. She hugged me back, fragile, like the tension in her joints might cause them to shatter. When we untangled, I held her hands for an extra moment, then she let them go. Sitting back down, she turned her attention to the ceiling. And we walked away.

"You okay?" Amanda asked. She could tell I was rattled. More than that. It was all my memories—good, bad and wrenching—flowing back at once.

"I'm not sure yet."

"Will she be okay?"

"She's survived being married to him for almost thirty years. I think a little while without him will be easier."

"How are *you* holding up?" she asked.

"Given the circumstances? Could be worse. I haven't had the nervous breakdown I was sure was coming when I saw her."

"Do you believe your father's story? About the gun? The money?"

I sighed. "Guess I have to. You know what's funny?"

"What?"

"I've never felt closer to him. Guess not too many sons and fathers can have being accused of murder as a way to relate to each other."

10

Amanda and I sat in the first row of the Bend County District Courthouse as my father was led into the room in handcuffs. My mother sat next to us, her eyes distant like she was viewing a movie, not watching her husband accused of murder. He was seated at a small wooden table next to a man in a natty suit, his temporary court-appointed lawyer, Douglas Aaronson. Once the case was transferred to New York we'd have to find him new representation. None of us could afford much of anything, so the best we could hope for was someone competent enough to either prove my father's innocence, or at least keeps things progressing until we could prove it ourselves.

Judge Catherine Rawling entered the courtroom. "All rise," the bailiff said. Everyone stood up. Aaronson had to prompt my father. He stood up awkwardly. Rawling was younger than I would have expected for a judge, late thirties, with close-cropped blond hair. Her face was emotionless as she took her chair. She looked at my father for a moment.

"Be seated," she said, averting her gaze. Chairs and

benches squeaked as we obeyed. "Counselor, I'm under the impression that Mr. Parker has agreed to sign the nonjudicial waiver. Is that correct?"

The lawyer next to my father stood up, hands at his sides. "Yes, Your Honor."

"Do you have that document present?"

The bailiff, a hulking bald man, approached the table and took the paper from Aaronson. He brought it up to Judge Rawling, who put on a pair of reading glasses and pored over the sheet. Once finished, she looked up.

"I now remand James Parker to the custody of the New York Police Department, who have a warrant out for Mr. Parker's arrest on the charge of murder in the first degree."

I shuddered as I heard those words. Though my father and I had this terrible thing in common, I'd thankfully never heard those words uttered. They seemed to affect him too, as he turned to the lawyer, eyes open, as though expecting the man to suddenly yell *surprise* and remove the handcuffs.

Rawling continued.

"Mr. Aaronson, am I also correct in the information that two deputies from the NYPD have arrived to take Mr. Parker into custody pending a grand jury hearing?"

"That is correct, Your Honor." So far Aaronson was doing a bang-up job.

"Bailiff," Rawling said, "please show them in."

The bailiff walked to the double doors at the front of the courtroom. He pulled them open, and nodded at whoever was waiting outside to follow him. When the bailiff reentered, there were two men trailing him. One was a young officer, couldn't have been more than twenty-four or -five, but with muscles that stretched out his blue uniform. And right behind him, wearing a standard suit, to my surprise, was Detective Sevi Makhoulian.

"Your Honor," the bailiff said. "Officer Clark and Detective Makhoulian of the NYPD."

"Thank you, Bailiff. I hereby grant transfer of this prisoner into custody of the NYPD for extradition to New York City." She looked at the two cops as she spoke. "From this point forward James Parker is under your responsibility and jurisdiction, in accordance with New York State. Gentlemen, thank you for your promptness in coming out here. Mr. Parker," she said, "you are remanded into the custody of these officers."

The bailiff approached. The three men took my father by his cuffs and led him outside. As soon as they did, Amanda and I got up and followed.

"Detective!" I shouted. Makhoulian turned around. He looked slightly surprised to see me.

"Henry," he said.

"My father's innocent," I blurted. I had no idea how he was supposed to respond to that. Maybe part of me was hoping he'd simply nod, smack his head and say, "Whoops, you're right!"

Needless to say, that did not happen.

"Henry, we can talk more in New York. For now, it's my job to get your father back to New York safely. All you can do is make sure that happens."

"How can I do that?" I asked.

"Stay away. Go home. There's nothing more you can do right now."

Then Makhoulian and Officer Clark took my father by his manacles and led him away.

"There's a computer in the courthouse library," Amanda said. "Let's change our flight home and get the next plane out of here. He's right. There's nothing more we can do here."

After a brief goodbye to my mother, we managed to book a red-eye from Portland to JFK. I would have thought that after everything we'd been through, the confrontation with my father, the arrest, the hearing, that I would have slept like a baby. And while Amanda's head rested comfortably on my shoulder while she slept, I was awake the whole flight, my eyes open, staring at nothing. Wondering how this had happened.

When the crew turned off the cabin lights to allow other passengers to sleep, I stayed up in the dark. Nausea had taken the place of normal functions, and a cold sweat had been running down my back for hours.

I couldn't understand it, not a word. That I had a brother to begin with, even one related only half by blood, was shock enough. That my father—that *his* father—was now accused of murdering him, that was enough to make my world stop.

And as I sat there, one image refused to leave my mind's eye: that of my father, clothed in dirty pants and a rumpled shirt, being led away from the courtroom in handcuffs. I'd grown up used to a sense of rage in the man's eye, a frustration and impotence that perhaps the world had left him in the dust. His voice and mannerisms were that of an animal who bore its claws at anyone who came close, and even when he seemed calm, the wrong look could turn him into a different man.

Yet thinking about him, head bowed, hands behind his back, he looked less like a beast than a small dog being led somewhere he didn't understand for reasons he couldn't comprehend. He looked defeated. Lost.

And I wondered if, somehow, my father didn't think that in some way he deserved it.

I thought about Amanda's line of questioning, and my father's answers. According to him, Helen Gaines had called him for money to help Stephen battle his addiction. My father said the money was for rehab, to help him kick the drugs. This was possible, I supposed, remembering the state Stephen was in when I saw him on the street. He looked like a man whose rope had been pulled as taut as possible, one more tug causing it to snap.

But my father had admitted to holding the gun, aiming it in such a way that his fingerprints would be found on the trigger and butt. For a jury to believe he did all of that—and that Stephen Gaines had coincidentally been murdered by a different man using the same gun on that same day—was pushing the limits of reasonable doubt. If I wasn't his son, if I hadn't lived with the man for eighteen years, if I hadn't been able to look into those eyes, I would doubt his innocence myself.

And deep down, a small part of me did doubt it.

When we landed, I had a message waiting for me from Wallace Langston. I hadn't spoken to Wallace since we left for Bend, and no doubt my father's arrest would be reported in local papers. The *Gazette* would have to cover it, as would the *Dispatch,* our biggest rival. I only hoped that Paulina Cole wouldn't get a hold of it.

Paulina Cole had actually been my coworker at the *Gazette,* but soon left for the more lucrative pastures of the *Dispatch.* There she became the paper's chief print antagonist, penning articles that were as loved as they were reviled, and always stirred up controversy. She'd slimed me in print numerous times, and had made it clear that her mission was to bring our paper down. Last year she'd penned an exposé on my mentor, Jack O'Donell, exposing his rampant alcoholism, shaming the man to the point where he'd left the paper and disappeared. I heard several rumors testifying to his whereabouts. They usually ran the spectrum of "he's in rehab in Colorado" to "he threw himself off the Verrazano Bridge."

I missed Jack deeply, the newsroom felt as if it were missing its most important gear with him gone. Yet I knew the man needed time to heal. I only hoped he would, and that the Jack O'Donnell who'd single-handedly brought the *Gazette* to journalistic prominence would return to his old, worn desk.

In my heart, I knew what I had to do. The cops had my father. They had physical evidence he was not only at the scene of the crime, but had actually handled the murder weapon. They had proof of his travel; no doubt airline bookings and credit-card receipts would show his travel plans.

And the most damaging piece of all, they had a motive.

Odds were my father would be made to stand trial by the grand jury, and he certainly wouldn't be able to afford a lawyer worth a damn. His freedom—maybe his life—would be in the hands of whatever public defender happened to have a clear docket. I'd like to say my contacts in the press might get my father someone with a little more experience, a little more court savvy, someone who would maybe even take a pro bono case or two. Unfortunately that wasn't so. Law-enforcement officials—except for a scant few—weren't big fans of mine. They still harbored a grudge for one of their own who died, and right or not, they blamed me for his death.

James Parker didn't just face an uphill climb, he faced a sheer cliff slick with ice.

When we landed, I called Wallace Langston at the *Gazette* and told him I'd be there within the hour. Amanda and I stepped into the taxi line.

"What are you going to do?" Amanda asked. I pocketed the phone as a cab pulled up.

"Only thing I can do," I said. "I need to prove he's innocent. And then find at who killed Stephen Gaines."

11

The newsroom of the *New York Gazette* felt like home. And after leaving Bend, a place I never truly thought of as one, I needed a new home. Many of the reporters I considered friends, and even those I clashed with, like Frank Rourke, had started to attain a certain grudging respect for me. I'd started here under the worst circumstances imaginable. Fresh out of college, anointed the golden boy right off the bat, and immediately embroiled in a scandal that threatened not only the integrity of the paper but my life. It's no secret which of those things most reporters considered of predominant importance.

I exited the elevator and made my way down the hall. Evelyn Waterstone saw me rounding the corner. I gave a halfhearted wave, and she snorted like I'd just pulled my pants down in the middle of the cafeteria. Evelyn was never one for endearing gestures.

Making my way to Wallace's office through the sea of dropped pens, smells of ink, paper and clothing still fresh from its wearer's most recent smoke break, I looked up to see Tony Valentine approaching.

Tony's face erupted in a toothy smile as he sped up

to meet me. I took a breath, prepared for whatever verbal bath I was about to get. Tony was wearing a blue pin-striped suit with a yellow tie. His face looked extra orange today. Either he'd fallen asleep in the tanning bed, or his mother had mated with a pumpkin.

That wolf's mouth open in a wide smile, perfect, gleaming teeth. Nobody in their life had ever been so happy to see me.

It was impossible to avoid him, so I sucked it up and prepared myself.

"Henry!" Tony shouted with the glee of a man who found a rolled-up hundred in his pocket. "Listen, my man, it's good to see you back here. I've heard some bad things about you and your pops, and you always assume the worst. So I'm glad to see you're okay, my man."

"Wait," I said, holding my hand up. "What did you hear about 'me and my pops'?"

"Oh, this and that," he said cryptically.

"Oh yeah? And who are these sources of yours?"

"Please," Tony said. "You have your channels of information and I have mine. Let's leave it at that. But listen, my man, I know a guy who knows a guy who knows a lawyer who reps all the celebrities when they, shall we say, stray on the wrong side of the law. Remember how Paris Hilton got released from prison after serving an hour for her DUI? That was my bud."

"Didn't she have to spend a month in there after the judge sent her back?"

"Wasn't my friend's fault. Judge was an idiot. Can't luck out every time, but you can pay for the best luck possible. Hey, and keep your head up, because they're salivating for scandal over at the *Dispatch*."

"That surprises me about as much as the sun rising."

This didn't come as a shock to me, since Paulina Cole had all but made it her duty to end my career. So far the only surprise was that it hadn't been plastered over the front page. Since my only use for Tony Valentine was as a font of information, I decided to play along.

"Out of curiosity, *my man,* why haven't they moved on the story?"

"Oh, they've moved on it all right," he said, running his hand flat along the air like a traveling car. "Right now it's buried on page nine. Word is Ted Allen is still basking in their Jack O'Donnell scoop. He thinks pouncing on you too hard will make them look vindictive and undercut their efforts to shut us down. So they're waiting until the trial gets under way, and based on how the evidence looks, they'll report accordingly."

I felt a knot rise in my stomach. Ted Allen ran the *Dispatch,* and since Paulina Cole worked for him, I was never far off their radar. The evidence looked pretty bad. Hopefully Tony didn't have sources at the police department that would spill details. I trusted the man as far as I could throw his veneer, but it was always good to be prepared for whatever came next. I had no doubt my father would get beaten in the press, but knowing what was coming could soften the blow.

I thanked Tony and continued on. I knew his direct line, just in case.

Waving hi to Rita, Wallace Langston's secretary, I walked into his office. We both likely knew what was coming, but that didn't make it any easier. At least I could be thankful that this would probably hurt us both equally. Wallace was wearing a brown sport jacket. I recognized the coat. A few months ago he'd chewed his pen too deep during a meeting and the blue ink spilled all over the breast. He'd gotten it cleaned the next day, but the stain didn't wash out fully. Now a small, quarter-size blue circle remained.

He didn't seem to care, and nobody else did. We all knew Wallace had much bigger things to worry about, and Lord knew how many other stains and abrasions existed where we couldn't see. Oddly enough, we respected him for that. To Wallace, the work was more important than the gloss, the ink more important than anything. So we didn't mention it.

Other than the occasional chewed-to-death pen we left on his desk as a friendly reminder.

Wallace looked up when he saw me come in. His lips were tight beneath the closely shaved beard. His eyes were bloodshot, as usual. He was hardly a peppy man, unless he was excited about a story. And bad news seemed to take him over like a death shroud. He wore his heart on his sleeve, and unfortunately I'd had far too many experiences piercing that heart.

I hoped it was strong enough for one more.

"I need some time off," I said.

Wallace nodded. I was right. He knew this was coming.

"I'm sorry about your father. But I don't think that's the right decision."

"He's innocent," I said. "I need to help prove it."

Wallace nodded again. Not at the information, but because he respected my feelings. "I imagine it might be tough to work under those circumstances."

"Probably right," I said.

"Might also help keep you focused," Wallace said. "I don't pretend to know everything about you, Henry. But I know what you live for. You take that away, even for a little while, you forget who you are."

"The past few days have shown me that *I* don't even know who I am."

"If you want time," Wallace said, "I can give you a leave of absence. Or, you can stay on the job. Do what you need to, but keep your nose to the grindstone anyway. Some of the best work reporters do is during times of crisis. If that's too much to ask, I understand. But it might also be good for you. Give you another outlet."

"I don't know," I said, considering what Wallace was saying. "I need to do what feels right here. And right now I don't know what that is."

"What's right to one man is wrong to another. You over anyone should know that by now. Every villain is the hero of their own story, Henry. If your father is innocent, somebody killed Stephen Gaines for a reason that they felt was justified. If you can aid his defense, that's a noble deed. I don't want to sway you. But I've seen too many young reporters get lost in the chaos. You have a great career ahead of you. You end up in the middle of trouble more than anyone I've ever known. And you can either use that, work with it, or you can let it consume you. You do what you want, Henry."

I nodded. Wallace was right. And in the past, he'd always stood by me. I'd like to think I'd earned his trust through hard work, and that even if I did get myself into the occasional—okay, regular—scrape, it would be because I was doing the right thing.

"With Jack and I both gone," I said, "that's a big hit."

"Don't I know it. Hey, I never said I didn't have the paper's interests in mind, too."

The way Wallace said it, he wanted me to know he had more on his mind than a simple lack of writers. The *Gazette* had been engaged in a bloodbath with the *Dispatch* over the last few years, each doing whatever it could to lure new readers into the fold. Our industry wasn't quite dying, but it was being forced to deal with innumerable obstacles.

Each reader was valuable. Each demographic worth its weight in gold. Jack had amassed a large and passionate readership over the years through his columns, his books and his numerous awards. Though I hated to think of myself as a quantity, I got enough letters from readers to know that there were quite a few people tuning in to our pages to see what stories Henry Parker had unearthed that day.

If I took a leave, I'd be pulling away one more tent pole that was keeping the *Gazette* upright. I owed Wallace. And Jack. I loved the *Gazette,* and if years from now I was still cranking away on my keyboard racking up bylines while my fake teeth were chattering around in my mouth, I'd be a happy old codger.

And yes, blood is thicker than ink. As little as I owed James Parker and Stephen Gaines, I owed them my best efforts. I had to help find Stephen's killer, to get my father out of prison. It didn't look like the cops were going to bend over backward to dig up new leads. They had their man, and likely enough evidence to send him away for a long time.

And perhaps send him somewhere a lot deeper than a prison cell.

"I'll stay in the game, Coach," I said. Of course, I couldn't be sure how effective I would be. I had no idea where the truth about Stephen Gaines lay, or where exactly to begin my search.

Wallace smiled.

"I'm glad to hear that. For both of us. You have my number, Henry," he said. "Keep in touch. Go fight the good fight."

"Thanks, sir," I said.

"I mean it, Henry. Keep in touch. It's not too much to ask for a good story, is it?"

"No, sir," I said. "Not at all. Thanks, Wallace."

Wallace nodded. "You're going through something not many do. Stay safe, Henry. And stay smart."

I said I would. But I wasn't sure if I meant it.

12

Leaving the *Gazette,* I endured a brief man hug–back slap from Tony Valentine. I ran my hand over my face and checked my clothes to make sure none of his spray tan had rubbed off on me. Some kind of sweet cologne did seem to have made my acquaintance, smelling like a mixture of citrus and the floor of a movie theater. A shower was my first order of business.

I called Amanda at work. She picked up on the second ring.

"Hey," she said. "How'd it go?"

"I just told the boss who'd supported me at the job of my dreams that I wanted to take some time off to look into the death of my half brother who was allegedly murdered by my father. Out of all the times I've had that conversation, I'd say this one went pretty well."

"You're funny when you're pissed off."

"Maybe I'm pissed off when I'm funny."

"No," she said. "Because you're pissed off fairly often, but you're really not that funny."

"Thanks for the pep talk," I said.

"Seriously, Henry. How'd it go?"

I rubbed my forehead. "Felt like crap," I said. "Wallace convinced me to stay on the job, but I can't help but feel he's disappointed in me. With Jack gone, they can't spare to lose a lot of writers. But he also knows how important this is. I can't let him down."

"So what are you going to do now?"

"Now?" I said. "Start at the beginning."

Gaines was found murdered in Alphabet City, near Tompkins Square Park, according to the papers. The park itself was bordered by Tenth street on the north and Seventh street on the south, and lay between Avenues A and B. It had a tumultuous history, dating back to the 1980s when it was a petri dish for drugs and homeless people.

An infamous riot occurred in 1988 when the police attempted to clear the park of its homeless population, and forty-four people were injured in the ensuing chaos. Since then the park had been closed several times for refurbishment, and between that and the increasing gentrification of the neighborhood, it was now a pleasant place to hang out, play basketball and just enjoy a nice summer day.

I took the 6 train down to Union Square, then transferred to the El, which I rode to First Avenue. First bordered Peter Cooper Village, or Stuyvescent Town, a woodsy enclave largely populated by recent college grads who liked the cheap rent, younger families who enjoyed the well-tended parks, and older residents whose rents were stabilized and who hadn't paid an extra dime since New York was the capital of the Union.

As I approached the park, it was hard to believe a murder could occur in such a pleasant area. Parks seemed to be the one place where all the stress and hostility emptied out of the city. Where families became instant friends, children ran around while their parents watched approvingly, and young men and women played sports and chatted without playing the stupid mating games that choked you to death at any bar.

I wondered what in the hell Stephen Gaines was doing here when he was killed. If he lived here, did his habit go unnoticed? When I saw him on the street, he looked as if he was on the tail end of a ten-year bender. In an area geared toward family, I could hardly imagine he was a welcome sight. Chances were if someone saw him stumbling around like I witnessed him doing, they'd call the cops.

I realized as I approached the park that I had nothing to show people. Not a photo identifying traits, or personality quirks. All I knew about Stephen Gaines was the image of him on the street, and then on the slab in the medical examiner's office. I hoped the trusty New York City newspapers were more up to speed than I was.

I stopped at a small bodega that had a cartful of newspapers out front. I bought three papers—the *Gazette,* the *Times,* and even the *Dispatch.* When it came to finding my brother's killer, I wasn't above supporting the competition if it meant getting the information I needed.

Thumbing through the papers, I was pleasantly surprised to find that the *Gazette* was the only one that printed a photo of Gaines. It looked like a driver's-license shot. He was looking straight into the camera, serious yet a little confused, as though he didn't quite understand what he was doing there. His hair was much shorter than when I'd seen it, and the man looked about ten years younger as well. Clearly he wasn't the kind to show up in a lot of photographs, and I had a feeling combing through MySpace and Facebook likely wouldn't yield many, either.

The article was brief. Though it did mention my father.

Stephen Gaines, 30, was found shot to death in his Alphabet City apartment late Monday night. At this time one arrest has been made in the killing, one James Parker of Bend, Oregon. Parker is alleged to be the estranged father of Gaines, though the police have not made any comment on Parker's motivation or why he was in New York City the night of Gaines's death.

Referred to Detective Sevi Makhoulian of the NYPD, the officer said simply, "I have no doubt that the district attorney's office will be prosecuting Parker to the fullest extent of the law. As for details of the case, those are pending and will become available as the trial progresses."

There was no photo of my father, and the snippet did not mention me. I wondered if the paper should have done so, or if this was another example of Wallace protecting me. I only hoped he knew I'd repay the effort.

I ripped out the picture from the *Gazette* and tossed the rest of the papers in the trash.

I was no detective. My career thus far had progressed almost solely on instinct. Seeing a thread, no matter how thin or frayed the strand, and pulling on it until something larger unspooled. At this point, though, I had no thread. There was nothing to pull on. No leads, no witnesses. Nothing.

So I started where any reporter or cop would when they had nothing.

When in doubt, talk to everybody.

I walked straight into Tompkins Square Park looking for young families and older pedestrians. I figured those were people most likely to come to the park because they lived in the vicinity. And if they lived nearby, there was a greater chance they might have seen Stephen Gaines at some point.

But what if they *had* seen him? That hardly meant they saw him being killed, or even knew who he was, what he did, or anything about him. Still, it was the best shot I had.

Walking around, I noticed a couple in their early thirties sitting on a bench. A baby stroller sat in front of them. I hated bothering nice people who looked like they just wanted to spend their afternoon relaxing with loved ones, but I hoped they'd understand.

Of course not too many people could sympathize with trying to hunt down the man who'd killed your brother, while your father sat in prison.

I approached the couple in as nonthreatening a manner as possible. Smiling, even. They paid no attention to me until I got closer and it was clear they were my targets. The husband looked up at me, and I noticed his hand slowly plant itself on his wife's leg. Guarding her. Nobody trusted young people these days.

"I'm so sorry to bother you," I said, putting my hand out in apology. "I was wondering if you happened to have seen this man in the area."

I showed them the picture from the paper. They looked at it long enough and with enough confusion to show they didn't know him.

The wife said, "No, I'm sorry."

I thanked them for their time. Then it was on to the next stop.

I approached an older black man sitting at a chess table. The other seat was unoccupied. He was studying the board, perhaps planning out moves in his head. I crouched down at the other side of his table, cleared my throat awkwardly.

"Excuse me," I said.

"Have a seat, young man," he said, his mouth breaking into a smile. He reached into his briefcase and pulled out a cloth containing numerous chess pieces. "Pick your poison. Speed chess? I've got a killer Danish Gambit, so hold on to your hat."

"I'm not looking for a game," I said somewhat apologetically. "I was wondering if you might have seen this man before."

He looked at the picture, a blank expression on his face. He said he'd never seen Gaines, and I believed him.

I spent the rest of the day questioning every person I could find in the park, until by the end people started to recognize me as having pestered half the lot and they began to move away before I even approached them. One couple I asked twice within half an hour.

Nobody had seen Gaines. Nobody had noticed him. He was a ghost in his own neighborhood. Or at least to these people.

When people asked what I was looking for, I

mumbled something about him having gone missing. If they knew I was looking into a murder, they'd clam up faster than a vegetarian at a barbecue.

The sun began to set. So far my efforts had yielded nothing. I took a seat on a park bench. Desperation had come and gone, and I was left holding a crumpled photo of a man I barely knew, who'd lived a life seemingly nobody had known. Several days ago none of this mattered. Work was good. My relationship seemed to finally be on stable ground. And now here I was, bothering strangers, hoping they might have happened, by some ludicrous hope, to have seen someone other than my father shoot a man in the back of the head. Or at least knew more about Stephen than I did which was next to nothing.

I was searching for a needle in the East River, with no clue which way the current was flowing.

I was about to give up, to try to think of a new angle to attack from, when a shadow fell over me. I looked up to see a young woman, late twenties or so, standing in front of me. She was reed thin, one arm dangling limp by her side while the other crossed her chest, holding the opposite shoulder. Her hair was red and black, mascara haphazardly applied. Perhaps twenty pounds ago she'd been attractive, but now she was a walking, painted skeleton. She was wearing a long-sleeved sweater, but the fabric was dangling off her limbs. It allowed me to see the bruising underneath. The purplish marks on her skin immediately caught my attention. My pulse sped up. Her lip trembled. I didn't have to show her the newspaper clipping. I knew what she was going to say even before she opened her mouth.

"I knew Stephen."

13

A cup of steaming tea was set in front of me. It smelled like mint. She offered me milk, which I politely declined. I watched her sit down, a cup of the same at her lips. She'd poured both from the same kettle, so I didn't have to worry about being poisoned. I began to think about how much more paranoid I'd become over the years.

"Thanks," I said.

"Don't mention it. I brew three pots a day."

I nodded, took a look around.

This woman, Rose Keller, had taken me up to her apartment after I told her who I was and what I was doing. She seemed apprehensive, but once convinced of my authenticity she was more than happy to help.

She lived in a studio apartment at the top of a four-story walk-up on Avenue B and Twelfth Street. The floor was covered with gum wrappers, the walls decorated with posters of vintage album covers and artsy photographs, usually of frighteningly skinny women shaded in odd pastel light. The room smelled like patchouli and cinnamon. Our tea rested on what appeared to be an antique trunk, covered in customs stickers from every corner of the earth. Portugal, Greenland, Syndey, Prague, the Sudan. This woman didn't look like she traveled much. Odds were she'd bought the pieces, stickers already applied.

The bed was unmade, and I noticed a large box sticking out from underneath. She saw me looking at it, said, "Clothes. I keep meaning to donate them."

She was lying, but I wasn't here to judge.

"So how did you know Stephen?" I asked.

"We used to…" She looked away from me. Then she pulled a lighter from her sock, took a bent cigarette from a drawer. "You mind if I smoke?"

"Go right ahead."

She took out a glass ashtray and set it on the table. It was crusted with old butts and ash. Flicking the lighter, she lit the cig and took a long puff, holding it aloft between two fingers.

"We used to get high together," she said.

"Used to?" I asked.

"I met him when I moved to the city eight years ago. Wanted to be on Broadway, you know? All that kicking and dancing. I was voted 'most likely to succeed' in high school. Starred in all the drama shit. Figured I'd come here and show those Rockette girls how things are really done."

"And then?"

"It's a tough gig," she said like a woman who'd given up the dream long ago and had come to peace with it. "Too tall. Too fat. Too short. Nose too big. Tits too small. There's always an excuse. So I started waitressing in Midtown, cool little Irish pub. Some of the actors used to go there for a drink after the shows. Then I'd come back here, get high and crash. That's how I met Stephen."

"How exactly did you meet him?"

"Funny story," she said, taking another long drag. "I used to call this guy named Vinnie when my stash needed re-upping. Well, his name wasn't actually Vinnie. It was kind of a global pseudonym that all the runners used, they'd all call themselves Vinnie. There were probably a dozen different Vinnies working at any given time, covering different parts of the city. So one day I'm outside on the stoop waiting, and another guy kind of ambles up and just stands around. I can tell from the way he's walking, kind of looking at the street, side to side, he was *definitely* a user. So I said hi. He said hi back. Vinnie rolls up half an hour later, this greaser wearing a hat turned sideways, couldn't have been a day over fifteen, and fills us both up. And since it's always more fun to see those bright lights with company, we went back to his place."

Rose's eyes flickered to the walls, then back to the table. There was sorrow and pain in her eyes that hadn't been there a minute ago. She was trying to stay cool, but I could tell she'd cared about Stephen.

"It was kind of funny, because Stephen and Vinnie had this little, I don't know, chat. Friendly, like two buds. I figured Stephen had used this guy before. You know how sometimes you order pizza so often, the delivery guy kind of becomes your pal? At first it's all tips and friendly hi's but then you're talking about the weather. One pizza guy actually asked me out once. That's when I knew I needed to learn how to cook."

"How long did you know Stephen?" I asked.

Rose sniffed, tapped out her cigarette until it stopped smoking. Then she placed it in the ashtray amidst a graveyard of used butts. She stared at them for a moment, like a woman who'd been trying for years to quit and realized just how addicted she was.

"Just about seven years."

"Were you two close?"

"Depends on when you mean," she said. Her voice had become a little more abrasive. She had feelings for Stephen, but there had been some bad times, too. I imagined that when two junkies got together it wasn't exactly Ozzie and Harriet. If a relationship between two such people could be thought of as "tumultuous," it was probably the best one could hope for. I'd had enough relationships that were able to find trouble on their own without the uncertainty caused by stimulants and hallucinogenic substances.

"Did you date?" I asked, hoping she wouldn't get offended at my prying.

"Again," she said bitterly, "depends on when you're talking about."

"Were you seeing each other when Stephen got killed?"

"Hell, no," she said irritably. "See, thing is, after a while you get tired of the life. It's one thing to be irresponsible and screwing around in your twenties. I mean, everyone does it. Most folks don't settle down by twenty-five and spend time worrying about a mortgage and a 401k. I didn't, and neither did Stephen. But then you hit thirty, and you're still renting a studio smaller than a shoe box, and guys like Vinnie stay the same age because whoever the dude is who supplies them just keeps hiring high-school kids. Funny. I must have had half a dozen dealers all named Vinnie, all under the age of twenty-one. You know how stupid you feel when you're thirty and some kid is selling to you, and you know he's still in high school and probably makes more money than you?"

"So you were looking to go clean," I said.

"Have been for a year now," Rose said. She stood up, picked up the ashtray and brought it into the kitchen where she tapped out the contents into a trash bin. She came back, put the tray back into a drawer like it had never been taken out. "Trying, at least. The hooks are a lot easier to dig in than they are to pull out."

"What about Stephen?"

Rose sighed, leaned back in her chair. A wistfulness crossed her face. "I thought he was trying to quit. He seemed like he was. See, I never really thought Stephen had that serious a problem. Just recreational crap. I mean, everyone smokes a bit. Shoots up a bit. It's all about keeping it under control. I did that, and then I quit. Stephen never quit. And in case you haven't noticed, addicts never stay even keel. They either get better or they get worse."

"And Stephen got worse."

"Like cancer," she said.

I looked again at the skin under Rose's shirt. I could see the bruises weren't track lines, but destroyed veins. Dark blues and black, yellow skin surrounding them. Perhaps even an infection gone untreated. Whether drug addiction started off as a disease I didn't know, but sure as hell once those hooks dug in, the virus swam around in your system until it ate you from the inside.

"What do you do for a living, Rose? I mean, all those drugs couldn't be cheap."

"Graphic designer," she said proudly. "I make eighty grand a year."

She noticed how impressed I was.

"And your employer, they…"

"Never knew a thing. Been working for a television studio doing Web site design for six years. They figure the geeks are wired differently than everyone else, and that we were all born in the same freaky nursery. So you come in with your hair messed up smelling like stale cigarettes and beer, they figure you were up late 'hacking.' Most people can't differentiate between a designer and a programmer. As long as you know html, you're golden. As if they even knew what the letters stand for."

"Stephen," I said. "What did he do?"

The moment I said it I felt a sadness. The more I learned about Stephen Gaines the closer I got to him. The more I despised having never known this man at all.

"I know he tried to write for a while. He wanted to do culture reporting, trend pieces…" Rose's voice trailed off.

"Did he get any published?"

"No," she said. "I'm not sure he ever really tried. He just talked about it."

"So how did he make a living?"

"You know," she said, furrowing her brow, "I'm not really sure. But at some point he stopped talking about writing altogether. The drugs got a hold of him worse than ever. It was all he could do to get up in the morning, and he looked like death when he did. I barely saw him after that."

"When was the last time you saw him?" I asked.

"A week ago," Rose said. She sighed again, but this time a sob cracked the noise. Her eyes began to water. As hard as this was for me, I didn't know Stephen at all. This woman had lost a loved one. A lover.

"He said he was going to get clean," she said, the cracks in her voice becoming more evident. "He promised me. He said he was going to get help. Rehab. We spoke on the phone. He swore on his mother. Then he stopped returning my calls."

Rehab, I thought. My father said Helen Gaines was looking for money to help Stephen get help. That part sounded like it was true. But unfortunately all it did in the eyes of a prosecutor was likely bolster my father's motive in Stephen's murder.

"Did you know Helen at all?" I asked.

Rose nodded. "They lived together. She was dirt poor, and Stephen seemed to make enough money to pay rent and keep food on the table. I met her maybe half a dozen times. Kind of quiet, like she was scared of life. Made good coffee, but never drank it with you, if you get my meaning."

"I got it," I said. "You wouldn't by any chance happen to have her contact information, would you?"

"I don't have a phone number or e-mail or anything like that. But when Stephen used to write, he'd always go to this cabin in the Adirondacks up by Blue Mountain Lake. I think Helen's parents left it to her or something. He went up there to work, and Helen usually went with him. She was quiet enough, and it's not like she had anyone else. Not exactly the kind of woman who liked to be alone."

The Adirondacks were about a four-and-a-half-hour drive northwest of the city. I'd never been up there, but knew it was a popular spot for camping, hiking and just getting away from the world for a while.

Something a mother might do if her only son was murdered.

"Rose," I said, "would you mind giving me that address?"

14

We finished the car rental paperwork by noon, then loaded the vehicle up with coffee, snacks and Amanda's iPod. I fought the good fight to bring mine, but lost despite a valiant effort. To be honest, it wasn't much of a fight since I learned early in our relationship that when it came to playing music, Amanda had the one and only vote. The only thing I could do was learn to love Fleetwood Mac and early Britney Spears. Though I did worry that listening to "Rumors" right after "Oops!… I Did It Again" might cause my head to distend like when you poured cold water on hot metal.

It was Saturday. Hopefully we wouldn't hit much traffic, the rest of the city either sleeping off hangovers or snacking on fried dough with powdered sugar at a street fair.

Luckily the car had an iPod dock built in. Amanda hooked it up and began scrolling through songs. I started the engine and pulled into traffic and headed toward the George Washington Bridge.

"You know, isn't there some kind of rule stating that whoever drives gets to choose the music?"

"I think that law was considered outdated in the 1970s. Now the female in the car gets to choose the tunes."

"What if there's more than one woman in the car?" I asked.

"Then it goes to the most dominant female," she said drily. "If need be you lock them all in a steel cage and whoever is the last one alive chooses the music. Kind of like Mad Max Beyond Thunderdome."

"Nice to know after all these years Mel Gibson still exerts influence over all realms of pop culture."

"Stop whining," she said. "Here. Try this one. And if I hear one reference to 'sugartits' you can walk upstate alone."

She pressed Play, and soon a familiar tune came over the speakers. It was Bob Dylan's "Not Dark Yet." It was a beautiful, melancholy song. I looked at her, confused.

"I know you like this song," she said, a sweet smile spread across her lips. "I figured we can split music choices. There's more stuff you like on there."

I stayed quiet, just smiled at her, listened to Dylan sing.

As we began the drive, we fell into a routine that was becoming familiar and comforting. Our conversations came easily. Each silence felt warm rather than simply because of a lack of topics to discuss. Being by this girl's side filled me up in a way I'd never truly experienced. Nothing between us had been forced. From the moment we met during the most stressful situation imaginable, there were a million moments when, if we'd not been stronger, things could have broken apart. Not too long ago I'd done just that. I thought I was being noble, chivalrous. Putting her life before mine. I learned quickly my heart didn't agree with that decision, and neither of us had rested easy.

When I contacted her for help on a story—that phone call as much for emotional help as professional—it was only a matter of time before we got back together. Amanda was smart, tough, resilient. Stronger than I was. And together we were more than the sum of our parts. If not for her, my father might still be sitting in an Oregon prison trying to simply wait out the legal process. At least now we had a chance to help set things right.

Of course, the one bad thing about being together was our tendency to snack. We went through two large coffees, a giant bag of Combos and half a dozen cookies by the time we hit I-95. If we kept going at this pace I'd have to ask Amanda to start hauling my big ass around in a pickup truck to talk to sources.

The scenery driving up was truly breathtaking. Pine trees studded the landscape as we passed numerous hiking and cross-country skiing trails. There was little up here for visitors other than what nature offered. I could see why Stephen Gaines liked to come here. As much as I loved the clicks and clacks of the newsroom, there was something about the peace and quiet this area offered that appealed to me.

It was six o'clock by the time we turned onto I-87 North heading toward Blue Mountain Lake. The city itself was nestled in Hamilton County, in the town of Indian Lake. After passing Albany and Saratoga Springs, we turned onto Route 28 toward Indian Lake.

The drive down 28 was breathtaking. The roads were

teeming with lush, green trees, small-town stores and crisp blue water. It was the New York that existed outside of what people commonly associated with New York. Nearly untouched by technology, commerce and industry.

About half an hour down 28, we passed a brown-brick building on our left. The sign read, Adirondack Museum. The lettering was burned into a wooden plaque, and unlike some other museums I'd seen in my travels this one looked remarkably well maintained. It was a shame, I thought, that I'd seen so many places yet actually experienced so few. When I traveled, there was always a reason. A story, something pulling me to a destination. There was never much time to enjoy my surroundings. I was here for business, and as much as I could admire the beauty of this place, I wouldn't—at least now—be able to lose myself in it.

We drove several miles down Route 28, the majesty of Blue Mountain Lake on our left. I could picture Stephen Gaines (or was it myself?) sitting in a chair by the water, writing in a spiral-bound notebook, listening to nothing but the world itself. It was a far cry from what I'd gotten used to in the city. Either I could love being here for the blissful solitude—or it would drive me crazy not to hear blaring horns and the music of the newsroom.

There were several unpaved roads, which, according to Rose, led to various cabins. There weren't many year-round residents up here, and most of the occupants were, like Stephen and Helen, city dwellers who came to get away from the hustle and bustle. Each house stood far enough away from its neighbor to allow peace and quiet, but were close enough that it did feel like somewhat of a community up here.

As we approached the turn onto Maple Lodge Road, on the northeast ridge of Blue Mountain Lake, I noticed a set of tire tracks leading up to the cabin that looked fairly recent, and another set leading away. They looked like the same type of tread. The weather reports said that it had rained here just two days ago, so whoever had come here had done so in between the time Stephen Gaines had died and now. And if, as Rose thought, Helen *had* come here, we would hopefully find her. The tracks leading away could have been Helen shopping, picking up supplies.

Amanda turned the stereo off. I could feel the breath become shallow in my chest. Helen Gaines had to have answers. Even if she didn't know who killed her son, she would certainly know what he might have been mixed up in that got him killed. She was our only hope, our only lead. My father's only hope.

We pulled onto the driveway and slowly entered the Gaines residence. The only sounds were the rustling of leaves in the slight wind. I could hear Amanda breathing beside me. I felt her hand on my elbow for reassurance.

As we got closer we could see the cottage. It was two stories tall, made from rounded interlocking logs. The front door was bracketed by six logs surrounding a makeshift porch. A chimney jutted from a roof lined with a green material. It looked as if some sort of moss or other plant life was growing on it. The chimney was static. I lowered the window, smelled the air. It was clean. If Helen was here, she hadn't made a fire recently.

"Henry," Amanda said, her hand gripping my arm tighter. "Look at that."

In the dirt driveway, we could clearly make out the tread markings from a second set of tires. These treads were marked with numerous crisscrossing lines, both vertical and horizontal in even patterns. Truck tires tended to have more grooves, deeper cuts, better for sluicing water and specifically designed for off-roading. These tracks likely belonged to a some sort of SUV. Our eyes followed the tracks back to a clearing in the woods. Whoever had come here hadn't used the front door. They'd come in a different way. They didn't want to be seen arriving. Who could have come here besides Helen? And what kind of person would have come not wanting to be seen? Clearly, whoever had come here knew they would be coming in through the woods, and needed treads that could handle it. Somebody wanted to not be seen using the front door.

"This can't be good," Amanda said under her breath. "What if someone is still there?"

She didn't need to say that that person might not be Helen Gaines.

I stopped the car short of the driveway and put it into Park. I kept the engine running. Just in case.

With the engine purring, we both unlocked our doors and tentatively stepped into the evening air. Wind swirled around us as we stared at the cabin. I couldn't see much inside, so I crept closer, hunched low to the ground. Dirt crackled under my feet as Amanda kept pace several steps behind me.

I crept up the front steps and up to the door. Both side windows were closed, and a drape prevented me from viewing what was inside. I gently knocked on the door. There was no doorbell.

"Miss Gaines?" I called. "Helen?"

There was no response.

I called louder. Waited a minute. Heard nothing.

I walked back down the steps, then decided to go around the house to see what we could find.

Heart pounding in my chest, I slid up to a side window, cupped my hands to the glass and peered in.

The room was dark. There was a long couch, and I could make out a television stand and what looked like a desk. Other than that the room was impeccably clean. Peering in closer, I could see a faint yellow glow emanating from a room beyond this one. A light was on somewhere on the first floor.

"Stay here," I said to Amanda.

"Like hell," she replied. That was the end of that discussion.

Staying low, we sidled around the back of the house where another window faced the forest. Off in the distance, I could make out a narrow road, paved poorly but wide enough for a car to fit through. It did not face the front of the house, and would be unseen by anyone who was not in this room at the time. The window was mere yards from the SUV tire tracks.

There was no doubt; whoever had come here had used that path to gain access to the house.

I approached the window. My breath was ragged, and I could hear Amanda panting behind me. Gently I stood up until my eye line was just over the windowsill.

I made out the top of a shower rod and a medicine chest. This was clearly the downstairs bathroom. Then I saw it.

The right medicine cabinet was open. Pills and makeup were spread out all over the counter. Bottles were broken. Things scattered everywhere.

That's when Amanda stood up, saw the entirety of the bathroom, and let out a bloodcurdling scream.

When I saw what she was looking at, it was all I could do to stifle mine.

A body was facedown on the floor. Her blouse was ripped and tattered. Her arms were splayed out in a horribly unnatural position.

And a pool of blood was spread around her head like a gruesome sunrise.

Without thinking, I ran to the nearest tree, propped my foot against a limb and pulled until I heard a crunch and the thick branch snapped off. Taking a running start, I brought the limb back behind my head just like when I played Little League, and slammed the branch against the windowpane. The glass didn't shatter, but a large crack snaked down the middle. Just enough. Two more whacks and enough glass had broken for me to clear the rest out with the branch. I carefully climbed through the window. The blood around Helen Gaines's head looked dark red, almost dried but not completely. A small piece of metal floated in the gore, but I couldn't tell what it was. I smelled the air, a faint but still noxious odor present. I looked closer. There was a chance she was still…

I gently moved her hair away from her neck so I could check her pulse. And that's when I realized that this woman was black. It was not Helen Gaines.

I pressed three fingers against her carotid artery, praying for a pulse. I felt nothing. I pressed again, this time on her wrist. Silent. Dead.

I looked at the body.

My hands shook as I reached into my pocket and pulled out my cell phone. Thankfully there was reception. My fingers fumbled and I had to dial 911 three times before getting it right.

"911, what is your emergency?"

"A woman's been killed at 97 Maple Lodge Road. Please get here quick."

"Sir, can you check her pulse?"

"There's no pulse. Please just get here."

"All right, sir, an ambulance is on the way. Do you know the victim?"

"No," I said, nearly passing out as I sat down on the rim of the porcelain bathtub. "I don't."

Sitting in the pool of blood, about two feet away from the body, was a tiny diamond earring, lying next to another thin sliver of what looked like gray hair. The diamond was a princess cut. One day, a few weeks ago, I was looking online at engagement rings. Thinking about whether I could see Amanda wearing one. I remembered seeing the name—princess cut—and thinking it was perfect. *A princess for a princess,* I'd thought.

But there was only one earring on the ground.

The other was either taken by the killer. Or still being worn by someone who'd escaped.

Then I looked at the body again. The victim's ears weren't pierced. Which meant the single earring on the ground had belonged to Helen Gaines. And she'd dropped it before she fled.

15

Her name was Beth-Ann Downing. She lived two floors above Helen and Stephen Gaines in their apartment in Alphabet City. She and Helen had been friends for fifteen years. She owned a Camry, which she parked in a garage on Fourteenth Street. A call to the garage confirmed that Beth had taken the Camry a few days ago and had not returned it. Beth-Ann Downing was fifty-three years old. Divorced. One daughter who lived in Sherman Oaks, California, Sheryl Harrison, who was on a flight to New York City to attend her mother's funeral.

Beth had worked as a bank teller. According to the police, gas and credit-card receipts showed she'd left the city with Helen Gaines the very night Stephen Gaines was killed. A waitress at a diner on I-87 recognized Beth and said she'd been eating with another woman. That woman fit the description of Helen Gaines, Stephen's mother. Beth was either fleeing from something, or was simply helping an old friend who *was* fleeing from something.

And last night she was killed when a bullet severed

her brain stem, fired from less than a foot away. Death was almost instantaneous.

Almost.

And I wondered if Beth-Ann Downing had even known what her friend was running from.

We'd given our statement to Deputy Reece Watts of the Indian Lake Police Department. I took a little extra time washing the blood off my fingers.

We told the police everything we knew. From early forensics, it appeared that an SUV or van of some sort approached the Gaines residence during the night, when both Helen Gaines and Beth-Ann Downing were asleep. They pried open the storm shutters and snuck in through the basement.

Beth had awoken, and went downstairs to check on the noise. She saw the intruders. The police confirmed there was more than one. Several pairs of footprints, they said. They chased her to the bathroom, where they shot her. In the confusion, Helen Gaines had escaped.

That's why we saw tire tracks leaving the cabin. Helen had fled while her friend was being murdered. Nobody had any idea of the whereabouts of Helen Gaines. She hadn't called the police. Hadn't stopped anywhere for help.

She'd just disappeared.

It might have just been me, but that didn't seem like typical behavior for a woman whose only son had just recently been killed. Especially when the alleged murderer was locked up awaiting trial.

I had no idea how this would play in regards to my father. Stephen Gaines was still dead. The police were still figuring out if anything in the cabin was missing.

If they could chalk it up to a burglary gone horribly wrong. Or if there was something else. Another reason the intruders had come to that cabin in the middle of the night.

Regardless of how the autopsy and discovery came out, I couldn't believe the murder was the result of a botched robbery. The killers had brought in weapons. For protection? Maybe. To scare any residents? Perhaps. Or maybe they brought them because they were there for the sole purpose of killing Helen Gaines. And Beth-Ann Downing just got in the way.

On the ride back from Blue Lake Mountain, neither Amanda nor I said a word. The iPod sat on the armrest untouched. We had no coffee, no snacks. It was just completely and utterly silent.

I parked the car on the street near my apartment. Amanda came upstairs with me.

Upon opening the door, I had a momentary burst of fear. I generally took my safety for granted, despite the fact that I'd been the recipient of some fairly severe beatings over the past few years. I had scars on my leg, my hand and my chest as a result of intruders. Yet I wanted to believe I was safe. With Amanda I usually felt that way. But tonight, after seeing how another person's life—a *helpless* person—could be invaded and snuffed out so quickly, it made me rethink the simple dead bolt that protected my apartment.

"Did you see," Amanda said, forcing the words out, "all that blood?"

I nodded. Went into the kitchen and poured us each a glass of water. Amanda gulped hers down while I sat there holding the cool glass in my hands, wondering just what the hell was going on.

It didn't make sense that Helen Gaines would be on the run. I had to assume my father did not kill Stephen Gaines. I also had to assume that Helen Gaines knew who the real killer was. And if that was true, she fled because she did not feel like contacting the police. She fled because of something she knew, either about her son or his killer.

She'd gone to upstate New York to hide from something or someone. And not just from her son's killer. From something larger. If you fear one person, that fear can be contained, limited. Controlled. You can seek the help of cops, lawyers. There are always people who can help.

What exactly was Helen Gaines fleeing from?

I thought about what Binks and Makhoulian talked about at the medical examiner's office. Binks said that Stephen Gaines was killed by a pistol likely covered by some sort of makeshift silencer. That insinuated the murder was premeditated. Of course, any prosecutor could make the claim that my father made up his mind to kill Stephen, that his death would allow my father to keep on living without paying the money Helen wanted, or exposing his bastard child to his family. The motive would still hold up.

But then I thought about seeing Beth-Ann Downing lying facedown in that pool of blood. The scene was gruesome and hard to look at, yet I'd trained myself to do just that. You had to divest yourself of any emotional attachment. Present the facts. They would tell the story themselves.

Beth was lying in a pool of blood. I remembered seeing something floating in that pool. A small piece of gray hair. I hadn't thought much about it then, merely processed it into my memory, but now I called it back up.

The strand was very thin, very short, almost a hair's width. But it wasn't hair—it was metal.

The conversation with Binks and Makhoulian came back to me. The silenced gun that was used to kill Stephen.

Most silencers were not professional. They were made from simple items. A pillow. Aluminum tubing.

Aluminum tubing filled with steel wool.

I looked up at Amanda.

"Steel wool," I said.

"What?"

"The gun that was used to kill Stephen—whoever did it used aluminum tubing filled with steel wool to create a silencer. They didn't find evidence at Stephen's murder scene, but the coroner said the wounds suggested a silencer. But it was impossible to tell what kind of silencer was used. When I saw Beth-Ann Downing, there was a piece of metal near her body. I'm positive it was steel wool. Which means the intruders knew where Helen was. And between the silencer and the offroad tires, they didn't want anyone to know they were there."

Fear grew in Amanda's eyes. "That means the same people who killed Stephen probably killed Beth."

"And are still after Helen," I said. "Not only that, but they're actually taking precautions during the murders. According to Makhoulian, no shell casings or bullets were found at Gaines's apartment. Whoever killed him took them to prevent analysis, but left the gun itself. Somehow I don't see my father on his hands and knees picking up spent shell casings, or digging a bullet out of the wall. And why would they leave the gun?"

"Someone out there has the answer," Amanda said.

"We need to find Helen Gaines," I said. "She has to know what's going on. And something has to be frightening her enough to stay away from the cops."

"If someone doesn't want to be found," Amanda said, "they won't be found."

"Not necessarily. If you have the resources, anyone can be found. The trick isn't going from point A to point Z. There are stops in between. Each one will lead you closer. We need to find the next step, even if it only takes us a little bit closer."

"So who knew Helen Gaines besides Stephen and Beth?" Amanda said. "And who knew Stephen besides Rose Keller?"

"The question isn't necessarily who knew Helen and Stephen," I said, "but who else knew Rose and Beth? Beth-Ann Downing had a daughter. Sheryl Downing, who now goes by the name Sheryl Harrison. She's thirty-five, and according to the Indian Lake officer who spoke to Sheryl, she and Beth hadn't spoken in nearly ten years, ever since Sheryl moved to California. For there to be that kind of estrangement, something had to have driven mother and daughter apart."

"But it could be anything," Amanda said dubiously. "Maybe Beth disapproved of her daughter's husband. Maybe Sheryl didn't like her mom's cooking."

"Or maybe there was something else," I said. "It

took a lot more than burned meat loaf to make me want to leave a burning trail of rubber when I left Bend."

"So how do you plan to get in touch with Sheryl?"

"She lives in Sherman Oaks. We have her name. She's on her way to New York, but will likely still be checking her messages. Give me one minute."

I went to my laptop and booted it. Opening Internet Explorer, I went to 411.com. I plugged in Sherman Oaks as the city, then entered the name Sheryl Harrison. The page loaded for a few seconds, and then three names popped up, along with their phone numbers.

"Let's hope this works."

I called each of the three numbers. The first Sheryl Harrison picked up. I told her I had a question about her mother, Beth. She said her mother had died years ago. I thanked her and hung up. Neither of the next two were home. One of them might have been the right one. I had no idea if they were, or which one. But I left them both the same message:

"Hi, Sheryl, my name is Henry Parker. I'm so sorry for your loss. I have a question about your mother. I don't mean to pry, and I know this is a difficult time for you, but I wouldn't be contacting you if this wasn't of the utmost importance. If you can, please call me back at the following number."

I left my number on both machines, and thanked them again for their time. One Sheryl would call me back. I had to believe that. And to believe that, all I had to do was wait.

After a quick slice of pizza, I threw off my clothes and stepped into the shower. I immediately noticed there were no towels hanging on the racks. Either we'd used them all and they were in the laundry waiting to be shipped off, or Amanda had purposely taken them all out so I'd have to beg for one. I had a feeling it was the latter. For some reason she got a kick out of seeing me open the bathroom door just a crack, then squirt through the apartment naked looking for something to cover myself up with. She called this game "hide and peek," and I'd be lying if I said she was the only one who enjoyed it.

For some reason, I was too scared to play it on her.

The water felt wonderful, hot and nearly scalding. A long shower would do my body good, just to take my mind off everything. We had to start up again soon, but every brief respite was a moment to be savored.

After that, I threw a pair of shorts on while I air-dried, then went to the bed and passed out. Amanda was already asleep, surrounded by enough pillows to build a fort big enough for both of us. No reason to ask where all my towels were. Sleep came easily.

It must have been several hours later when a shrill ring woke me up from the darkness. I blinked, noticed Amanda was no longer on the bed. I groped around for the phone, forgetting where I'd placed it. Then I heard Amanda from the living room.

"Henry, your phone is ringing!"

"Who is it?" I replied, picking crust from my eyes. "Check the caller ID."

"I don't know, but it's an 818 area code."

Eight-one-eight. That was a California area code.

I leaped out of bed, toppling half a dozen pillows onto the floor. I was wearing nothing but a towel. Not like whoever was calling would notice. Then I bolted out of the bedroom—stark naked, the towel fluttering to the floor—and made a beeline for the phone.

Amanda was standing there, holding it in one hand while trying to stifle a laugh with her other.

"Sweet dreams?" she said, looking south.

I scowled at her, crossed my legs, grabbed the phone, looked at the ID and pressed Send.

"Hello?" I said, hoping I'd made it in time.

"Is this…Mr. Parker?" It was a woman's voice I did not register in my memory.

"Yes, who is this?"

"Sheryl Harrison. I had a voice mail from a Henry Parker asking to call back at this number. Something about my mother."

"Yes, Mrs. Harrison, thank you *so* much for calling me back. I was wondering if I could talk to you about your mother, Beth. Do you have a few minutes?"

"I'm leaving the church right now. My mother's funeral is tomorrow. I have an hour before my appointment with the florist, that's all the time I can give you. If you can meet me on Twenty-seventh and Third, you'll have whatever time is remaining before my appointment."

"I'm leaving right now," I said, looking around to see where I put my pants.

"Just so we're clear, I know who you are, Mr. Parker. You're a reporter. To be honest, I really want nothing to do with you, and you're not going to get much more than a 'no comment.'"

"This isn't for my job," I said. "It's personal. It's about my father. He's linked to this crime. You'll understand when I see you."

"Is that right. So none of this will end up in print."

"Not a word."

"In any event, everything that passes between us is officially off the record."

"I understand," I said. "You have my word."

"So if any word of our conversation ends up in print, I'll own your newspaper, your apartment and every pen and pencil you've ever held."

"I swear on my life, this is personal."

"We'll see." She hung up.

I looked up to see Amanda standing there holding a pair of slacks and a clean blue shirt.

"If you're not out this door in three minutes," she said, "I'm going down there to meet Sheryl Harrison in your place."

16

The good and bad thing about New York is that if you don't have time to sit stuck in traffic while your cab racks up forty cents every one-point-two blocks, you can pick from myriad transportation options. There are dozens of subway and bus lines that crisscross the city like a drunk doctor's stitching, and even if the Second Avenue subway remains a figment of the city's imagination, there's always a way from point A to point B.

Of course, even though there happens to be a large public transportation system, it was still as spotty servicewise as your average Wi-Fi connection. Which is why I stood sweating in a dank station for nearly half an hour before the 4 train rumbled to its stop. By the time I took a seat across from a heavily tattooed couple playing tonsil hockey like they were trying out for the Rangers, my nice blue shirt was soaked through with sweat and my pressed slacks looked like they'd been crumpled in a ball in a Russian steam bath for a week.

Thankfully, the one place in New York that was air-conditioned was the subway cars, so when I transferred to the 6 and got off at Twenty-eighth and Park, my clothes looked only mildly rumpled. I couldn't decide whether this appearance would make Sheryl Harrison more or less skeptical of my motives.

Hustling over to Twenty-seventh and Third, I saw an attractive black woman standing on the corner. She was finishing the last of what appeared to be a sandwich or a wrap, and held a gigantic iced coffee in her other hand. The smart yet subdued suit she wore seemed to work for someone in mourning, yet keeping her appointment book up-to-date.

Just as I approached, she strapped her purse to her shoulder and began to walk away.

Sprinting across the street, I yelled, "Miss Harrison! Sheryl!"

She turned to look at me, the expression on her face unchanging. Panting, I caught up to her, composed myself. "Mrs. Harrison, Henry Parker, so sorry, the subway, I—"

"I'm on my way to the florist. I don't have time to stop and chat. You're welcome to walk with me, but as soon as we get there we're done."

"I understand," I said, falling into step with her.

It was a dry, sunny day, and pretty soon I wasn't even thinking about the trip down. Sheryl Harrison walked west down Twenty-seventh, and I followed.

"I'm sorry for your loss," I said.

"I doubt that," she said. "Though the police did tell me you found her. Is that right?"

"That's right," I replied. Sheryl nodded, kept walking. She was tall, about five-ten, with an almost regal walk. Her hair looked professionally done, her makeup highlighting her natural features rather than trying to add some that weren't there. She took long, gallant strides, and though I wasn't a short guy I found myself expelling quite a bit of energy just to keep step.

To my surprise, Sheryl did not ask a follow-up question. Not about the circumstances in which I found her mother, if she had any last words, nothing. If she was in mourning, she hid it. If she had any feelings for her mother, they were worn far below the sleeve.

Without Sheryl prompting, I told her about Stephen Gaines, about my father's arrest for his murder. I also told her how Rose Keller had pointed me in the direction of the cabin at Blue Lake Mountain, and how I was working to prove my father's innocence. She listened without saying a word. I couldn't tell if she was merely aloof, distracted with everything that had gone on, or, more distressingly, not surprised at all.

"Were you two close?" I asked. A rhetorical question, but what I hoped would be a baby step in finding out more about Beth-Ann Downing and her relationship to Helen Gaines.

"I hadn't spoken to my mother in almost ten years," Sheryl said, her gaze straight ahead. She spoke as if I was asking her about her previous employment. And I noticed she used the past tense—*hadn't*. Most people, when discussing a recent death of a friend or family member, would slip up, say *haven't* as though the person was still alive. Somehow I got the feeling this was a day Sheryl Harrison was prepared for.

"Did she ever try to reach out to you?" I asked. "Or mention friends, associates, anyone?"

"Mr. Parker," Sheryl said, a hint of annoyance creeping into her voice. "I answered your question. My mother and I were not close. Not even before I left the city. Yes, she did try to reach out once or twice. I didn't return her phone calls."

"Why not?"

"Perhaps you're too young to have experienced this, but when someone hurts you so badly—I'm not talking about a faulty relationship or bad argument—I'm talking about hurts you in such a way that decimates you, your confidence, your life in such a way that the only chance you have to life is by cutting off a diseased limb, you don't care or make an effort to reconnect. If anything, you stay away from it."

"What did your mother do to you?" I asked. This came out less incredulous than expected. If I didn't grow up with a father whose mission in life seemed to be to alienate his family, this kind of revelation from Sheryl might have taken me aback. Instead, I understood, maybe even empathized with her.

"What didn't she do." Sheryl sighed.

"When you left," I asked, "was it one act that drove you away, or did the camel's back suddenly give out?"

"A little of both," Sheryl said. We turned right on Madison, began to walk uptown, my legs growing sore with the exertion. I was in good shape, but Sheryl Harrison looked like she was ready to compete in the Olympics. "But if there was one thing that I could point to that destroyed my relationship with my mother," she continued, "it was the drugs."

I stopped for a moment. Sheryl did not stop with me, so I had to jog back to keep pace.

"Drugs?" I said, surprised. "What do you mean?"

"Well, when I left it was still the crack," Sheryl said

with the blank expression of a clinical diagnosis. "I'm sure there were a few other things mixed in there— meth, weed—but it was the crack that burned her humanity from the inside out."

"She did this while she raised you," I said.

"I don't think she was as heavily into it while I was a child, but by the time I got to high school it was like coming home to a woman who'd turned into a fun-house mirror."

"Jesus," I said.

"I don't think Jesus smoked crack," Sheryl said. For the first time, I heard a lightness in her voice, as though she was amusing herself. "And all those people who call you late at night to ask if God has a plan? I tell them God didn't have a damn thing for me. He gave me a treasure map to a pile of dog shit, and I had to clean up after it myself. Finally I got tired and moved on."

"How long did your mother do drugs?" I asked. "Was it something she picked up?" I felt slightly off kilter with this line of questioning. Growing up, I'd experienced many forms of addiction of personal evils, both in my family, my relationships and my friends. I'd lived through Jack O'Donnell's alcoholism. I'd seen first-hand what external poisons could do to a person internally. One thing I'd never been exposed to on a personal level was a habitual drug user. Yet both of us had left family behind to free ourselves from their trappings.

"Let's see…how long did my mother use? My whole life," Sheryl said. "You know you can pretty much make your own crack pipe using household materials. My dad died when I was a baby. One of my first memories was seeing all these pretty flowers my mother, Beth, used to keep around the house. Pretty flowers inside this metal tubing. One day I brought one to school, and I got a belt across the back because of it. Turns out those little roses you buy at any gas station are actually crack pipes in disguise. You just take off the foil and remove the rose, stuff about an inch of Brillo pad into the tubing. That's your filter. Take a rock and put it on the Brillo pad, then run a lighter over it, constantly rolling the tube between your fingers to make sure the rock burns easily. Some kids learn how to build sand castles, braid hair, make macaroni necklaces. I learned how to build a crack pipe."

"Do you know if your mother was still smoking it when she died?"

"I'd be shocked as hell if she wasn't," Sheryl said. "And I remember there were days when my mother forget to pay her electric bills, and rather than own up, she'd just go with Helen up to that cabin. Don't get me wrong, Henry, in some way I loved my mother. But I saw her death coming from miles away. It was only a matter of time before her life ended, and ended badly. But one thing I do know, that lovely Ms. Helen Gaines? She was the biggest enabler my mother ever had."

The words struck me like a punch. Helen Gaines? I knew Stephen had a habit, but Helen?

"Don't look so surprised," Sheryl said. "Based on where they lived during that time, Alphabet City in the '80s? Would've been a surprise if they didn't end up addicts. I mean, I remember this WASPY-looking young punk always coming by the house to drop off whatever my mom had ordered. Remember his name too, Vinnie."

"Vinnie?" I said, the surprise in my voice evident. Rose Keller had said that whenever she needed a new supply she would call some delivery system where they'd send over a guy named Vinnie. I had no idea how many Vinnies there were, but it was clear this system had been in place over a decade and was likely still in business today. This wasn't just some petty drug deal, but something much larger.

"Take that British singer, Amy Winehouse," Sheryl said, "then multiply it by ten and that's how bad my mother was. So my guess is this. If my mother was killed while hiding out with Helen Gaines, I'd bet my husband's Infiniti it's got something to do with drugs. And Stephen Gaines must have crossed some damn unpleasant people."

17

Rose Keller was home. This didn't quite surprise me—most graphic designers worked freelance. So I figured she wasn't the kind of person who woke up to an alarm clock at six forty-five, got dressed and grabbed a tall latte on the way to the office. When I called at eight in the morning, it was no great shock that Rose Keller sounded like a bear awoken from hibernation.

Actually, she kind of reminded me of what Amanda sounded like before her first cup of coffee.

One thing I learned early on when talking to sources: get them early, or get them late. During the day, everyone was at work. There was always an excuse not to talk. I hate to say this, but often a source would agree to talk to you if only to prevent you from ever interrupting their private time again. Probably the only time I would compare my profession to that of the noble telemarketer.

"I need a favor," I said to Rose. I put the statement bluntly, accentuating the word *need*. Not want. Need. And since she was close to Stephen, and aware that I was tracking down his killer, she might be more apt to accept the rather large, not to mention illegal, favor I was about to ask of her.

"What can I do?" she replied. Good start.

I filled her in on the details of Beth-Ann Downing's murder, and the disappearance of Helen Gaines. I told her about my conversation with Sheryl Harrison, and the confession that her mother had maintained a ruthless addiction her whole life. The silence on the other end told me that Rose was well aware of why I was coming to her.

When I finished, I asked if I could fill her in in person. She agreed, and I was on the next subway downtown to meet her.

Before turning on to Rose's block, I stopped at an ATM and withdrew two hundred dollars. I had no idea how much I'd actually need, but I figured better to have more money and not need it than need more money and not have it.

When I got to her building, I buzzed up and she rang me through. She opened the door wearing a tank top and pajama bottoms. Her eyes were weary, deep bags settling under them like squished blueberries.

"Morning," I said.

"Is it morning already?" she asked.

I noticed the shades were all drawn, and there were no clocks in sight. Half a dozen wrapped candy bars were strewn around, as well as what looked like a month's supply of Red Bull. It looked like the apartment was stocked and prepared for a bout of hibernation. "It's almost 9:00 a.m.," I said.

"Huh. Didn't realize it."

"Listen," I said. "I have a favor to ask of you. A big one."

"You said that already. What gives?"

"I need you to order something from Vinnie," I said. "I want to know who he works for."

Rose sat back in her overstuffed leather couch. The confident woman I'd just met looked like she'd just been swallowed up whole.

"I've been clean for a long time," she said. "I've put that behind me."

"I don't want you to use anything," I said, attempting to clarify things but wondering if that mattered at all. "All I need is for whoever's playing Vinnie this week to come here so I can follow him."

"So why don't you call him yourself?"

"They won't know me," I said. "They'll trust you. I'm willing to bet that whoever these Vinnies work for, they keep a record of addresses, customers. The runners might be idiots, but their bosses never are. I intend to follow this guy, see where he goes, and I don't want to chance being recognized. They know you."

Rose shook her head violently, as though shooing away demons that were swirling around. A pang of guilt thudded in my stomach, and I wondered if my one-track mind in finding Stephen's killer could hurt others as well. The last thing I wanted to do was encourage Rose to relapse, but...I didn't know where else to turn. And I needed to know where the stream started. Or at least needed to find the next level.

"I'll do it," Rose said. "But I won't order anything stronger than weed, and I won't pay for a cent of it."

"Fair enough," I said. "What's the smallest amount you can order?"

"You don't want the smallest amount, trust me."

"Why not?"

"They'll know my phone number. Let's just say back in the day, I never ordered the smallest amount. Not to mention I haven't ordered in a long time. If all of a sudden I call up and ask for one tab of ecstasy, they won't believe me. Somebody who comes back to the stuff after such a long layoff, it's because they fell off the wagon. Hard. We want to make the order sound realistic. You order a dime bag of schwag, he'll laugh in your face and tell you it's not worth his time. And then he'll never take my call again because he'll assume I'm turning on him. Cops on stakeouts are cheap. You want a real delivery, an ounce of decent weed will probably run you a hundred fifty or so, though I've been out of the game for a while so, you know, inflation and everything."

"Really? Inflation affects drug sales?"

"We live in the United States, don't we? You think people will pay more than four bucks for a gallon of gas but won't pony up a Ben Franklin to get high with their friends? A gallon lasts until the next exit. A good high will give you stories that'll last for years—if you can remember it. I'd go with this—order a quarter ounce of mids. Decent enough stuff, probably run seventy-five bucks. Enough so it's worth the trip for them, but it won't put a big crimp in your discretionary fund. That work, champ?"

"Whatever you say. You call and order. When Vinnie buzzes up, just send a text message to my cell phone. I won't respond, but that's the signal that it's the right guy. Then send me one more when he leaves, just to be sure." I took out my wallet, peeled off two hundred dollars and handed it to Rose. "In case it's more than you expect. Or you need to, like, tip him."

"Tip the drug dealer," she said, laughing. "Right. I'm sure he'll take it back to the Dairy Queen and divide it up among his colleagues. What are you, some kind of nitwit? Didn't you smoke in college?"

"Once or twice," I said, "but I don't think anyone ever trusted me to handle the business transactions. I just assumed you tip people in the service industry."

"All right," Rose said. "But after this, no more favors. I told you everything I know and then some, and now you have me risking my sobriety for you."

"It's not for me," I said. "It's for Stephen."

"Are you sure?" Rose asked, one eyebrow arched. "'Cause I've been around a lot of users before, every kind of drug you can imagine. I've seen too many friends die because of the pipe or needle. But not every addict smokes or drinks or inhales. A lot of them get off on other things. I see a little bit of that in you, Henry. You're a bit of an addict, too."

I didn't know how to reply to this, but something about it didn't feel good. Rather than respond, I simply thanked Rose for helping, and went outside.

I was still thinking about what she'd said when I found a park bench to sit on that afforded me a full view of her building's entrance.

Addict. I repeated the word to myself. It was a cool, sunny day, and if I weren't tracking a drug dealer I could envision myself sitting here with Amanda, watching the families play. Young children growing up in a city that seemed to offer them brief pockets of respite, small guarded sanctuaries in between the playgrounds for millionaires.

Addict.

It was an ugly word, one I never associated with myself. Yet when Rose said it, I felt an angry fire burning inside me. I wanted to argue with her, but somehow felt it would have strengthened her point.

Addict.

I watched the children play and wondered if she was right.

My eyes stayed fixed to the building entrance. Every time someone entered—old, young, white, black, Hispanic—I would place my hand over the pocket holding my cell phone. It was set to vibrate. Every few minutes I would take it just to make sure I hadn't missed anything. Nothing yet.

An hour and a half passed, when a man wearing a Yankees hat approached the doorstep. He pulled out a cell phone, checked it, then went up the steps. He was young, maybe nineteen or twenty. He wore baggy jeans and a chain looped around from his belt to his back pocket where he kept a wallet. And most importantly, he was carrying a backpack.

As he went to press the buzzer, another man walked up to the steps. He was wearing a dark suit with slicked-back hair and sunglasses. An expensive-looking briefcase was in his hand. He was a few years older than hat guy, maybe twenty-four or -five, but looked like he lived in a totally different world. Not to mention bank account. Funny, I thought, that he was standing there next to a drug dealer and didn't even realize it.

They both pressed the buzzer and waited. When they were rung through they both entered, the nicely dressed guy holding the door for the young punk.

Ten minutes after the door closed, I felt my cell

phone vibrating. I took it out, looked at the call log. It was Rose. Jackpot.

Adrenaline began to course through me. As soon as hat guy came through the door, I was prepared to go wherever he did. My hands were sweating. I was ready.

Then the front door opened, and a man stepped through. Only it wasn't the young guy with baggy pants and a backpack that looked sketchier than a forty-year-old at a dance club. It was the young-executive type.

I looked at him with intense skepticism, debating whether to wait until the other guy came through. This guy didn't look anything like a dealer. He looked too well off, and I doubted most drug dealers bought their briefcases at Coach.

It couldn't be. The guy was young, looking like he'd just stepped out of his b-school graduation. He was about five foot ten, in terrific shape. There was a small, moon-shaped birthmark on the front of his neck, and he gripped the briefcase so tight it looked as if it could crumble in his hands.

Then, as the man began to walk away, I saw him stop, look at his briefcase. He picked it up, clicked a loose clasp into place, then walked away.

Then my cell phone vibrated. The screen had a text message from Rose. It read

Gordon "Vinnie" Gekko has just left the building.

That sealed it. This man about town was Vinnie.

Waiting until he was half a block ahead of me, I began to follow. He walked north to Fourteenth Street, when he stopped for a moment to look at his cell phone.

I stopped as well, retreating into the shadow of an electronics store. When he put the phone back in his pocket, he began to look around. His eyes caught something, and suddenly he turned and jogged across the street. He zigged between several cars, making it impossible for me to follow him without drawing attention to myself. Instead, I watched in between traffic as he approached a pay phone. I saw him put money in the machine and make a call. He hung up less than fifteen seconds later.

No doubt he was calling whatever number had just come up on his cell phone. Briefcase man had another delivery to make.

He turned West on Fourteenth Street and made his way to what I assumed was the Union Square subway stop.

I picked up the pace, narrowing the gap between us to thirty feet or so. I wanted to remain behind him, but if he was heading for the subway, losing him in the bustle of pedestrians was a chance I didn't want to take.

He went down into the subway, paid his fare and headed for the 6 train. I followed.

He went down the two flights of stairs onto the 6 train platform. I followed ten feet behind. He walked halfway down the platform then stopped and waited. I stopped two car lengths away, and hung out behind a steel column, peeking out every now and then to make sure he was still there.

The 6 train rattled into the station. My heart was pumping. I wanted to run up and grab this guy, make him give up everything he knew. But that would cut off my only source of information. And unless I killed him, he would tell whoever he worked for what happened, and the whole thing would clam up faster than a mute on the witness stand. And while I was willing to do a whole lot to figure out just what exactly happened that night at Helen Gaines's apartment, murder wasn't on my approved list of actions.

The man stepped into the car, and I got into the adjacent one, making sure I could see him through the separating window. For a moment I had a sense of déjà vu, remembering that it was not too long ago when I was on the subway running from two men who wanted me dead. Funny how the tides turn.

The doors closed, and the man took a seat. That likely meant we were traveling a few stops. I stayed standing, not wanting to lose sight due to a bad angle. This was slightly awkward considering there were half a dozen open seats and I was the only person standing in our car. Still, I'd rather be considered an antisocial weirdo than lose the rabbit.

Every stop I braced myself in case my target left. Finally as we approached the Seventy-seventh Street subway stop, I saw him stand up, check to make sure his briefcase was still looped around his shoulder and approach the door. I didn't move.

When the train stopped, a mass of passengers exited. The Seventy-seventh Street stop was right by the entrance to Lenox Hill Hospital. This Upper East Side location was right near a large residential area. Though heavily populated, it wasn't as crowded as Union Square or one stop higher, Eighty-sixth Street.

The man walked east across Seventy-seventh. I followed him. Between First and Second Avenues, he went up to a brick town house, stopped in front of it. I sat on a small brick outcropping and pretended to tie my shoe. He took out his cell phone, looking like he was double-checking something, then went up the stairs and pressed a buzzer. I heard a ring, then he said something but I couldn't hear what. He opened the door and walked in.

I retreated around the corner, peeking back every few seconds to make sure I didn't lose him.

I only had to wait five minutes, then the man was back outside and walking west, toward me. My heart raced. If he was dealing—or delivering—drugs, this seemed to fit the profile. Short and sweet. No chitchat. Just in and out, over and done. Pay the man his money.

And the bulge in the briefcase even seemed to have gone down a little bit.

I bought a bottle of water at a corner store as he walked past, then I got back into our familiar pace. I needed to see how many stops he made, see if anything interesting presented itself. I decided to follow him the rest of the day. I took out my cell, and sent Amanda a text message.

Got a lead. Will call when I can.
Don't wait up.

If I were a girlfriend and my boyfriend sent me that kind of text, I'd probably scour the city looking for him, half expecting to find him in the arms of some illicit lover. But I trusted Amanda. And after everything we'd been through, I believed she trusted me back.

My phone vibrated. I took it out, checked the message.

Go get em, Tiger.

God, I loved this woman.

The man with the briefcase made four more stops the rest of the day: 124th and Broadway, Ninety-eighth and Broadway, and then back downtown to Fourteenth between Fifth and Sixth. Each time I noticed the bag on his shoulder became a little easier to carry. It swung at greater arcs as he carried it. As his stash grew lighter, the bag weighed him down less.

During his journey, I decided that I would follow him home. I had no idea what to expect, or what I would say to this man. But I needed to know where someone like him lived. And I needed to know where I could find him again.

It was nearing eleven o'clock. My legs were getting heavy. Vinnie had just downed his third bottle of water of the day. So when I followed him to the N train, the night having fully descended over the city, I hoped this would be our final ride of the day.

Vinnie rode the N train to the Canal/Broadway stop. He looked weary, his eyes fluttering open and closed as his breathing grew deeper. I knew how he felt. My muscles felt sluggish. Private detective work was certainly not a calling I was prepared for. Spenser I was not.

Where he sat, Vinnie opened his bag and dug through it. He pulled out an MP3 player, then scrounged around some more. He seemed unable to find something. Then he turned the bag upside down and shook it. A thin white wire fell out. He picked it up, plugged one end into the MP3 player and took the two earbuds and fit them into his ears. Then he pressed a button on the player and relaxed.

No doubt this was the last stop. When he turned the bag upside down, not a thing fell out. No bags, no foil, no vials.

Vinnie was heading home.

I followed him out of the station. At this point I probably could have walked right next to him and he wouldn't have noticed or recognized me. He walked two blocks west and one block south before approaching a row of town houses. He was walking slowly, but then all of a sudden his head perked up.

Another young man was walking down the street in the other direction. He looked to be the same age as the guy I was following, maybe a year or two younger. He was wearing loose jeans, sneakers, a Mets cap with the brim turned sideways. The other guy's head snapped up, too, in a familiar greeting.

These two men knew each other. They slowed down as they approached. I slipped behind a wall, out of sight, but easily able to hear every word they said.

"S'up, Scotty?" the other man yelled as they got closer.

"SSDD," my guy, apparently Scotty, yelled back. Same shit, different day.

As they got closer, their voices lowering, I heard Scotty say, "What'd you pull in today?"

"Four-fiddy. Would've been more but these trust-fund princesses thought they could get a taste for free if they shoved their tits in my face. Don't need to tell them I can get that on my own. How 'bout you?"

"Five-twenty," Scotty said, a note of pride in his voice. "And that's *after* the man takes his cut."

"Better than serving lattes," the other guy said. "I'm cleaned out for the night. Gotta re-up in the morning."

"Same here," Scotty said. "How's your moms doing?"

The other guy shrugged. "Her hair hasn't started falling out yet, but the docs say it's a matter of time." He scratched his nose. "She's strong as a bull. Wouldn't mind moving out on my own like you, but not while she's like this."

"Give her my best, bro'."

"Will do. Hey, meet on the corner tomorrow morning at seven? Go over together?"

Scotty nodded. "Sounds like a plan. 'Night, Kyle."

"Later, Scotty."

The kid named Kyle kept on walking, as Scotty entered his building.

I stood there stunned as Kyle passed by me.

Re-ups tomorrow morning. I knew what that meant. They'd both cleaned out their stash today, and would need to restock tomorrow to make more deliveries. It meant they weren't working for themselves, and they didn't keep any drugs at their houses. Somebody held them for re-upping. And there was enough to resupply at least two soldiers.

Which meant that if Scotty and Kyle were going to meet at seven, I would be there waiting for them.

_18_

I was standing on the corner of Broadway and West Sixth Street at 6:30 a.m. I didn't know what corner Scotty was referring to when he and Kyle made plans to meet, so I wanted to make sure I had my eyes on him from the moment he left his apartment. I was on my second cup of coffee when, at six fifty-five, the front door opened and Scotty came out. He was dressed just like the day before. Natty suit, hair combed, a briefcase slung over his shoulder.

He yawned and stretched, and I watched while wondering if this was a morning ritual. Whether he and Kyle met every day, or only on re-up days. He began walking east, presumably toward the corner.

I walked half a block down and watched as he stopped on the corner. Scotty checked his watch, dawdled for a bit, then turned around and nodded his head at someone I couldn't see. A minute later, Kyle joined him on the corner.

Last night when I saw Kyle he was loose, relaxed. This morning he and Scotty looked like twins.

Gone was the baseball cap, and a mop of red hair was

slicked back into place. He was wearing a navy blazer and slacks. Kyle, too, had a briefcase in his hands.

They spoke for a minute, and I saw Kyle pass Scotty a stick of gum. I retreated into a deli as they passed, then fell into line.

They entered the N train at the corner of Canal and Broadway. Again I took the adjacent car. They conversed as though they'd known each other a long time. Neither wore a wedding ring. They were just two young guys, mid to late twenties if I had to guess. Much the same as thousands of other young men in the city, dressed and ready for a day at the office.

Only I knew that their work entailed something much darker than punching a clock.

At the Fifty-seventh Street station, Kyle and Scotty left, went upstairs and began walking north on Seventh Avenue. I had no idea where they were going, but when they turned on Fifty-eighth and headed toward Sixth, I noticed both Kyle and Scotty cock their heads in that familiar "what's up" way that insinuated they saw someone they knew.

I picked up the pace. Felt my pulse quickening. Then I saw something that nearly made me stop dead in my tracks.

At least half a dozen young men were approaching from the opposite direction. All of them were well dressed in business suits. All of them were smiling and jeering at Kyle and Scotty.

And all of them were carrying briefcases that were most certainly empty.

"S'up, bitches!" Kyle yelled at the oncoming group. Kyle and Scotty joined the other young men as I hung back, dumbfounded. They'd stopped outside of what appeared to be a small office building. I wrote down the number and address in my notepad. I couldn't get any closer without arousing suspicion.

After a minute of horseplay, all eight men entered the building, like a troop of bankers ready to conquer the world. When they'd gone inside I ventured closer until I could see. They were writing their names down at a security station, and giving a good-natured ribbing to the guard on duty. He was laughing and playing along. He must have known them.

Then, just like that, they were gone.

Could all of these men have been going to the same place for the same reason? Were they all part of the same crew? Were they all dealers?

As I stood outside weighing my options, several more young men entered the building, stopped by the security station and went upstairs. A few of them chatted with the guard. I assumed they were part of the same crew as Scotty and Kyle.

I decided to wait. I couldn't go inside in case Scotty or Kyle came downstairs. Thankfully, I didn't have to wait long, because within twenty minutes a veritable crush of young, well-dressed men came pouring out of the front doors. Their pace was quick. They offered pithy "laters" and "rake it in, boys" goodbyes to each other.

And, I noticed, all of their briefcases looked full.

I waited another fifteen minutes to be sure, then I walked inside the building. I pretended to act confused, reading the directory on the wall.

"Help you?" the guard asked.

"Yeah," I said. I went up to his station, saw the logbook open. I pretended to be thinking while I scanned the log.

And there, right next to each other, were two names:

Scott Callahan
Kyle Evans

Scotty and Kyle. And by the company line they wrote "718 Enterprises."

"Actually," I said to the guard, "I'm in the wrong place."

Walking back into the lobby's atrium, I stopped by the company directory listings. Scanning the names and floor numbers of the companies that were housed here, I could find no listing for 718 Enterprises. Strange.

Where were all these young men going?

And what the hell was 718 Enterprises?

I figured I'd ask someone who might know. I walked up to the security guard and said, "Hi, sorry to bother you again. I'm looking for a company called 718 Enterprises. I'm pretty sure it's here, but I can't find it in the directory and I forgot the name of the person I'm supposed to meet."

The guard looked me over. He was in his late fifties, heavyset, with big wide eyes that looked like they believed me as far as he could shove me down his throat.

"No, you didn't," he said.

"I didn't?" I said incredulously.

"No. You're not. I don't know you, friend." He averted his eyes to the crossword puzzle on his desk. I stood there for another moment, until the guard's eyes came back to mine. He put his hand on the phone at his desk and said, "Do I have to call the cops?"

I apologized and walked outside.

Standing there outside the building, I tried to piece this together. Those young men who filed into the building, who knew each other and were all dressed alike, I'd be willing to bet they all took on the moniker of Vinnie during their day job. And I'd also be willing to bet that whatever 718 Enterprises was, it was some sort of supplier.

I still had no idea what, if anything, they had to do with the deaths of Beth-Ann Downing or even Stephen Gaines. But it's all I had. As thin and transparent as this thread was, it was the only one I had to pull. And I'd had thinner ones that ended up unraveling a great deal.

As I stood outside the building pondering my next move, a lone straggler exited the building wearing the telltale suit and carrying a bulging briefcase. He was thin, younger-looking than his cohorts, and had a gangly walk that told me he hadn't been at this very long. He began walking north. He took a cell phone from his pocket, checked it then dropped it into his briefcase.

A thought crossed my mind. Suddenly it occurred to me what I could do. What I *needed* to do. I certainly wouldn't feel good about myself…but my father's freedom was at stake. Finding a killer was my justification. I silently apologized for what I was about to do.

I began to walk faster, the young kid in my line of sight. I was ten feet behind him. Nine. Eight. Seven.

I began to jog to keep pace, my pulse quickening. The subway was just a few blocks away. I'd make it…

Pushing off my back foot to get a burst of speed, I

lunged forward and grabbed the briefcase off the young guy's shoulder. It was loose with surprisingly little effort, and suddenly, to my surprise, I was standing there in the middle of the street holding a young man's bag that I'd just stolen.

He twirled around to see what was happening, and just before I could react, he locked eyes with me. His were light green, a mixture of anger and horrific fear in them. He knew what he stood to lose.

I didn't wait another moment. I turned around and began to run as fast as I could, whispering, *I'm going to hell, I'm going to hell,* as my legs churned.

"Stop! Thief!" I heard a high-pitched voice scream. An arm reached out for me but I shrugged it away.

The N train would be too obvious and too close. If the train took a long time to pull into the station, I'd be dead. I could outrun this kid. I had to.

I sprinted east down Fifty-eighth Street as fast as I could. The kid was screaming behind me. I peeked over my shoulder, feeling a surge of adrenaline as I saw my lead increasing. Once I got to Sixth Avenue, I turned south and saw the entrance for the B and Q trains ahead of me.

Pulling things into fifth gear, I leaped down the steps into the station, fumbling as I got my MetroCard out. I swiped it, went through, and took a millisecond to decide to head for the downtown B train. I figured if I was caught, at least he wouldn't know the direction where I lived.

The platform was all but empty. Bad luck for me. But there was a red light in the tunnel signaling an approaching train. It couldn't come fast enough. I walked quickly toward the end of the platform, the weight of the bag pressing on my shoulder.

As the train rumbled into the station, my breath caught in my throat as I saw the kid clamber down the stairs approaching my platform. I hoped he hadn't seen me.

When the doors opened I slid into the car, peeking out once more.

The kid was on the platform, peeking into each car.

The train began to move. Faster and faster, it was bringing me right toward him.

As the train passed where the young kid was standing, I saw his eyes meet mine. His mouth dropped open, and I could have sworn I heard a stream of profanity. Then I was gone, into the darkness of the tunnel.

I transferred at the next station onto the uptown B, then rode it until the 125th and Frederick Douglas Boulevard station. From there I walked home, the bag on my shoulder burning a hole.

I was tired, weary, trudging up the stairs, my blood still pumping, however, with my prize. My guilt had been overcome by my curiosity.

When I opened the door, I saw Amanda sitting at the dining-room table eating a bowl of cereal. I forgot how early it was, that she hadn't even left for work yet.

She was wearing a formfitting tank top that accentuated her amazing figure. Her hair was held together in a ponytail, and her shapely legs disappeared beneath her chair. I smiled, and she returned it.

"Whatcha got there, sweetie? A present for me maybe?"

I sat down at the table opposite her. I stuck my hand in the outside pocket and came out with a cell phone. The same one the young kid had been using.

Then I unlatched the brass buckles on the outside. When the bag was unlocked, I folded back the top and turned it upside down.

Out poured five white bricks the size of VHS cassette tapes, as well as several thumb-size bags of the stuff. It also contained a dozen small bags of marijuana with varying quantities, and several pieces of tinfoil. I didn't want to open or touch anything I didn't need to, so whatever was in those packets would remain a mystery for now. Chances were, it was either coke or crack.

One package, though, was half-open. Sitting on one loose piece of foil were three small off-white stones that looked almost like sugar cubes. But I knew exactly what they were. Rocks of pure crack cocaine.

"Wow," Amanda said, staring at the mass of drugs. "Remind me to buy my own birthday present next year."

I reached for one of the packages, but Amanda grabbed my arm. I looked at her to see what was up, and she was shaking her head like she was scolding a child about to eat paste.

"Do you really want your fingerprints on those?" she asked rhetorically. "Don't we have enough problems with fingerprints where they didn't belong? I assume at some point we're going to have to get the police involved, and we'll have a much easier time convincing them if it doesn't look like you were rolling around in the drugs beforehand."

My arm shot back. The girl had a point.

"This is unreal," I said, the words not even doing

justice to the feeling of seeing all the drugs spread out on our table. My college never offered a Drug Dealing 101 course, so I had no idea what the value of the narcotics were. Though, based on the amount of stops Scotty had made yesterday, and the money Rose Keller claimed to have shelled out over the years, it had to be several thousand at least. And if I factored in all the different suit-wearing carriers I saw this morning, there had to be at least a hundred grand making its way around the city *every single day.*

"What do we do with this?" Amanda asked. The truth was I wasn't sure. If I delivered it to the cops with the story, I'd have to explain the stolen briefcase. And then I'd have to explain how I got there, how I'd followed Scotty, and why I was doing all this in the first place.

The goal, of course, was to find Stephen Gaines's killer and free my father. That would likely have to wait until I had the full picture. If I went in with half a bird in hand and the other half hiding in the bush, they'd laugh me off and then possibly arrest me. Neither of which sounded particularly appealing.

I picked up the cell phone. It wasn't as fancy as mine or many of the newer models, and didn't look to have photo or video capacity. There was no flip top, just a dimly lit LCD screen and chunky buttons that looked old and worn. Clearly, this phone was meant for one thing, and one thing only. And whoever was using it didn't need all the excess accoutrements.

The phone was still on. The screen said there were five missed calls. I checked the log, and saw they'd all come from the same number. I didn't recognize it, and rather than a name popping up it was just the number.

Most likely it was the kid whose briefcase I'd stolen calling from a pay phone, praying someone would pick up. It was only a matter of time before the phone was disconnected.

Though somehow I didn't think there was a high probability of the owner calling the cops to report it.

On the LCD screen, there was a "contacts" line directly above a flat, rectangular button. I pressed it.

Immediately a roll call of the kid's contacts came up. I scrolled through the names, hoping for something. Then I saw two names that *did* ring a bell.

Scott Callahan and Kyle Evans.

Scotty and Kyle from this morning.

It didn't shock me that they were listed in the kid's contacts list. They did share the same "occupation," and odds were Scotty and Kyle had this kid's number in their database as well. I kept scrolling.

Then a name appeared on the list that made me catch my breath.

"What?" Amanda said. "What it is?"

I showed her the phone, my finger underlining the name.

"Oh my God," she said. "Why would he be…"

I looked at her. We both knew why he was there.

Halfway down the lists of contacts was the name Stephen Gaines.

"He knew my brother," I said. "Wait a second…"

I exited the contacts list and returned to the main menu. I knew what I was looking for but didn't know if it was there.

I hoped it wasn't.

I pressed the send button to bring up the list of the

most recent calls from this cell phone. There were several from a name marked Office. I clicked edit to see the number. It was from a 646 area code in Manhattan. I wrote it down, then kept on scrolling.

None of the names were recognizable.

But then, at the very end of the list, was the one name I'd hoped not to see.

"He called Stephen," I said to Amanda. "He called my brother the night he died."

19

The next morning, Amanda and I took the subway to 100 Centre Street, which housed the New York County Correctional Facility. My father was being held there before his grand jury hearing, and we were on our way to show support, discuss his court-appointed lawyer. And ask him some questions to which I hoped he would hold the answers.

Amanda and I had spent the previous night talking and thinking about the Gaines family, Rose Keller and Beth-Ann Downing. Drugs seemed to be the only link between the four people. Two of them were dead, Stephen Gaines and Beth-Ann. And the stash of narcotics from the stolen briefcase was hidden inside my laundry hamper. I figured if anyone were to break in, the stench itself might deter even the most hardened thief.

Stephen used to date and party with Rose Keller. She claimed they'd met randomly. But I had to wonder. Stephen's name was in the kid's cell phone I stole. Which meant one of three things.

First, the two were merely friends. Which was highly unlikely.

Second, that Stephen was the kid's client. That one was a possibility.

Third, and perhaps the most frightening yet the most plausible, was that Stephen Gaines was a dealer himself.

Perhaps Stephen, before he died, was one of the faceless suit monkeys who entered that office building in midtown for re-ups. Perhaps had I gone there another day, I would have seen my brother enter with an empty briefcase and exit with a full load of narcotics.

Helen Gaines had somehow befriended Beth-Ann Downing after relocating from Bend to New York City. They both had children—though I had no reason to suspect Sheryl and Stephen had met, unless Stephen happened to have sold to Sheryl's mother. Sheryl was likely gone by the time Helen and Stephen settled in. And at some point along the line, both Helen and Beth-Ann had developed drug addictions.

Chances were Stephen discovered the path to his own demise through his mother. Anytime you grow up in a household in which such evils were not only common but encouraged, it was just a matter of time before you followed in step.

In my relatively short time on this planet, I'd learned that there were two types of people. Those who were doomed to follow in whatever footsteps had been laid out for them, and those who were strong enough to carve their own path.

Amanda and I were lucky. I could have turned out like my father, with a general disregard for decency and an attitude toward women that could be described as combative on a good day. Amanda could have been swallowed by her grief as a child, stifled by the tragic deaths of her parents. She never grew close to Lawrence and Harriet Stein, her adoptive family. She feared that she would never truly be close to another person again. She began to write in diaries. There were hundreds of them, each one chronicling every waking moment of her life, cataloging every soul she met on her aimless journey. A moment-to-moment timeline of loneliness. After we met and later began seeing each other, she stopped writing in them. I like to think that, in each other, we found a path through the darkness. She found someone who would be with her every night and every morning, and I found a woman strong enough to show me my weaknesses as well as my strengths, beautiful enough beneath the skin to make me want to smooth over the rough edges.

And there were a lot of them.

Stephen Gaines never found that path. He'd never had a chance. Between his mother and her friends, the darkness was too much for him to bear.

I gripped the handrail tight as I approached my destination. My childhood memories of my father were of this great and powerful man who never feared anything. He was an omnipotent tyrant, a man unconcerned with convention or emotion. I never saw him cry, never saw him beg. Even when I knew our finances were dwindling and my mother was as distant as the sunset at dusk, he stood rock solid, impenetrable. Seeing him today would be the opposite of everything I knew as a child. He was the negative in my life's photograph. And I wasn't sure if I was prepared.

The New York County Correctional Facility had several outlets, and as a prisoner your stay was largely dependent on a combination of luck and just how many criminals were waiting their turn before your case came to the docket. Some ended up on Riker's Island, but many, like James Parker, were relegated to the facility known affectionately as the Tombs.

The Tombs had actually been the name for several locations over the years, beginning in 1838 back when it was called the New York Halls of Justice and House of Detention (or NYHOFJAHOD for short. No wonder they called it the Tombs).

After numerous successful escapes and the deteriorating quality of the cells themselves, the old building was merged with the Criminal Court building on Franklin Street, separated by what was called the Bridge of Sighs.

In 1974 much of the old Tombs had finally been shut down due to health concerns. Currently the Tombs consists of two facilities connected by a pedestrian bridge, with a prisoner capacity nearing nine hundred.

Ironically, in 2001 the Tombs were given the official name of the Bernard B. Kerik Complex, though in 2006 after Kerik pled guilty to ethics violations (including several violations of infamous book publisher Judith Regan in an apartment near ground zero that was supposed to be used for the rescue effort) the moniker was removed.

Currently my father was awaiting a grand jury hearing on the charges of first-degree murder. According to Amanda, the prosecution was surely in the process of collecting evidence to convince the jury that there was "reasonable cause to believe" that my father might have killed Stephen Gaines. We both admitted the likelihood of a trial at this point, so time was becoming more and more precious. We had interlocked several pieces, but we couldn't see the whole puzzle.

The 4 train took us to Canal Street. For some reason, passing by the massive pillars and intricate scrollwork adorning the Supreme Court building reminded me I hadn't yet served jury duty since arriving in New York a few years ago. I could already imagine the tremendous sense of irony I would feel upon signing that jury slip. Maybe if I was lucky it'd be juror appreciation day. Get a free coffee mug and everything. Leave this mess with something memorable.

The Manhattan Criminal Courthouse towered above the city skyscape, with four towers encircling a larger center with floors in decreasing size, as though you were viewing a staircase to the sky. In front were two massive granite columns, and the whole structure was designed in an art deco-style.

We entered the lobby through glass doors and made our way to the security stand. We showed our identification, which the security guard scrutinized intensely and matched to his logbook before writing us passes. After that we passed through a series of metal detectors and, after a search of my bag and Amanda's purse, we were headed toward the Manhattan Detention Complex, aka the Tombs.

A tall guard in a neatly pressed blue uniform accompanied us to an elevator that looked like it was built into a brick wall. I noticed he did not have a gun on his holster. Instead, there was a Taser, a can of Mace and a thin cylinder about a half inch in diameter and six inches long. The guard noticed I was staring at it.

"Expandable baton," he said. "Officers have been complaining about the longer ones for years. They're heavy as my mother-in-law and an incredible nuisance. These puppies are compact and pack a hell of a punch."

"Can I try it?"

"No."

We got on the elevator and the guard pressed Down. We waited just a few moments before the doors opened up.

"Not a lot of elevator traffic," I said.

"Anytime I see the elevator going up from the lower levels and I'm not in it," he said, "we've got problems."

"I hope that's not a regular occurrence."

He didn't answer me. I'd begun to get used to people tuning me out.

By staring straight ahead I wasn't sure if he thought that was a stupid statement, or one that struck a nerve. As much as I hated embarrassing myself with silly comments, I hope it was the former.

Once the elevator opened, the guard led us through a long, musty tunnel. At the end was a series of metal bars, not unlike those on an actual jail cell. Beyond we could see several more guards, and the unmistakable orange of prison jumpsuits. The guard took a key card from his pocket, slid it onto a keypad and unlocked the door. Opening it, the guard ushered us into a smaller room lined with metal benches. Guards took both of our bags and patted us down. Guards with shotguns and handcuffs adorned the walls, their eyes traveling the length of the room and back again, dispassionate. Security cameras with weapons.

We sat down at a table at the end of the room. There

were two other people seated at a table twenty feet from us. An older balding man wearing an orange prison jumpsuit, thick glasses and a thick paunch sat, chin in his hands, while a bejeweled woman many years younger (with many half-priced plastic surgeries under her belt) rattled on about something the man couldn't have seemed less interested in. In fact, he looked slightly relieved that he would end the night in his cell as opposed to in bed next to her.

We sat waiting. I wanted to take Amanda's hand. Felt like I needed to hold on to something that was right. Being here in this place accentuated my simple need to feel like I was a part of something wholesome and decent. Amanda represented everything I had in that department.

Soon I heard a jangling of chains, and my father appeared behind a set of metal doors. Two guards were poised on either side of him. They looked somewhat disinterested, but the tense muscles in their forearms told me differently.

They led him over to our table, hands under his elbows as he struggled to walk with chains binding both his wrists and ankles.

Finally he took a seat across from us, and I could see what this place had done to him.

My father looked pale. Thin, reedy. He was never a very muscular man, but any tone he had seemed to have dissipated over the last week. His hair was stringy and looked unwashed. His eyes wandered around the room. They looked scared, as though he expected something or someone to jump out of the shadows.

I wondered just what kind of hell this man was enduring here.

Part of me, and man I wished I didn't feel this way, wondered if it was penance.

"Henry, good to see you, son." He smiled weakly as he said this, and I knew he meant it. Those were the warmest words my father had spoken to me since…I couldn't recall when. And it was a shame they came under these circumstances.

"How you holding up?"

He made a *psh* sound and leaned back. "S'not so bad. You see all those movies where guys get gang-raped in the shower and they're all getting stabbed waiting on line for food."

"Nobody's tried to hurt you, have they?" Amanda asked.

"No…well, one guy did get stabbed in the shower, but I didn't know him."

My mouth dropped as Amanda looked at me. "We need to get you out of here," I said.

"Well, what in the hell is taking you so long?" he shouted. The other couple turned and started. I heard a rustling as two guards moved closer. He looked at them and shrank back. Suddenly the warmth was gone. This was the man I grew up with. But that didn't mean he was a murderer.

"We're working on it," I said.

"How's your attorney?" Amanda asked. "Has he been to see you regularly?"

"He's been down here two or three times. How the heck should I know if he's any good?" my father seethed. "I mean, he knows more about this legal stuff than me, but so does the janitor here. He could be the smartest damn lawyer in New York or the dumbest and

I wouldn't know the difference between him and the Maytag repairman."

"What's his name?" she asked.

"Marvin something. Marvin Fleischman."

She shook her head. "Don't know him."

"Have you spoken to Mom?" I asked.

"Once," he said. "Her sister drove in from Seattle."

"She didn't want to be here?"

"I wouldn't let her be here," he said.

"If you're worried about the money, she could stay with me," I said.

"She's not here because I don't want her to be. The house won't take care of itself. Bills don't send their own checks."

"People can help you and her, Dad."

"We don't need people. We're fine."

"Clearly."

"These public defenders," my father said. "Do they know their ass from their elbow?"

"Depends," she replied. "A lot of lawyers go the PD route because they believe everyone deserves a fair trial and good representation. Believe it or not, a lot of lawyers enter the profession for the nobility of it. Of course, a lot of them go the PD route because it's a guaranteed paycheck, as opposed to private practice where you run the risk of getting stiffed on your bill by a client who can't pay. And…" She trailed off.

"And what?" James Parker said.

"And some of them, well, let's just say that government work does not always attract the best and the brightest." My father slumped into his chair. I got the feeling he thought this Marvin Fleischman fit the latter category. "But seriously, Mr. Parker, every lawyer is different. You could get great representation from a PD."

"So," I said, "let's hope you got a guy who graduated from Harvard Law with a summa cum laude in nobility."

The noise my dad made said he wasn't quite expecting that to be the case.

"Listen, Dad," I said, "we've found out a lot. About Stephen, his family. I think he was mixed up in some pretty bad stuff."

"You're telling me. Remember, I knew that mother of his."

I didn't have the heart to tell him that unless Helen Gaines was a junkie back in Bend, she'd only gotten worse. Two peas in a pod, her and James Parker.

I filled him in on what we did know. About Helen and Beth-Ann Downing. About Rose Keller, and the Vinnie brigade.

"We need to know more about the night you saw them," I said. "We know Helen wanted money from you, and she told you it was for rehab, but I don't think that's the case. Think about your conversation with Helen. Specific words. Gestures. Clues that might give us a lead as to where the money would actually be going, or what was running through Helen's mind when you saw her."

He rubbed his head, either thinking very hard or working very hard not to think. "Henry, it was a rough night. I remember the big things. The gun, this woman I hadn't seen in years looking like she was hopped up on something."

"Like what?"

"I don't know, I'm not a doctor. But her eyes were

red as all hell and she had a bad cough. That girl was not in good shape."

I looked at Amanda. That would jibe with the possibility that Helen was still using.

"Anything else?" I asked.

He tapped his thumb against his cheek, tongue flicking against his upper lip. "One thing seemed strange," he said. "Helen."

"You mean besides the jitters and the gun? What about her?"

"She was a mess, but she was scared, too," my father said. "And not of me. Kept looking around, like someone could burst through the door at any moment. I could tell from her eyes something was wrong. Now, does that make sense? She wants to check her son into rehab, seems to me that'd be a cause to have hope, you know, these two chuckleheads finally getting their act together. But Helen wasn't like that. When she didn't think I was going to give her the money, she just… freaked out."

"Maybe that's why she took the gun out," Amanda said. "She was worried that if she didn't get the money from you something terrible was going to happen."

"What?" my father asked.

"I don't know, but you're right about her being scared. Granted, I've never been to rehab, but you'd think fright isn't the number-one emotion running through a mother's head when helping her son. Unless she was scared of you. Is that possible?"

"Oh, she was scared of me at the end of the night, I'll say that, but this was there when I got to the apartment. Something else scared Helen."

Amanda said, "I'd be surprised if what scared Helen didn't kill her son."

We both looked at her, knowing she was on the money.

Turning back to my father, I said, "Please, Dad, think hard. Did she say anything, anything at all that could give you a clue as to what she was afraid of?"

My father raised his head, his eyes red. His breathing grew labored. Immediately I recoiled and Amanda looked at me. I could see my father's teeth, bared through his lips. I'd seen this before. It was rage boiling inside him, ready to explode. It was how he would get when my mother or I upset him. It was how he looked before a rampage, before he made us too scared to live in our own home. It was the rage and confusion of a man who couldn't do anything to stop his world from spinning on an already tilted axis. So all he could do was force that energy outward onto the people closest to him.

I watched this from across the table as he simmered for several minutes. Then the rage subsided, his breathing returning to normal. He realized there was nowhere for the rage to go here. No outlet for it. He was an animal surrounded by barbed wire.

I finally realized that what it took to subdue my father was not him seeing the pain he caused others, but him seeing the pain he could cause himself.

"There was a notepad," he finally said quietly. "At one point Helen went to the bathroom. I took a look around the apartment, just curious. So I see this lined pad she must have just been writing in."

"What was on it?" I said.

"First thing she wrote, weird as hell, was 'Mexico' and 'Europe.'"

"Any specific country in Europe?"

"No, just Europe."

"Maybe those were rehab spots Helen had in mind. Cheaper ones since she couldn't afford the tony places in the States. What else?"

"Next she wrote '$50,000,' with a question mark after it."

"Thirty years' back child support," Amanda said. "That could add up to fifty grand. Maybe that's what the number represented."

"The last word she wrote was—" my father thought for a moment "—fury."

"Fury?"

"It was capitalized, like a name. And she underlined it. A few times. With another question mark at the end."

"We can guess what the other words represented," I said. "But what does the 'Fury' mean?" I asked the question, but a small chime went off in my subconscious. Like I'd heard the word before. And not in relation to its standard usage. Something more specific. But I couldn't conjure up just what it was.

"What if," Amanda said, "they had nothing do to with rehab facilities or resorts. What if Stephen and Helen were trying to get away from something?"

"Like what?" my father asked.

"I don't know, but that kind of money seems kind of high for a rehab joint, especially when he could probably just check himself into detox. It would, though, be just enough money if you wanted to disappear."

"Fifty grand might get you somewhere," I said, "but is it enough to start a new life?"

"Maybe not," she said. "But it might be enough to survive."

20

We arrived back home feeling like we'd taken a few too many punches to the head. So many thoughts and ideas were swimming around in there—mixed in with the fear and apprehension of what my father was going through—that I wished we could just curl up in bed, fall asleep for a month or two and wake up with everything back to normal.

Even if we did manage to prove that my father didn't kill Stephen, James Parker would go right back to Bend where he would reenter that joke of a life. My mother hadn't even come because he refused to let her. He wouldn't be seen like this. Chained. Weak. And knowing my mother, she wouldn't question it.

I wondered if it was worth it. Saving him. Maybe the universe was a little more right with James Parker in jail. Maybe I was saving a man who didn't deserve to be saved.

Yet here I was, doing what needed to be done. Trying to find the proof that would free him. I wondered if he would do the same for me. The answer was fairly obvious.

I thought about the money Helen Gaines had asked for. Amanda was right. If Stephen's aim was to check into rehab, fifty grand was overkill. It could have been for more drugs, I supposed, but if the two of them had subsisted for nearly thirty years to this point, it didn't make sense that they suddenly needed a lump sum to sate their cravings.

From what it seemed like, the dealers I'd seen the other day had more than enough business to keep them going. True, on the surface the ones I saw looked far more put together than my brother. Scott Callahan and Kyle Evans barely looked like they touched the stuff. What was the old drug dealer's maxim—never get high on your own supply?

These two, as well as their well-heeled cohorts, looked as if they were in this game to make as much money as possible. With the exception of the kid whose briefcase now sat in my living room, they all looked like red-meat alpha males, the kind of guys who would normally be braying on the floor of the stock exchange rather than riding the subway to dole out dime bags.

Thing is, the cocaine in the briefcase made it clear that not all of their scores were small-time. Any company built its business on a combination of small revenue streams mixed with larger ones. The larger ones took more effort and paid higher dividends, but the smaller ones tended to be the most dependable, the ones that would always be there.

With the economy tanking the way it was, with people watching their wallets to a degree I'd never experienced in my lifetime, it wouldn't surprise me if disposable income for recreational drugs—like it was for all other consumer products—was being severely limited. Especially since coke was a favorite amongst bankers, financiers (i.e., high-salaried types). The kind of people whose livelihoods were being dashed against the rocks as the economy tumbled.

Maybe Stephen and Helen really were trying to start a new life. After all, Helen had desired nothing more than to raise her son with James Parker (why on God's green earth she would want to do this is an entirely different matter. One I'm not sure had a satisfactory answer).

Leaving the country would enable them to start their lives anew, to begin fresh somewhere they weren't known. Where demons and drugs wouldn't follow them.

But that last word…Fury. I still didn't know what it meant, if anything. It might have been a spasm, something Helen Gaines wrote while her mental faculties bounced around like Ping-Pong balls.

I put it on the back burner. If it was relevant, it would come up again.

The apartment felt warm and inviting, though compared to the visitation room in a correctional facility an icebox would have felt warm and inviting. We both stripped off our clothes, Amanda jumping into the shower while I pulled on a pair of shorts and a T-shirt. Before long, steam was pouring through the slat in between the door and the tiling.

I approached the door silently, then knocked gently. There was no answer. I knocked again, and when there was still no reply I knocked again, louder.

One more knock and I heard the water turn off.

"What is it, Henry?" She sounded annoyed.

"Just wanted to say hi," I said. "Go back to your shower."

"Gee, thanks."

The water came back on. Good thing there was no lock on the bathroom door.

I gently turned the knob, the cool air flowing into my face. I could see Amanda's body hazy behind the shower glass. She hadn't seen me yet.

I stripped off my shorts, flung the T-shirt onto a chair. Then I pulled open the shower door.

Amanda spun around, shampoo in her hair. The look on her face quickly went from annoyance to surprise to pleasure. She pushed the door open and I joined her, wrapping my body around her, feeling her warmth surround me.

We kissed, and then our bodies were clinging to each other, skin on skin. Pain and hurt and everything else melted away as we touched. My body was on fire as I kissed her neck, Amanda throwing her head back as she sighed. I kissed her up and down her body, feeling her skin tingle below my fingertips. Then I pressed myself against her, hard, and she moved in perfect rhythm with my body.

We touched and held and moved against each other under that beating stream for a long time, until the heat became so unbearable that we ended up in bed, naked, clinging to each other like we always did when we wanted the world to melt away for a little while.

I left Amanda sleeping in bed and crept into the living room. Booting the computer up, I poured myself a cup of ice coffee from the jug we kept in the fridge. I took a sip. Stale. It'd probably been sitting in there close to a week. I checked the freezer, but we were fresh out of grounds. Instead, I poured a healthy dollop of milk, added enough sweetener to make my teeth chatter and sat down.

Our Internet connection was spotty at best, so it was a sigh of relief when my home page came up. I'd changed my preferences so that the *Gazette*'s page would load whenever I opened my browser. I took a moment to read the latest stories, then went to Google and began my search.

I typed in the name "Scott Callahan." To no great surprise, over four thousand entries came up. To refine the search, I added "New York."

That narrowed it down to under a thousand. There were a few wedding notices and Web sites for law offices, but unfortunately none of them had any pictures. I scrolled through a few dozen pages hoping for something that would perhaps be linked to the Scott Callahan I followed the other day, but nothing came up.

I went back to the Google home page and typed in "Kyle Evans" and "New York." Two thousand entries came up. I sighed, having no choice but to slog through.

Nothing seemed to be terribly interesting until the fourth page. The page title was "Dozens laid off in wake of financial collapse." I clicked the link.

The article was from a financial magazine, dated about six months ago. It was a feature on the recent meltdowns of several financial institutions and the decision to lay off massive numbers of workers, some of whom had just graduated from business school. The author had interviewed several recently fired employees, including one man named Kyle Evans.

The section read:

> Kyle Evans expected to pay off his student loans in a matter of months, having taken a six-figure job right after receiving his MBA. Yet within weeks of his first day, Evans, a twenty-seven-year-old Wharton graduate, was unemployed and unable to find a job.
>
> "Between undergrad and Penn I owe about a hundred thousand dollars," Evans said. "I was going to have a bitch of a time paying it back anyway, but now what do I do?"

Though the article was posted on the Web, there were several photos taken of its subjects. They were small thumbnails, and according to the site these were exclusive and had not been printed in the physical magazine.

And there, in a group of three other men and woman his age, was the very Kyle Evans I'd seen on the street the other day. His hair was shorter and he was about ten pounds heavier, but there was no doubt it was him.

Suddenly Kyle's career choice made more sense. With no income, and training for jobs that didn't exist anymore, Kyle had decided to take another route to paying off his loans, joining an industry that didn't have as many down cycles. One that could afford him the same lifestyle. The same money.

It was a fair assumption that Scott Callahan—and maybe some, if not *all*, the other briefcase men—were victims of the same circumstances as Kyle. If you thought about it, who would make better drug couriers? These people were young, energetic, highly motivated, perhaps by money above all else. And, most of all, they *owed.* And if they owed enough, they'd be willing to take a few risks, break the law for a while before they found their footing. But who was employing them? What was 718 Enterprises?

I pulled "718 Enterprises" into Google, Yahoo! and half a dozen other search engines. Less than a dozen hits came up, none of them looking as if they had anything to do with a company of that name or with any relation to New York. I twiddled my thumbs. I'd never been a thumb twiddler, but at this point I wasn't quite sure where to go or who to talk to. And we still had no idea where Helen Gaines was.

I opened up the music player on my computer, took a pair of headphones out and put on some Springsteen. Something about the Boss always made me think a little more clearly. There was honesty in his voice that was often missing from popular music, and his earlier works were like pure blasts of adrenaline. That's what I needed right now. An energy boost to carry me along. There were half a dozen threads in this story, and I had no doubt that when unravelled they would all lead to Stephen's killer. I just needed that one connecting thread that told me how the story would all play out.

I sat there for half an hour, shuffling between songs. "Dead Man Walking" came on. It was a haunting tune, composed for the movie of the same name where Sean Penn played a character named Matthew Poncelet, on death row for the murder of two teenagers. The film was based on a book by Sister Helen Prejean, and Poncelet

was actually a composite of two men Prejean had coun-
seled. Prejean grows closer to this man many viewed
as a monster, trying to understand the humanity beneath
the inhumane crime. The music was simple, tragic, and
the lyrics filled my head as my eyes closed, the sounds
enveloping me.

All I could feel was the drugs and the shotgun
And the fear up inside of me

Suddenly my eyes opened. I stood up, the headphones flying off my head and clattering on the floor.

Drugs.

The Fury. I knew that word had sounded familiar, in
a context that, if I was right, made terrifying sense.

We kept a bookshelf in the living room, spines three
deep and nearly pouring out onto the floor. I'd bought it
used for seventy-five bucks from a thrift shop. It was
maple, still in good shape, with one large crack running
lengthwise down the side. I figured a good book was one
read so often the spine was cracked, a good bookshelf was
one that was cracked as well. That might have been justification for the piece's condition, but it made sense to
me.

Sometimes when I'd finish a book I'd bring it to the
office, drop it in the Inbox of a reporter who I thought
might enjoy it. Sports books went to Frank Rourke,
trashy celebrity tell-alls went to Evelyn Waterstone. I
knew the gal had her soft spot.

There were some books, though, that would never
leave this shelf. And no matter where I moved, or what
life planned for me, they would never be far away.

Without a second thought I pulled a pile of books
from the middle shelf and sent them toppling to the

ground. The noise was loud, and soon Amanda entered, bleary eyed, clearly wondering what was making such a racket. I must have looked half-crazed, throwing books on the floor, looking for that one book I knew was there.

But I couldn't find it.

I threw more books on the floor, the shelves emptying, my frustration growing. Where the hell was it? I knew it was here, somewhere.

"Henry," Amanda said, the patience in her voice surprising me. "I'm not going to ask. I assume there's a good reason for this. What are you looking for?"

"A book," I said stupidly, still rifling through the few books left. I told her the title and author. She looked at me, then walked back into our bedroom. I figured she'd had enough, would try to go back to sleep. But a minute later she came back holding something in her hands. And when my tired eyes focused, I saw what it was.

Through the Darkness, by Jack O'Donnell.

"I was reading it, remember?"

"You are so freaking beautiful," I gushed, standing up and taking the book from her.

I opened the cover, thumbed to the table of contents. There it was, chapter eight. "The Unknown Devil."

I began to skim, looking for that one word, that one phrase I knew existed. It was the link, what Helen Gaines was talking about. What she and Stephen were running from.

Then I found it. Midway down one page. I read the paragraph, feeling a chill run down my spine.

As the '80s came to a close, police were baffled by a string of homicides occurring at seemingly random locations at random intervals. Between August 1987 and October 1988, two dozen men were found murdered execution-style, often with one or two bullets emptied into their heads. These men were notable because they had previously been either arrested or identified as drug dealers, peddling primarily crack cocaine (among other narcotics).

It was felt, both by the law enforcement community as well as within the criminal element itself, that these murders were part of a larger consolidation of Manhattan's drug trade. Whispers began to grow about a man presumably responsible for the carnage, a ghost whose identity nobody could confirm, and details about whom nobody would (or could) go on the record about.

In fact, the only evidence there was to this man's existence at all was at the murder scene of one Butch Willingham. Willingham had been shot twice in the back of the head. The wounds were catastrophic, though miraculously, neither bullet was instantaneously fatal.

The autopsy concluded that Willingham had lived between five to ten minutes after the shootings, though the terminal damage to his brain prevented him from moving, speaking or doing anything to save his own life.

Apparently the bullets did not completely deprive Willingham of all of his motor skills during that brief period he remained alive, because while Willingham lay dying, his skull shattered by the slugs, he scribbled two macabre words on the floor of his apartment, using only the blood leaking from his own body.

The Fury.

21

I spent the rest of the night rereading *Through the Darkness*. It had been several years since I'd last read it, and the sense of awe I gained by reading Jack's work was tempered by the sudden knowledge that a forgotten passage from the book was somehow relevant to two murders today.

Most of the book came back to me, like seeing a good friend after a long absence. Amanda woke up, kissed me on the cheek and left for work, knowing how important this was. There were no other explicit references to the Fury, no other mention of who it was, or whether or not he or she even existed. People say some strange things when they've been shot in the head.

I opened up the search engine on my computer and looked for any old interviews Jack had done for the book. Unfortunately most had either not been archived digitally or they'd been lost, because only two came up. Neither mentioned the Fury in any way.

Working at the *Gazette,* Jack's presence was missed on a daily basis. Now, his absence felt like a hole in my stomach, an emptiness. I needed to talk to him, to see

what he knew, what he remembered. But Jack was recovering from his own battle with alcohol, and I
couldn't bring myself to interrupt that. There was one
person, though, who might be able to help. Thankfully
he worked long hours, and started the day early.

Wallace Langston picked up on the second ring.

"Henry," he said. "I was wondering when next I'd
hear from you. You do still work here, right?"

"How are you, Wallace?" I figured I'd ignore the
question.

"I'm doing well. Henry, what's up? Or did you just
call to make sure I'd had my morning coffee?"

"Actually, that's why I called," I said. " Seriously, I
need some help. Listen, Wallace, I need to ask you a
question. It's about Jack."

There was a moment of hesitation on the other end.
"What is it?" Wallace said curtly.

"I'd rather we talk face-to-face. It's not about my job
or the paper. You can say no if you want…but I need to
know. It's kind of personal."

"My door's always open, Henry. As long as you're
honest with me about what you want and why you need
it."

"You have my word. I'll be there in forty-five minutes."
I was putting on my shoes before I even heard the dial tone.

The newsroom was loud, boisterous.

I heard Frank Rourke shouting at someone over the
phone, something about a report that the Knicks were
about to can their coach. I heard Evelyn Waterstone
chewing out a reporter who'd misspelled the word
borough on his story. All of these sounds make me

smile. Who would have thought this kind of chaos could be an antidote to everything that had been going on?

I made my way down the hall, toward Wallace's office.

"Henry, what's shakin', my man?"

I turned slowly, eyes closed, my stomach already feeling sick. Tony Valentine was standing in the hallway, a goofy grin on his face. At first something looked different about him, then I noticed how unnaturally smooth his forehead looked. And not many people could smile without creating smile lines. I wondered if he had a Botox expense account as part of his salary package.

"Listen, Parker, I got something for you. I know you've got a girlfriend—don't we all? But there's this actress... can't tell you her name, but it rhymes with Bennifer Maniston. She's a good friend of mine and she's in town for a few days. I was thinking the two of you could go out to dinner. Nothing special or fancy, but tomorrow it's in my column. You get great press for canoodling with a star, she gets good press for dating a nice young reporter who won't ditch her for a costar. Sound good? Say the word and you've got reservations for two at Babbo."

I stared at Tony for a minute, then said, "Goodbye." I turned around and headed for Wallace's office.

He was sitting down, elbows on his desk, papers splayed out in front of him. "Henry, sit down," he said. The last few months had been tough on Wallace. Jack's departure had hit the paper hard, but Wallace personally. Harvey Hillerman, the publisher of the *Gazette,* had been eyeing the bottom line closer than ever.

Whether Jack had lost a few miles of his fastball was

to some extent irrelevant. He still brought readers to the paper, and he knew New York City better than anyone alive. His name off the masthead hurt our readership, bit into our circulation and took a bite from our advertising revenue. There was no replacing him. We were all praying for his recovery, but Wallace was praying for more than that. He needed Jack for the paper. For his job. For all our jobs, in a way.

I envisioned myself as the kind of reporter who could ease the *Gazette* into the next generation, but I never saw that happening without Jack. He wasn't someone who simply disappeared. He had to leave on his own terms, when he was ready.

And having known Jack for a few years, having gotten close enough to him for the man to confide in me, I knew that before his battle with the bottle nearly killed him and his reputation, he had no desire to go quietly into that good night.

"Thanks again for seeing me."

"No problem," he said. "My door is always open."

I laughed. "So I wanted to talk about Jack. Specifically something he wrote a long time ago."

"Shoot."

"It wasn't for the paper."

Wallace leaned back, curious.

"What is it then?"

"Twenty years ago, Jack wrote a book called *Through the Darkness*. It was about the rise of drugs and drug-related violence. Do you remember it? Jack was working at the *Gazette* when it was published."

"I sure do. O'Donnell took a year off to write that book, and after it came out and became a bestseller none of us expected him back. We figured he'd take the money and work on books full-time, especially when Hollywood came calling. But the news runs in that man's veins. Leaving never even occurred to him."

"It still hasn't," I said. Awkwardness choked the room. I had no idea if Wallace had even been in contact with Jack since he left, but the man's downcast eyes let me know he was happy to talk about Jack's past, but less so discussing the man's future. Part of me felt as if Wallace and Hillerman bore some responsibility for Jack's condition. They knew his alcoholism had been getting worse, but other than a few halfhearted Band-Aid measures they'd stand by, let him turn in substandard material, drinking Baileys with his coffee during war room meetings at nine in the morning. Perhaps they let it slide because they didn't want to believe it could destroy a man with his reputation. Or maybe they turned their backs because they needed to. Needed him.

"So what about the book?" Wallace asked, his voice sounding less patient, a little less happy I was there.

"Butch Willingham," I said. "He was a street dealer killed in '88. His death would have gone unnoticed—like most of his colleagues, if you will—except that unlike the others he survived his execution for a few minutes. He had just enough time to write two words, using his own blood. Do you remember what those words were?"

"No, I can't say I do. I haven't read the book in at least a decade."

"I remember," I said. "Not too often you forget something like that. The two words Willingham wrote were 'The Fury.' Do they ring a bell now?"

Wallace sat there without taking his eyes off me. I waited, unsure of what he was going to say. Instead, he just sat there, waiting for the blanks to be filled in.

Since Wallace's memory didn't seem to be jogged much, I pulled a copy of the tattered paperback from my pocket. Moving around to the side of Wallace's desk— and realizing I hadn't ever viewed the room from that perspective before—I showed him the passage it came from.

"Look at this," I said. "Tell me if you remember anything about it, or Jack writing it."

Wallace took a pair of thin reading glasses from his desk drawer, slipped them on and read the passage. After a few seconds, he took the book from my hands and began to read further. I could tell from his eyes and intense concentration something was coming into focus. He was remembering. Excitement surged through me. This was something, I knew it. It had to be.

"The Fury," Wallace said. "If I recall correctly, it was a big nothing."

I stepped back around, sat down, confused. "What do you mean?"

"I remember when this happened, the Willingham case got a little press for a day or two, mainly over the gruesome details. You're right, it's not too often someone writes words in their own blood while dying, and the press, present company often included, loves the chance to hyperbolize and scare people to death with Stephen King–style visuals. O'Donnell did look into this, interviewing dozens of dealers, punks and scumbags."

"And?"

"For a while he was convinced that there was

an…entity…I guess that's what you could call it… named the Fury. It was the kind of word that existed only on the lips of people involved in drugs, mainly dealing. The Fury was some kind of mythical demon, some kind of human being so cold-blooded and cruel that nobody dared cross it."

"All those people killed during those years," I said, the picture coming into view. "Jack thought this Fury was behind it all. I have no idea if that's a person, an organization or a code for something else. But it's in there for a reason."

"That's right," Wallace said. "If I recall, the first draft of this book was a good hundred or so pages longer, but Jack's publisher balked at a lot of what he'd written about in the chapters on the Fury. There were no eyewitness accounts. It began and ended with Willingham. Nobody was willing to talk. They felt Jack was stretching too far with the blood angle, and by printing chapters about some boogeyman, some all-powerful kingpin, it weakened his other arguments. Made him look like he was aiming for sensationalism rather than good, solid journalism."

"Who won the argument?"

"Well," Wallace said, "you see how long your edition of the book is? It was going to be another hundred or so longer."

"So why did he leave that one part in?" I asked. "If everything else relating to this was taken out, why did they let him leave Butch Willingham writing that before he died?"

"If I remember—and you'll forgive me if my memory bank doesn't access twenty-year-old information as readily as it used to—Jack threatened to pull the plug on the whole book at that point. They'd already paid him, I believe a good six-figure sum, quite a penny for a book back in those days. And if they'd refused to publish, they wouldn't have recouped a penny since they would have been in breach of contract. So they allowed Jack to keep that one bit in. Kind of an appeasement. Jack considered it a footprint that couldn't be erased by time. And because what Willingham had written was in the coroner's report, it was a matter of public record and could stay in. Everything else, they felt, was conjecture."

"So Jack thought there was more to the Fury, then."

"I believe so, but again I'm speaking from what I recall twenty years ago. Jack and I haven't spoken about that book or that story in years. He's written half a dozen books since then, most of which made him a lot more money than *Through the Darkness*. And with no new leads to track down, no other proof or witnesses, it was on to new matters. In a city where new stories materialize every day, if you spend your time hoping a fresh angle will pop out of the ground you'll miss everything going around right beside your head. Jack's a great reporter, but he's not stupid."

"He's not a coward either," I said. "He kept that bit in there for a reason. Like you said, a footprint."

"Maybe he did," Wallace said.

"I need his files," I said.

"Henry," Wallace said, folding his hands across his chest. "You know better than that. Besides, company policy states that any work, research or otherwise, done on books is kept outside of the office."

"He must have something here," I said. "I've seen Jack's apartment. He barely had any furniture, let alone files. Please, do me a favor. Let me see Jack's files. I know there's a storage room here. I swear I won't take anything that doesn't pertain to the Willingham case. And I'll even do the digging for you."

"I can't let you do that," Wallace said. "But I'll meet you halfway. I'll go through it myself and send it over to you if I find anything. I'm going to err on the side of caution, though, so don't expect much."

"Thank you," I said. I stood up, prepared to leave. Then I saw a copy of that morning's *Gazette* on Wallace's chair. I looked up at him, raised an eyebrow.

"Go on, take it," he said, grinning. "But after today you don't get diddly-squat for free until I see your name below a story."

22

The subway was hot and humid as I went back uptown. I had no idea how long it would take for Wallace to get me those files. The man had been gracious enough to offer, and frankly I didn't expect much going in. I desperately wanted to know what Jack knew, what else he knew about the Willingham murder. And what, if anything, it had to do with Stephen Gaines.

The strange thing was, the deeper I looked into this, the further away it seemed to go from Gaines. From him to Beth-Ann Downing, from Rose Keller to Butch Willingham, there seemed to be a pattern of behavior that went back twenty years. I had no idea how long, if at all, my brother had been dealing. But I was damn sure that it had somehow gotten him killed.

Now, I've read the books. I've seen the TV shows. I read as much news as I can take until my eyeballs hurt. I'm well aware that pushing is not a profession made for duration. People get into it hoping to make a quick buck, usually because they have no other options. They have neither the education to get a job punching a clock, nor the desire to work for a corporation that can terminate them without a moment's notice. There was something romantic about the notion of a drug dealer, something that went against the system. But when I saw Stephen Gaines that night on the street, I did not see a man defiant in the face of unspeakable odds stacked against him. I saw a defeated, emaciated, broken-down young man. A man scared of something. Something he felt, for some reason, I could help with.

I was a newspaper reporter. Nothing more, nothing less. I sincerely doubted Gaines came to me because I was his flesh and blood. He'd had years to try to reach out. He came to me because something about my profession, my line of work, could have helped him, thrown him a lifeline.

I sat down, my butt immediately becoming stuck to the seat by a clear substance I hadn't seen before. The joys of traveling on the MTA. Unfolding that morning's copy of the *Gazette,* I put all thoughts of Gaines and Willingham out of my mind until I got home. Perhaps good old-fashioned newspaper reporting would help me out. Clear my mind.

But when I saw the story on page eleven, I nearly threw up.

Man, 27, Shot to Death in His Apartment

A photo accompanied the article. I recognized the man in the shot. I'd seen him just recently.

It was the guy whose briefcase I'd stolen. He was found last night, murdered, shot twice in the back of the head.

23

I couldn't think of any words. My mouth was dry, my head throbbing. Amanda and I were sitting in a cold room in the Twenty-eighth Precinct on Eighth Avenue between 122d and 123d streets. On the table in front of us were several items: an empty briefcase, several thousand dollars' worth of various types of narcotics; and one cell phone.

The man's name was Hector Guardado. He was twenty-seven years old. Lived alone in Spanish Harlem. According to police reports, Hector had less than a thousand dollars in his bank account. But upon searching his apartment, they found nearly fifty thousand dollars in cash stuffed underneath a fake floorboard in his kitchen.

Hector was not some young kid with no education dealing to make ends meet. He had an MBA. A freaking business degree. Yet despite the degree, despite the hundred thousand dollars he spent to attain it, Hector Guardado had not been able to find employment since returning to New York City, his hometown.

The other day I'd stolen Hector's briefcase to learn

more about his dealings, to learn more about this group of misfits that my brother may or may not have been a part of. And now the man was dead, murdered in cold blood. Another young man killed like a piece of meat, shot twice in the back of the head, surely by someone who knew him.

Because of that, I called Amanda the moment I got out of the subway. Stopping at the apartment first to pick up the briefcase and its contents, I headed straight for the police. No more clandestine detective work. No more hiding my hand until all the cards were dealt. A life had been taken.

It made me sick to my stomach to think that Hector Guardado's life might have been taken because of his stolen briefcase, but two days ago he was alive. Two days ago the briefcase, along with the drugs and his cell phone, were in his possession.

And now today he was dead, and the drugs were in police custody. I wasn't willing to write it off as a coincidence.

"You okay?" Amanda asked. I didn't nod. I wasn't the one on a slab somewhere, or being written about in the newspaper. She seemed to get this, because she didn't ask again.

Soon the door opened and a familiar face walked in: Detective Sevi Makhoulian.

Makhoulian sat down in a chair across from us. Looked me over, then looked at the items on the table. He took a pair of rubber gloves from his pocket, spread open the black folds of the suitcase and peered in.

"This everything?"

I nodded.

"And this was all in Guardado's possession when you took it from him."

I nodded again. "You can fingerprint it," I said. "I never touched the stuff." I nudged Amanda slightly with my elbow, giving her a silent thanks for the advice.

Makhoulian sighed and leaned back in his chair. He folded his arms behind his head as though deciding what to watch on television. He didn't look the least bit concerned with anything.

"What are you going to do?" I asked.

"Frankly," he said, "I'm not sure yet. Unfortunately we can't charge you with theft, because Mr. Guardado would have been our only witness, and frankly it would be a waste of time. Because, though I don't know you that well, anytime a person willingly brings half a pound of weed, a fourth of a kilo of cocaine and enough crack rocks to keep Flavor Flav's teeth chattering for a year, they're not the ones using it."

"We're not," Amanda said. "We weren't."

Makhoulian nodded, then thumbed his lip. "Look, Parker, I know you think your father is innocent. If I was in your shoes, I'd want to do anything I could to help him, too. And if he is innocent, he'll be found as such by a jury of his peers."

"The case hasn't even gone to the grand jury yet," Amanda spat.

"True, but we all know that's a mere formality. We have his fingerprints. We have his receipts from his trip to New York. And we have a motive."

"Does the name Butch Willingham ring a bell?" I asked suddenly.

Makhoulian looked confused. Said, "No, why?"

I believed him. "Nothing," I said. "Just a guy who was killed a long time ago."

"And you bring it up, why, as a brainteaser?"

"I'm not sure why," I said. "Just wondering if I'm the only one who thinks there's a lot more to this than a simple case of a guy murdering his son. Since, you know, another young man was just killed in the same manner as Stephen Gaines."

"The investigation into the death of Hector Guardado is under way," Sevi said. "You're a reporter, Henry, right? Can you tell me how many murders were committed in New York City last year?"

"Not the exact number, but I believe it was under five hundred."

"Four hundred and ninety-two," Makhoulian said. His eyes were riveted on mine. This was not a history lesson or an attempt to belittle my knowledge. "Now, first of all, that was the lowest number of murders committed in Manhattan in over forty years. First time it's been under five hundred since 1963, to be precise. Thing is, even though that's low for our standards, that's still an awful lot of homicides. Now, think about that word. *Homicide.* These four hundred ninety-two people were killed by someone else. They didn't step into open elevator shafts or pee on the third rail. They were killed. Murdered. Now, you are a reporter. So it's part of your job to report crimes that are extraordinary. Like Sharon Dombrowski, the elderly woman on Spring Street who was so convinced she was being targeted by a robber that she hooked up an electric cable to her door, so when her poor landlord came by to check on a leak and knocked he was electrocuted to death. Or Percy

Whitmore who bought a studio in Little Italy using a loan from his father. Only when he didn't repay in time, Percy's dad came over and smacked his son across the face so hard ol' Percy fell and cracked his skull open on his bookshelf. Accidental? Maybe. But homicides nonetheless."

"What's your point?" I said.

"See, you write about these instances because they're one in a million. Like a shark attack, they're so gruesome and out of the ordinary that people want to hear about them just like how they slow down when passing a car wreck. What doesn't get that press are the boring murders. The two taps to the back of the head." Makhoulian mimicked pointing a gun to his cranium, cocking his trigger finger twice to illustrate the shots. "You know how many of those nearly five hundred murders were the result of gunshot wounds? Four hundred and twenty-eight. Now, I'm not a mathematician, but that's somewhere between eighty and ninety percent. So you're going to come in here and tell me, *definitively,* that these two murders are the result of some vast conspiracy that I'm too dumb to see?"

"I'm not saying you're dumb. But Hector called my brother that night."

"According to Verizon, the phone call lasted eight seconds. You know how long eight seconds is? Long enough to realize you've dialed the wrong number before you hang up. There are no other records of these two having ever corresponded, no other calls between the two."

"You don't see these killings as two pieces to—"

"Pieces my ass, you're reading too much James

Ellroy. Know what they teach us in the academy? The rule of *lex parsimoniae*. Since I'm guessing you're not exactly fluent, what the Latin translates to is 'entities must not be multiplied beyond necessity.' Boil down the translation, what that means is if a man is murdered, and the fingerprints on the gun belong to someone he knows, who has access to him, and who has a *motive* to kill him, I'd be willing to bet my badge, my wife, my mortgage and my iPhone you put that killer in cell block D you've got the right guy."

"You said usually," I replied. "You said eighty to ninety percent. Well, it's my job to find the exception to your rule. I've told you everything I know. I'm hoping when I walk out of here you do something with it, and don't piss it all away because of what you read in a damn textbook. Because I *find* that extra few percent, Detective. Father or not, brother or not, it's just what I do."

Amanda and I stood up. Waited for Detective Sevi Makhoulian to say something. When he didn't, we waved at the camera so the observers in the other room would unlock the door. Makhoulian nodded, a click signaled that the door was unlocked, and I left to prove to the detective I was a man of my word.

And as I walked down the hallway, Amanda's unsteady hand locked in mine, I could feel the detective's eyes on my back.

24

I was dialing the number before I even left the station house. He picked up right away, his voice not even attempting to hide the boredom that had no doubt settled in over the past several months. Though I still harbored some guilt over what had happened, every time we spoke he'd forbid me to show any pity, either for myself or for him. To Curt Sheffield, being wounded in the line of duty was something to be proud of. He'd never wanted to be anything but a cop—and he was a damn good one at that—and he wasn't going to let some pissant reporter wallow in a pint over some spilt blood.

"Officer Sheffield," he said, practically moaning. Curt had taken a bullet in the leg last year while helping me investigate a series of child kidnappings. The slug had nicked an artery, and it took a few surgeries to repair the wound. He'd probably never run in the Olympics, but while he wouldn't accept anyone's pity he had told me on several occasions the injury had done wonders for his sex life. Guess chicks really do dig scars. I'd have to ask Amanda if that's why she was still with me.

"Hey, man, has your ass spread at all today?"

"S'up, Henry? Matter of fact I've been doing butt blasts at my desk. Docs won't let me go to the gym, but I think it's a trick to get me to keep coming in so they can charge my insurance company. I swear my ass looks like the victim of an attack of cottage cheese."

"I don't want to think about anything involving your butt. What do you say to a drink after work? On me."

"I don't know man, I feel like I gotta lay low a little bit. Last time I brought you in here I caught hell from the chief of the department. You don't have a lot of friends around here these days, especially considering what's going on with your pops. At least you can be happy you got the deep end of the Parker gene pool."

"I'll let that one slide. No work talk," I said. "Just conversation. All I ask. Okay, maybe one or two questions, but that's it."

Curt went silent, but I could tell he was checking his watch. Sitting behind the desk for Curt was like keeping a racehorse stalled behind the starting gate. He was born to walk the streets, not type up reports. That's likely why I felt the most guilt; it was one less great cop protecting the city.

"Gimme one hour. Mixins." Mixins was a cheesy singles bar primarily frequented by law and finance professionals who felt eight-dollar beers and weak cosmos were part of the mating ritual. The bar had undergone a total renovation over the last few years, mainly due to its predilection to serving underage girls. A friend of a friend who used to drink there said the waitstaff would grossly undercharge young women, naturally in the hopes of luring free-spending men to the bar. Soon enough the cops caught on. Though rumor had it they didn't so much as catch on, but an off-duty detective saw a group of girls walk directly to the bar once after finishing class on Friday.

The bar had been shut down, but underwent a classic change in management, and now you'd be hard pressed to find someone holding a glass who didn't take home close to six figures. Neither Curt nor I pulled in anywhere in the universe of that salary, but Curt enjoyed it because, in his words, finance girls were workaholics in every aspect of their lives. They kept their minds and their bodies sharp, and even though he seemed to always be in a serious relationship—sometimes several at once—he enjoyed having nice views at the bar. When I asked him about it, his answer was simply that I wasn't pretty enough to hold his attention through more than one round of drinks.

I got to the bar before he did, took a seat and ordered a Brooklyn Lager. The bartender, a tall, rail-thin guy wearing a tight black T-shirt that ended right above his veiny pelvic area, served it to me then recommended putting his elbows on the table and looking tortured. The stools by the bar were never full here. It wasn't the kind of place one went to for a quiet drink.

A few months ago I'd gone through a rough personal patch. When Amanda and I were separated for a while. Being apart from her led me to drink too much and seek out my own solitude. Losing a part of your life can be the most accurate barometer of what matters most. If you love something, being apart from it will haunt you. If it doesn't, it can't have mattered all that much to begin with.

Being apart from Amanda was a miserable experience. I slept at my desk at the *Gazette*. My personal hygiene fell a rung below your average wino's. I wondered if I was simply the kind of guy who always needed to be in a relationship. Before Amanda, I'd been with my previous girlfriend, Mya, for several years. We also ended badly, and after suffering brutal injuries at the hands of a maniac, she seemed fully recovered, her life back on track. I was happy with Amanda, and I knew the difference between a good and a bad relationship. Learning it had nearly killed me, but it was worth it.

After waiting fifteen minutes and downing half my beer, Curt strode into the bar. He was tall, black, in great shape, though his recent sedentary work life had softened the edges just a bit. He was wearing a dark shirt made of some shiny fabric. Certainly not what he wore on the job, unless the NYPD was far more fashionable than I'd thought.

Though his posture was perfect and he betrayed no sense of pain, there was still a slight limp evident in Curt's walk. I remembered seeing him lying there in a pool of blood, holding back the pain, unwilling to let anything get over on him. It was as though he was disgusted at himself for showing weakness, taking the maxim "never let them see you bleed" quite literally. If he was limping at all, he was probably in more pain and discomfort than he let on.

We shook hands, and Curt ordered a beer. The bartender poured it from the tap, eyeing Curt while letting the foam pour over, a thin smile on his thin lips. Once he'd set the glass down and moved away, I said to Curt, "Now batting for the other team…"

"Don't even start, Henry."

"What? That's a compliment. Any man who can attract players from both dugouts is doing something right. Besides, wearing that shirt, I wouldn't be surprised if a few new dugouts spring up."

"You know, Parker, I don't even know what the hell you're talking about sometimes." Curt sipped his beer.

"How's the leg?" I asked, slightly apprehensive. It would have been easier to ignore it, to pretend he'd never been shot and there was nothing holding him back. It would have been easier to sit here, drink and carry on, pretend he wasn't limping.

"It's getting better," he said. "Takes a while for the muscle strength to build up, since they had to slice through some muscle to repair the damage to the artery."

Just hearing this made me wince. "Does it hurt?"

"When it's cold out, yeah. Gets a little stiff on me. Plus, it's a little numb by my toes, on account of them having to go through some nerves, too. Docs aren't sure that'll ever come back. Not a big deal, though."

I wanted to scream at him and ask how that could not be a big deal, but I supposed if you took a bullet in an artery and that was the worst-case scenario, you tended to think on the bright side of things.

"Tell you one thing," Curt continued, "I'm going to have to start wearing gloves, they got me filling out so many forms. Feel like I'm a supporting cast member on *The Office* or something. The black dude who stands in the corner with paper cuts on every finger. How's Amanda?"

"She's doing well," I said. "Been a huge help on this thing with my dad. Without her he'd probably still be sitting in an Oregon prison claiming not to be James Parker."

"She's a good one, my man. Glad you finally made amends for all that crap you pulled breaking up with her."

"It wasn't like I was just breaking up with her," I said, taking another pull on my drink. "I thought I was doing the right thing, being noble."

"Nobility isn't about telling someone what you think is right for them. It's doing the right thing, period. Girls's a grown woman, she can make her own decisions. What you did was selfish, and it was to alleviate your own guilt over what happened to her and Mya. You felt like if you broke things off, you could feel as if you were protecting them. Just not so. I don't claim to be Mr. Perfect Relationship, but there's give-and-take. You're with someone, you're their partner. It was selfish, bro, own up to it."

"Maybe you're right," I said. "And trust me, I know I screwed up. And I'm atoning for it."

"How?"

"For starters, I cook every Friday night."

"You a good cook?"

"If by 'good' you mean she's able to swallow one forkful without gagging, then yeah, I'm a good cook."

Curt sipped his drink, then shifted his weight, a small grimace spreading over his face. It was a brief reaction and certainly unintentional, but for some reason it made my stomach feel hollow.

"Can I ask you something?" I said.

"'Course, man. You sound serious all of a sudden, you got a month to live or something?" he said, laughing.

I smiled, drank. "You ever feel like I do more harm than good? As a person?"

Curt looked at me. He could tell I was serious. "Not quite sure why you say that," he said. "But it feels to me like you might be having a little pity party."

"It's not that," I said. "I'm over all that. I just feel like over the last few years…I mean, look at it. Mya. Amanda. You. My dad. Just feels like all these people I'm supposed to be close to get hurt. Not to mention this guy who got killed the other day."

"What guy?' Curt asked.

I filled him in on the details of Hector Guardado and the briefcase. He sat there, focused, listening intently. He nodded when I brought up Detective Makhoulian, said he'd met the guy once or twice and that he seemed like he was on the up-and-up.

Often it took a good cop to recognize a good cop, so it was reassuring to hear Curt say that.

Though my first few months in the city I'd been distrustful of cops—and who could blame me since two of them tried to kill me for erroneous reasons—recently I'd begun to settle back in, believing that guys like Makhoulian were truly here to serve and protect. Just because most of them didn't like me didn't mean I didn't have respect for them.

"And you think this guy Guardado is somehow tied in to your brother's death?" he said.

"Probably not directly, but I caught Guardado coming out of a building where I saw a bunch of other drug couriers signing in to a company called 718 Enterprises. I couldn't find much on them, but I'm pretty sure Stephen might have worked for them at some point."

"Selling drugs," Curt said.

"That's right."

"And what's the name of that company you mentioned? 718?"

"718 Enterprises," I repeated.

Curt scratched his nose, downed the rest of his beer. "Not sure why, but for some reason that name sounds familiar."

"That means it's likely not a good thing," I said.

Curt shook his head, thinking. "Give me some time tonight, I'm going to go back and dig into some of the files, ask around."

"Curt, you don't have to do that, I—"

"Don't even start. I need to get some action, so don't look at this as a favor from me to you, but an excuse for me to get back on the horse."

"Then giddyup, cowboy," I said.

"You know damn well there were no black cowboys, and no, I don't count Mel Brooks movies."

"Actually I think there were," I said. "I know a little about the Old West."

"You being cute with me?" Curt said.

He stood up. We'd finished just one beer, but I could tell he was motivated. And since his motivation might answer a few questions, who was I to stop him?

"Keep your cell on, I'll give you a call tonight," he said. We shook hands and gave an awkward fist-bump man hug that I always felt silly doing but practiced nonetheless.

We both left the club, Curt hailing a taxi while I headed toward the subway. I hadn't known Curt to spend money on cabs too often, he preferred to walk or use public transportation. That he was willing to spring for a cab meant his leg was bothering him enough to forgo the walk to the bus stop.

I arrived home a little past nine. Amanda greeted me with a hug and a kiss and a plate of cold spaghetti. She was wearing an oversize gray sweatshirt and a pair of light blue boxer shorts, and looked absolutely adorable. Even the rumples of the sweatshirt couldn't hide the body beneath, and I made sure to squeeze her extra tight during our hug.

Changing into shorts and a T-shirt, I sat down at the table and dug into the food. She'd sprinkled a light sheet of parmesan over the tomato sauce.

"I can warm that up for you," she said.

"It's actually good like this," I said. "I ran some track back in high school and always ate cold pasta before meets. It always tastes better cold than reheated."

I proved this by shoveling another forkful in my mouth and grinning.

As I finished the meal, I couldn't help but think about how just yesterday a briefcase full of drugs had occupied the tabletop. Now the owner was dead, and it frightened me to think that whoever Hector Guardado was working for, his life was expendable compared to the contents of the briefcase.

And I wondered, again, why my brother's name was in a dead drug dealer's cell phone. And why Hector Guardado had called him once and only once, the night Stephen was murdered.

And as I sat there chewing and thinking, my cell phone rang.

Rummaging through the pile of laundry on the floor,

I pulled the phone from my pocket, clicked Send. I recognized the prefix as coming from Curt's precinct.

"This is Henry," I said.

"It's Curt."

"You find anything?" I said, beginning to feel that familiar rush of apprehension and excitement. Then I remembered what I'd told Wallace, promising that my mind was still with the paper. I had to think about all this information both as a son and a reporter.

"You could say that. Now I know why the name 718 Enterprises sounded familiar. You sitting down?" he said.

"Yes," I lied.

"Your boys Gaines and Guardado, they're not the only ones."

"What do you mean?"

"Five bodies, Henry. Christ, what have you gotten into."

I stood there, listened, feeling dread pour through me.

Curt continued, saying, "Five young men murdered, the coroner's reports all suggesting the use of a silenced pistol. All gunshots from close range, all execution-style. Assumed that the victims knew their killers. So if that's true, these guys were all killed just like Stephen Gaines. Which means all five people were somehow connected to this 718 Enterprises. And all of them killed in the past three months. It's not just Gaines and Guardado, man. Somebody is systematically taking out everyone who works for that organization."

25

When I was finally able to wrap my head around what Curt had just told me, I sent an e-mail off to Wallace Langston informing him of our conversation and what I'd learned. There had to be some sort of story in what Curt had told me, and I wanted to let Wallace know my mind was still sharp, I was still committed to the *Gazette,* and that at some point I'd have a hell of a page-one exclusive for him.

As always Wallace showed excitement for the possibility of the story, but again expressed concern that I was too often finding myself in situations where uncovering a story would put myself or others in harm's way. The fact was I'd never been to Iraq, never reported on a war from the trenches, so neither he nor I could state that any danger I found myself in could compare. Bad things happened to find me. So be it. If I was still reporting about cute kittens and big ugly metal spiders— I mean, *works of art*—I would have impaled myself on a number-two pencil by now.

And as much as it energized me to think of this as a

story, I knew it helped distract from the apprehension I had over finding the truth.

Five young men murdered, all with connections to 718 Enterprises. I had no idea what the company did, but the name and address were clearly a front for something. And somehow, after Helen Gaines brought him to New York, my brother had begun to work for them.

If only he were alive today. If only I'd waited on that street corner. If only I'd heard what he had to say.

According to Curt, when the dead mens' bodies were investigated, a phone number attributed to 718 Enterprises was found on their call lists. When dialed, the numbers led nowhere, and in fact each man's cell had a different number credited to 718. This cemented my feeling that Stephen Gaines's murder was one part of something much bigger, much broader, and that not only did my father's freedom and his son's killer hang in the balance, but potentially much more.

Amanda was asleep. Nights like this I would often find myself sitting on the couch in our living room. No music playing, no television. No noise at all beyond what the city offered.

It took a few minutes to realize it, but it began to dawn on me just how strange my world had become. Nearly ten years ago I'd left the confines of Bend, Oregon. In part because my ambition drew me to more crowded, deeper waters. I was tired of living in what I felt was a small world, confined to a small house made even smaller still by the discomfort of being around my parents. I longed for adventure, mystery.

I wanted to make a name for myself, and thought nowhere better to do that than in the city that never sleeps.

Now, however, I found myself glad for any quiet that nighttime offered. The fact that my windows weren't soundproof and I could hear car horns and alarms all hours of the night only made the feelings more intense. On those rare nights when I could hear nothing but the hum of my air conditioner, night as I knew it reminded me of those old days in Bend. Those quiet nights I lay restless in my bed, longing for noise that proved I was somewhere, had *become* someone. Having been on the front page, having people know my name and my face, it was everything I wanted but nothing I'd expected.

Not for the first time I wondered if perhaps I'd be happier elsewhere, if Amanda and I lived in a place where I could report in a town where the media wasn't the focus of the media itself, where good work could be done out of the spotlight.

Where nobody else would get hurt.

News was in my blood. Had been for a long time. But was this what I wanted, what I'd dreamed of? At first it had been. That first day at the *Gazette*, seeing Jack O'Donnell at his desk, the first time I read my own byline, each of these was one of *those moments* in your life that you remember for years. What was happening now, though, I didn't want to remember. But if my father was going to survive, and if Stephen Gaines's killer was going to be brought to justice, I sure as hell couldn't forget.

It was only a few days before my father went in front of a grand jury. That jury would more than likely indict him for the murder of his own estranged son. No doubt once that judgment was passed along, my father would go through the same ringer I did when I was wrongly accused of the crime. Only for him, he would be incarcerated, a slab of meat lying in a cage for the wolves to pick at whenever they chose. Even though I escaped with a pierced lung, my ordeal never made it to court. I had to get my father out before that took place.

There was one person who had knowledge of 718 Enterprises. One person who likely knew both Hector Guardado and my brother. One person I knew enough about to make him listen.

I had to wait about eighteen hours before I could confront him.

It was going to be a long day.

I sat on the front stoop sipping from a cup of coffee, one of those great, old-fashioned cups that were made of cardboard and had cute little illustrations of mugs with wings on the side. Coffee cups these days seemed to be tall, sleek models that looked more like tubes of enriched uranium than something you drank to wake up in the morning. The deli I got this from had no logo, no branding, and the bag they gave it to me in had one of those cheerful I♥NY slogans on the side. Those were the bags you gave out when you didn't have a Web site, and didn't have spontaneous MP3 downloading capability.

There was no definitive time when he'd be home. I'd arrived at 7:00 p.m. on the chance it was an early day. So far it had not been. Around eight-thirty I went for a quick walk up and down the block to keep my blood flowing, and to make sure people in the neighborhood didn't get suspicious.

Finally at eight-thirty, just as I was beginning to feel the need to pee, I saw him walking down the street.

He carried the briefcase lightly. It was clearly empty.

As he got closer I could see that his suit was wrinkled, stained through with the sweat from a day spent going house to house, subway to subway.

When he got close enough to the point where he could see me, I stepped out onto the sidewalk. Right in front of him. He was bigger than I remembered, and the ill-fitting suit didn't fully stretch enough to hide the muscles in his arms. The shock of black hair that had surely been neatly combed that morning now sat askew on his head, beads of sweat traveling down his forehead and nestling in the collar of his formerly white oxford shirt. The man stopped for a moment, eyed me curiously, defensive, as though he half-expected me to take a random swing at him.

"Scott Callahan?" I said.

"The hell are you?" Scotty replied, taking a step back.

"My name is Henry Parker," I said. "And you're going to want to talk to me."

Scotty walked in front of me the whole way, like a prisoner heading toward the electric chair, knowing there was no chance of reprieve. On the street, Scotty had told me to go to hell. I responded by telling him everything I knew, how I'd followed him the other day. How I'd observed him going into each of those houses, how I knew he was selling drugs.

I had to leave out my stealing Hector Guardado's briefcase. He didn't need to know I was so close. I wanted to have leverage on Scotty, but put too much weight on a person and rather than talk they'll simply buckle. If Scotty thought I knew so much to the point where I could incriminate both him and 718 Enterprises, he'd feel no reason to talk to me. He needed to feel there was a way out. If there was a chance at survival, there was a chance to talk his way out of it.

I told him my name, my job. That he could end up on the front page of the *Gazette* tomorrow. Naturally I didn't tell him this was a personal investigation, but chances were Scotty Callahan would not be the kind of guy who'd consider filing a suit for libel.

We went into a 24-hour coffee shop, somewhere quiet where we wouldn't be disturbed and didn't have to worry about being kicked out. Scotty walked with his head down, and for a moment I felt sorry for the guy. He was still in his rumpled suit, still carrying the same briefcase. As he walked, the case flopped against his side like a fish running out of air.

I led him to the back of the restaurant, where we took a booth. A waitress came by and dropped two menus on the table with a *thunk*. One good thing about New York coffee shops, they took the food from every menu in the city and crammed it under one roof. You could order anything from a BLT to baby back ribs to sushi. Though I wouldn't recommend coffee-shop sushi.

Scotty slid into the far end of the booth. He looked tired, and I could imagine that this was literally the very last place on earth he wanted to be. After a long day delivering house to house, I was sure a cold beer and a warm bed were the next two items on his agenda. They'd have to wait a little while.

"You're making a big mistake," Scotty said. "I don't know anything."

"See right there," I said, pointing at him. "That's how I know you're lying. Anyone who says 'you're making a big mistake' knows a whole hell of a lot."

"Great, so you're a mind reader. Read my palm and let me the hell out of here."

"You stand up before I say you can, and you know what the front page of the paper says tomorrow?" I held up my hands as though spelling out a movie matinee for him. "It says, 'Scott Callahan, drug dealer.' Now, I don't know what your dreams and ambitions are, Scotty, but I'm going to guess you'll have a tough time finding gainful employment after that happens. So we're going to sit here, I'm going to have a big-ass chocolate milk shake, and we're going to talk. Then, maybe, if I feel like you've been honest, you can go."

"And if not?"

I held up my hands again, framing the marquee. "Then consider yourself Spitzered."

"You're a classy guy."

"Yeah, and how's the drug-dealing business going?"

"I'm not a drug dealer," Scotty said. The anger in his voice told me he actually believe what he said.

"Now, I'm not sure what the actual term 'drug dealer' is in Webster's, but I'm pretty sure that if you go door to door selling drugs, you'd find a picture of yourself next to that definition."

The thing was, I had no proof of Scotty being a dealer. I could link him to 718 Enterprises, and Hector Guardado, and possibly even my brother, but I hadn't actually witnessed him doing it. Thankfully by denying it with such vehemence he proved it for me.

"I'm not a dealer," he said. His voice was quieter this time. I wondered if Scotty had ever sat alone in the dark thinking about what he was doing, what he'd become. The softness in his tone told me he had. "That's not what I do."

"Then, please," I said. "Enlighten me."

He looked at me suspiciously, his eyes traveling over my shirt, my chest. Then he leaned over and peered under the table.

"Can I help you?" I said.

"Are you wired?"

I shook my head. "I'm not. This is between you and me, for now. I'm not looking to bust you. That's the truth. I just want some answers and I know you have them. You help me, I help you."

"How do you help me?" he said.

"By keeping my mouth shut."

"And how can I know I can trust you?" he asked. "I have a family, man. I have friends. They all think I'm living on a sweet severance package."

I sat for a moment. "You know what guys usually say in the movies when someone asks how they know they can trust them?"

"No."

"They say, 'because you have no choice.' So right now, you have no choice but to trust me. I'd be happy to strip down to my George Foreman underwear, but I don't think that's a scene either of us needs."

Just to show him I was on the up-and-up, I stood up, flattened out my jeans and did a quick flip-up of my top.

Sitting back down, I could tell Scotty was far from satisfied, but he also knew if motivated, I could cause him a world of trouble.

"They're not my drugs," he said. "I never wanted to do it. I mean, you're a reporter, right?"

"That's what my business card says."

"So you've got a job. And even though everyone's saying newspapers are going in the tank, you're still getting paid, right?"

I wondered where this was going, but nodded.

"I had my life planned out. I was gonna have my MBA by twenty-six," Scotty said. "So much for that. Three-point-nines all the way through college. Paid my own way through school because my parents could barely afford to buy the clothes I took with me. And right before I graduated, I got a six-figure job with Deutsche Bank structuring CDOs. That's the American dream, right"

"CDOs?" I said.

"Collateralized debt obligations. Basically you have a lot of banks giving out hundreds of thousands of loans. These loans are packaged into what's called a security. Then a bunch of securities are piled into what's called a CDO. Then when the crisis hit, we all got screwed."

"Still not quite sure I follow."

"Think about it like you were selling eggs," Scotty said. "There are dozens of chickens laying hundreds of eggs. Those eggs are taken from all different chickens and put into one carton, which is then sold. But what happens if the whole coop was diseased? Every egg in the carton is basically worthless. That's pretty much what happened. We ended up with a bunch of packaged loans that were in essence worthless. And once the economy got turned upside down, everyone who worked in that branch got the ticket out of there. I was at Deutsche Bank less than a year when I got canned."

"I'm guessing you didn't live with your parents while you were working."

"No way. Bought me a sweet two-bedroom for three-quarters of a mil. Between salary and bonus, I could afford the payments while paying off my student loans. But then I lost my job, couldn't make the payments, and took a hundred-thousand-dollar loss selling the apartment."

"Wow," I said. "I think you lost more on that pad than my apartment is worth."

"Don't be too sure. There's always someone willing to overpay for Manhattan real estate. If I could have waited six months I would have found a good buyer, but I couldn't afford my mortgage anymore and it was either that or live on the street for a while."

"And now?"

"And now what? I live with my parents. They still think I'm gonna be some financial genius. Warren Buffett or something. That's why you gotta keep this quiet, man. They can't know. It'd kill them." Scotty was starting to breathe harder, red flaring up under his collar. He was getting angry just talking about this. "You know what that feels like? You work your ass off for ten years, you pour every penny you have into your future. And then just when things seem like they're going your way, the rug is pulled out from under you and you're left with nothing but debt, bad credit and a crappy old bedroom that wasn't big enough when you were in high school."

"So you start dealing. To make ends meet."

"It's not permanent," Scotty said. "Things will turn around. There are peaks and valleys in every time cycle. In a year or so I'll have the job of my choice, back in a sweet-ass apartment. Living the dream."

"You tell that to all the people you're poisoning?"

"Screw yourself, Mr. High-and-Mighty. I'm doing what I need to do to survive. I owe fifty grand on my tuition, and even if I do get another job, who knows how long that'll last. You're a reporter, right? You ever think about all those people you feed bull to day in and day out? All those magazines telling women how they can doll themselves up, get sliced open just to be prettier? So maybe they can look like whatever anorexic slut you shove on your cover? Don't tell me about poison, man. You think I'm any worse than you are, you're deluding yourself."

"I don't need to defend myself. I know what I do, and I know what you do. If you can even compare the two, you're the delusional one, Scotty."

A waiter came over. He took a notepad from his pocket, licked his thumb and turned to a fresh page. "Can I get ya?"

"Pastrami and rye," Scotty said. "With Swiss and mustard. And a cream soda."

"Chocolate milk shake," I said. "And a side of fries."

The waiter nodded, walked off. I turned back to Scotty.

"When did you start?" I asked.

He sighed, for a moment saying nothing. He was steeling himself up to talk. "'Bout a year ago," he said.

"How? Who introduced you?"

"I went to my buddy Kyle's house one night a week after I got laid off. It was a few of us. Kyle's girlfriend, some chick I'd been seeing for a month who dumped me a few days later when she realized I couldn't afford tables at the China Club anymore."

"Wow, that's a sob story if I ever heard one. Let me call up Larry King for you."

"Dude, you're missing the point. Do you have any idea what it's like, how utterly fucking hopeless you feel, to live your whole life working for something only to know it can end—" he snapped his fingers "—just like that?"

Scotty sat there, leaning across the table like a life coach trying to convince me of the path to righteousness. Though Scotty and I had almost nothing in common—not our clothes, not our upbringing, not our vocation—something about what he said hit home for me. With my industry seemingly scaling back by the day, not to mention the far too often times my life was endangered by that chosen vocation, I knew how tenuous things could be.

"Your friend Kyle," I said. "Go on."

"We stayed up late, drank a lot. I think our girls were starting to get pissed off, feeling like we were paying each other more attention than we were them. And they were probably right. At some point I start jonesing for a toke. I used in college a bit. I asked Kyle if he knew where we could get some good stuff, and he kind of looked at me and laughed."

Our food came, and Scotty tore into it before mine had even been set down. The pastrami and rye disappeared in several ravenous bites, washed down with a chug of cream soda. When he finished, Scotty smiled and said, "Best sandwich in the world."

My chocolate milk shake looked a little silly in comparison, but I took a long sip and felt like a kid again.

He wiped his mouth, placed the napkin gently on the table and continued. "Kyle just got up, went into his bedroom and came back with what looked like an eighth of great bud. At first I didn't ask questions, I was just looking forward to the feeling. When we were good and baked—and man, that stuff baked us *quick*—I asked him where he'd got it. Know what he told me?"

"What?"

"He said, 'leftovers.' I didn't know what the hell that meant, so I asked him. He said times were tough, and he'd been dealing a bit on the side. His mom just got diagnosed with cervical cancer and she didn't have health insurance. So he was dealing to help her out with the bills. Kyle's dad died about ten years ago, drank away every penny they had, even gambled some that they didn't. So I asked him who set him up with that, and he said he'd met a guy who was kind of like the head recruiter. Kind of like Ben Affleck in *Boiler Room*, the grand pooh-bah of the game. The guy you want to talk to if you want in."

"So Kyle set you up with this guy."

"Yeah. Kyle said he was at some party where a guy named Vinnie came and sold the host some coke. Kyle was curious about making some extra coin, so he pulled Vinnie aside. Vinnie gave him a phone number, and that's all she wrote."

"And how did you get involved?" I asked.

Scotty chugged more of his cream soda, a frothy

mustache trail on his upper lip. He saw me staring, and wiped it away. "After a few weeks, I noticed Kyle was coming home later and later, and then I saw him with this sweet watch, a Movado. Brand-new, bought from the store. He said he was pulling down two, three grand a week easy. And that was just the beginning. So I asked if Kyle would introduce me to his man, this recruiter guy. Kyle tells me this guy is the one who makes all the decisions, the guy who's in charge of *everything*. Kyle sets up a meeting, I go in and talk with this guy for an hour, maybe two, and a week later I'm on the street."

"But not really 'on the street.'"

"Nah. Anyone who thinks dealers in NYC sit on street corners waiting for crackheads to come up to them is watching too much HBO. This is a *business,* run and worked by businessmen. There's no room for street hustling or stupidity."

"Any women?" I asked.

"Not that I ever saw."

"Guess it's not all that different from finance after all."

"No," Scotty said with a laugh. "Guess not."

"So you say this whole thing is run like a business, streamlined and thorough. So let me ask you this…how did I find you?"

Scotty shifted in his seat. "I don't know."

"This recruiter you're talking about. The head honcho. You say you met with him."

"Just once," Scotty said. "After I had my…interview I guess you could call it, I was always dealing with middlemen after that. Guys lower on the food chain."

"Are they the ones who give you the re-ups at the office in midtown?"

Scotty's eyes shot up, and for the first time a sense of fear crept into them. "Who told you that?"

I said nothing. Just stared at him. He needed to know he wasn't dealing with an amateur, and that if I'd come this far there was surely a lot more to dig up.

"Yeah. The Depot, we called it. The main guy was never there, it's kind of like as soon as we met him, he disappeared into thin air and stopped existing. We had his phone number just in case, but if anyone called it without a good reason, we knew they might not come in to work the next day."

"Did you ever hear anyone mention someone or something called the Fury?" Scotty looked at me, confused.

"No, not that I can think of." He seemed truthful.

"So Mayor McCheese. The Big Kahuna. The Big Boss. The recruiter. Who was he?"

"Just some guy," Scotty said. "We never really learned anything about him."

"I mean what was his name?"

Scotty had to think for a minute, then he said. "Gaines. Yeah, that was the dude's name. Stephen Gaines."

26

"You're a liar," I said. Panic and rage cut through my body like a hot blade. My stomach churned, the milk shake feeling like it could come back up at any moment. "Stephen Gaines can't be, he's…dead." The last word came out empty, hollow, as though I was arguing with thin air.

"I know that," Scotty said. There was no emotion in his voice. He was simply telling me the news as he knew it. "But what do you want me to say? You asked."

I had no energy to argue with him, and no argument to counter the claims. How the hell would Scotty even know my brother's name unless…unless…

It was too terrible to even think of. Was it possible that my brother was much higher up on this food chain than I'd thought? Not just one of the lower men, the Vinnies, the ones who carried tinfoil and Saran Wrap around the city like some alternate-universe grocer, but someone who actually was responsible for a piece of the action. Perhaps much more than a piece.

Was it possible Stephen Gaines *was* the Fury?

No, I thought. That was impossible. Somebody

killed him. He was innocent. A man with demons, sure, but not somebody who deserved to die.

The only way you're murdered in that kind of business is if somebody bigger than you thinks you're hindering the operation, preventing someone more ambitious from carving a larger slice of the pie.

Unless…what if he was knocked off by a smaller dealer, somebody whose eyes simply got too big for their head? Somebody who felt scalping my brother would give them street cred, a trophy, to assume the mantle for their own?

What if my brother wore a target on his back?

Immediately my mind went back to that night. The night Stephen found me at the *Gazette*. His face filled with fright, his body wracked with pain from the drugs and some secret he was carrying. Is it possible he knew he had a death wish, and simply needed help? If Stephen was so powerful, what could I possibly have done for him?

I'd seen men and women whose lives had been destroyed by drugs, by alcohol. Hell, my idol, Jack O'Donnell, was hidden away somewhere trying to drain the poisons and impulses from his body. Jack had been on the sauce for years, yet during that time he'd risen to the highest ranks of his profession. There were numerous examples of functioning alcoholics, drug addicts, people who achieved despite carrying the disease. I mean, I lived and worked in New York, which probably had the highest ratio of functioning addicts in the world. It would only make sense that if a person worked in that industry, they would be corrupted in some way, body or soul or both.

When I saw Stephen Gaines outside of my office building, his face pale, sweat streaking down his gaunt frame, it was clear he'd been wasted away by both.

Scotty Callahan sat there holding his glass while I tried to force his words from my mind, trying to will them to be false. Scotty didn't seem to care one way or another. Now that I had the information, it was no concern to him what I did with it.

And I could tell by the way he sat there eating, drinking, staring at his food, his mind completely oblivious to the anguish building inside me…this was not the face of a man lying to save his ass. There might have even been a slight catharsis in telling me.

Stephen Gaines wasn't just some random junkie, but in fact one of the leaders of this organization—718 Enterprises. No doubt Stephen knew what that stood for, who worked in it, how widely it reached. Perhaps that's what he wanted to tell me. It's what I would have heard had I stopped. It's what he would have done that night, while a killer roamed the streets waiting for him to come home.

"You only met him once," I said to Scotty. "Just once."

"Just once," he said, holding up one finger. Then he burped, and a shred of pastrami tumbled over his lower lip. He slurped it back up.

"What about Kyle?" I said. "How much does he know."

Scotty put down his drink. He leaned over until I could smell the meat on his breath. His eyes narrowed, and for a moment my anger and frustration was replaced by the possibility that this guy might take a swing at me.

"You leave him the hell out of this," Scotty said. "His mom is sick. He brings home enough to pay her bills, and doesn't want or ask for any trouble. None of us are trying to get anyone hurt. You want to drag me through the mud, tell people I'm dealing, it'll suck but maybe I deserve it. You screw with Kyle's life, it's not just him but his family. I don't know you, Henry, but you'd have to be one heartless son of a bitch to do something like that."

"I need to know what he knows," I said, my voice trying to explain without any hostility. "It's my family, too. My father was arrested for the murder of Stephen Gaines."

Scotty sat back at though slapped. The breath seemed to have left him. For a moment he said nothing, then he shook his head. "I'm sorry," he said softly.

"Thanks," I replied.

"So that's what this is really about," Scotty said. "Finding the truth to get your pops off the hook."

"That's right."

"Then I don't know what to say. I meant what I said about Kyle. I'll tell you anything you want. I know Kyle didn't know Gaines any more than I did. He met him once, for an interview kind of thing. And we both have to check in at the office, make sure our receipts match up with what we're selling."

"Can you give me the name of whoever handles that?" I said.

"It's always different," Scotty said. "And they never tell us their names."

"What happens if you screw up?" I asked.

Scotty sighed, said, "I guess you should ask Stephen."

We said nothing, as I processed what Scotty had said and he finished off the last of his cream soda. My milk shake sat lonely and untouched. If he was desperate enough for money to resort to drugs, I guess he valued a free meal when it came his way.

After the plates had been cleared and I'd taken care of the tab, we both stood up and headed toward the door. I followed him, my legs feeling rubbery.

The air outside was warm, the night sky a lovely dark blue. Sometimes I hated the towering skyscrapers of New York and how they totally obscured the horizons. But nights like tonight I could stare at the pinpricks of light, the behemoths sparsely lit, and admire the grandeur of it all. This was a magnificent city. One that almost seemed to beckon you to claim it all for your own, to rise up one of those towers and stand out over the masses, arms spread, taking it all in. All for yourself.

And maybe that's what seduced Stephen. And got him killed as well.

The streetlight turned green, the red Stop hand switching to the white "happy walking" person.

"That's my signal," Scotty said. I nodded stupidly, unsure of how to end our little gab session. "Listen, Henry, I respect what you're doing. If the guy was a dirtbag, it might not be worth your time if you didn't know him. I know better than anyone that sometimes you have to do things you're not proud of to make ends meet. You tell yourself it's okay, because it's the only way, and it's only for a short time."

"If that's what it takes to help you sleep at night," I said.

"Judge all you want. At some point you'll have to

make some tough choices too. And you gave me your word about this being off the record. I know some bad people, people who don't really give pink slips."

"Your name won't come up and won't appear in the paper."

"Good. And maybe ten years from now you can look back and know you did the right things because they were the only things available. I—"

And then Scott Callahan turned and walked away.

I stared at his back, hands in his pockets, hunched over, acting like the weather was far colder than it actually was. And then he turned the corner and was gone.

Sometimes people forget about the weight on their shoulders until you point it out.

My legs felt weak, and I debated just hailing a taxi. Then I remembered how long it would take to get back uptown, that I'd probably have to take on a second job to pay for it, and headed toward the subway. Considering prices of everything from milk to movies had skyrocketed in New York to the point where you had to hit an ATM just to buy coffee and a doughnut, you had to conserve wherever possible.

I couldn't wait to see Amanda, to hear her voice, to feel her arms again. Then I remembered she'd promised Darcy Lapore a night on the town and realized it would be several hours before that would happen. But it wasn't all bad. Amanda didn't go out all that often, and had never been a big drinker, but Darcy was dangerous. Her husband was a high roller and the one time we'd double-dated with them he took us to some club with a kinky name where he plunked down four figures for a table and two bottles, and we proceeded to get completely obliterated. In New York, when someone pays a grand for you to drink, you drink your money's worth.

Anyway, because of Amanda's relatively light drinking habits, she tended to get drunk rather easily. Which had two results: the first that she would have a wicked hangover the next day, but second that she was frisky as all get out when she got home. One night a month ago, she came home from a night out with Darcy, and upon arriving home she proceeded to give me a piece of her mind. The reason for chewing me out? I was still wearing pants.

God, I loved that woman.

The train ride was uneventful, and I wondered what my father was doing at that very instant. I'd only been to see him once since his incarceration in the Tombs. Every part of me wanted to see him released, to go back home and live out the rest of his life with my mother in whatever happiness the two of them could muster. I wanted to believe that, if he was released, he would treat her the way a wife deserved to be treated. Loved. Cared for. Respected.

But I knew none of that would happen. Chances were, things would not change. He would not suddenly become the husband he should have been years ago. That ship had sailed.

But it didn't mean he deserved to be treated like a murderer. And like I told him that night two years ago, while I was holed up in a crummy building as three men were approaching to kill me, I used my father's shortcomings to fuel me. Because of him I wanted to be to Amanda what he'd never been to my mother. I'd gotten it wrong once, with Mya.

I steadfastly believed that a person became who they

were by choice. They achieved or they did not. They were decent or they were not. Those choices might be harder depending on the worldviews they are subjected to. The climb might be more difficult, but being a good man, working at my craft, those were possibilities that were attainable to me.

I was born with ability. I knew that. But it took everything I had to wrench myself away from the grips of this man, and I was happy to forget him. And in the years since, I'd found a few times where that anger could be reversed. Where the climb became more manageable because it lifted me.

Amanda, Mya.

We were all recovering from our injuries, emotional and physical. Mya's would take longer, but inside the girl she'd become was the girl I once knew. She would move on.

I'd moved on eight years ago. Now I wanted to be everything James Parker was not.

I wanted to be strong. Anger was a powerful tool. And I wanted my anger to be used for the right reasons.

I stopped at a corner deli. The manager recognized me. He was a burly Arab man, very pleasant, who'd seen me once with Amanda and now greeted me with a humorous "hubba hubba" whenever I was alone.

"Large coffee," I said. "Cream and three sugars."

"Cream?" he said, surprised. "Usually you take it with milk."

"I need the extra jolt tonight," I said. He nodded, understanding.

"Where's your ladyfriend?" he asked, moving toward the pots.

"Out tonight," I said with a smile.

"That lady, whoo, hubba hubba," he said, pointing to the coffee. "Fresh pot, plenty hot," he continued.

"Just the way I like it," I said.

He poured me a full cup, steam rising off the top, and added the cream and sugar. I paid him, thanked him and left.

The coffee, cream and sugar would be enough to get through the night. Or at least keep me awake until Amanda got home. Sipping it as I approached my apartment, I set it on the call box and searched my pockets for my keys.

Staring ahead as my fingers felt around for the familiar metal, suddenly my body froze.

The door to our building was glass. Through the illumination of the lamp on the corner, I could see the reflection of the street behind me. And what I saw was a man approaching holding what looked to be an unopened switchblade.

He was a few inches shorter than me, white, with a scraggly beard and loose-fitting clothes that had surely been bought when he was a few pounds heavier. In that light, he looked scarily like my brother had the night I saw him.

Slowly I reached up, picked up my coffee cup, took a small sip. My fingers trembled as I pretended to be unsure of where I was.

Then I heard the chilling *snick* and saw a long, thin piece of metal protruding from the man's hand. His blade was now open.

My heart hammered. In just seconds he would be behind me. And I would be dead.

Then I saw the man's hand rise above his head, the knife pointed down, ready to bury itself in my neck. I had one shot to do this right, or I'd feel that knife point inside me, the cold steel lodging itself in me.

I spun around, startling the man, and swung the entire cup of steaming-hot coffee into his face.

He shrieked, his hands clawing at his face. The knife clattered to the ground, and I kicked it as far as I could before he could react. It skittered away and stopped beneath a parked car thirty feet down the block.

While he was still pawing at his face, I swung an elbow that hit him right in the chest. It connected solidly, and he went down in a heap, still moaning, his face red from the scalding liquid. He was curled into a fetal position, so I knelt down on top of him, spreading his arms wide.

Once his arms were spread I placed my knees inside the crook of his elbows until his upper body was pinned underneath me. His legs thrashed as he screamed like he was the one being attacked.

I raised my fist, ready to rain blows upon the man's head, but then when I saw the fear in his eyes, the utter helplessness of him, I relented. Keeping my knees pinned on his arms—just in case he had another weapon handy—I placed my palm under his chin and forced him to look at me. My other hand fished in his pockets to see if he had any more weapons. I found none. I patted him down—legs, ankles, even pressed an elbow into his crotch just to be sure. The squeal he let out was very satisfying. Then I dug back in his pockets until I found his wallet. I flipped it open, saw credit cards, a few crumpled singles and a driver's license.

Rule number one of attacking someone, never carry picture ID.

Suddenly I felt him rock forward, making me tilt slightly back, then he thrust his entire body weight forward. I lost my balance, toppling over. I could feel him squirm out from under me as my head smacked against the pavement.

I tried to stand up, but a kick to the side of my neck made me fall back over, the breath leaving my lungs for a moment. The man stood back up, then looked around, trying to locate the knife. He couldn't find it, and by that point I'd managed to prop myself up. I took my keys from my pocket, inserted them into my fist, each key sticking out from between my fingers like a makeshift pair of brass knuckles.

The man saw me do this. Looking around once more for the knife, he took one step toward me and said, "You don't watch out, your ass is a ghost. And if that doesn't bother you, maybe we'll stick one in your old lady, too."

Then he sprinted away and didn't look back.

I lowered my hand. Watched him go. I got lucky. If I hadn't seen him, I could be lying in the street bleeding.

I remembered that I'd taken his wallet and removed the license. The man's name was Trent Buckley. His license stated that he was six foot one, a hundred and ninety pounds. According to the address, Buckley resided in Boulder, Colorado. The license was dated 2002, so it was likely that Buckley had moved to New York from Colorado.

Who sent him here? And how did he know where I lived? And who was Buckley referring to as "we"?

Paranoia seeped in. I looked around, checking out the

abandoned street, wondering if someone else was waiting to pounce.

Then my mind went to one place.

Amanda.

My "old lady." Did they really know who she was or where to find her?

If someone was after me, they could very well know various ways to get to me.

I knew where she was. Knew what I had to do.

Calling 911 was a priority, but I had a more pressing one right now.

Taking the keys from my pocket, I unlocked the front door and pressed the elevator button. It took a moment for me to notice that an Out Of Service sticker was pasted over the jamb.

I sprinted up the stairs, my lungs burning, until I reached our apartment. The door was locked, but I opened it with the caution of a man who'd previously wandered into his apartment only to find a psychopathic killer waiting. When I was convinced there was nobody hiding in the closet, I grabbed the biggest suitcase I could find and began throwing clothes into it. I had no idea what garments were most important to Amanda, so hopefully she'd forgive me if in my haste I couldn't put together a matching outfit.

Once the bag was full with clothes, I jammed it shut and zipped it closed. Then I dragged it carefully back down to the lobby, burst onto the street and began waving my hand in the air. It took only five minutes for a cab to see me and pick me up.

"The Kitten Club," I said breathlessly.

The driver nodded, and off we went.

The Kitten Club held a lot of memories for me. As well as being the hottest nightspot in the city, it was where blond diva Athena Paradis was murdered. Strangely, once the investigation had ended and the club had reopened, its cachet as the most exclusive club in the city skyrocketed. Not only was it *the* place to be, it was basically a city landmark now. Lines that once stretched around the block looped each other. Darcy's husband was an old fraternity brother of Shawn Kensbrook, the Kitten Club's promoter, so they were able to hop the line. All that for the privilege of spending five hundred bucks on a bottle of Smirnoff.

The lights of the Kitten Club pulsated as the cab drew near. I lowered the window. The smell of cologne, perfume, cigarettes and sweat permeated the air. Naturally there was a line snaking all the way out the door and down the block, and that it was three people deep led me to believe it would be a two-hour wait just to get in.

But I wasn't planning to wait in line.

As the cab pulled up in front of the club, I threw him a twenty and hopped out, dragging my heavy luggage behind me. A few people waiting in line noticed my odd appearance—jeans, a short-sleeved shirt, sneakers and a massive Samsonite—and pointed me out to their friends. A few laughed. The rest looked slightly worried, as though they expected me to be lugging a bomb or a body in the suitcase.

I had to shove my way through the line to get to the front. A massive bouncer with biceps veins thicker than his waist blocked the way. He looked at me and rolled his eyes.

"Line starts over there," he said. He jerked his thumb in the opposite direction of where I *thought* the line started. Based on a rough calculation, the people at the end of the line would be allowed in right around the Rapture.

"I need to see Shawn Kensbrook," I said.

"I need a blow job," the bouncer said.

"One of those is going to be much easier to achieve than the others," I replied. "Listen, tell him this is about Darcy Lapore and her husband, Devin. He'll know who you're talking about."

The bouncer looked me over, trying to see if I was for real. Then he picked up a walkie-talkie, pressed a button and spoke into it.

"Yo, Byron, some kid out here with a damn suitcase says he needs to talk to Shawn. Says it's about some chick named Darcy."

"And Devin," I added.

"And Devin." He clicked off the walkie-talkie and waited for a response. Then he said, "You be messing with me, I'm a make you give me that blow job."

"I don't think either of us would enjoy that very much."

Then a crackling sound came over the talkie, and a voice said, "Hold tight, he'll be right there." The bouncer nodded, clicked it off. "Guess you won't need that mouthwash after all."

A minute later, a man came through the door and walked right up to me. He was wearing an Armani suit and sunglasses, and looked like a white, slightly less bulky version of the bouncer. His cuff links were sterling silver, and I could see his belt buckle was engraved with the letters SK.

Shawn Kensbrook walked up to me and said, "You've gotta be him."

"It's me," I said. "Henry Parker. You must be Shawn. I left you a few messages last year while I was covering the Athena Paradis story."

"I didn't talk to any reporters after that happened."

"I can understand. I know you two were close."

"Cut the crap. What do you want to do with Devin?"

"Long story short. My girlfriend, Amanda, is with Devin and Darcy right now. She's in trouble. I mean, big, bad, lives-on-the-line trouble. I don't have the time to wait on line, I just need to see her. You let me in, I grab the girl, and we're gone. Simple as that."

"How do I know you're not messing with me?" Shawn said.

I didn't know what to say. Then I thrust out the suitcase and said, "A deposit. I'm not back in ten minutes, you keep this. Some nice stuff in here. I know because I bought it for my girl's birthday. Plus, Captain Shower Rape here can have his way with me."

Shawn looked at the bouncer, confused. The guy shook his head like he didn't know what I was talking about. Shawn turned back to me, the light from the neon signs reflecting in the shine of his suit.

"Even if you're on the level," Shawn said, "you're dressed like a homeless person and you have a freaking *suitcase.* I let you in, I might as well go around Central Park inviting all the assholes sleeping on benches in."

"I didn't want to mention this," I said truthfully, "but I know Tony Valentine."

"Valentine," Kensbrook said, trying to remember why he knew the name. "You mean the gossip hound, right?"

"That's the one. I work with him."

"No BS?"

I pulled out my business card, showing Shawn that I, like Tony Valentine, worked at the *New York Gazette*. Shawn eyed the card, his head clearly filling with the possibility of getting a good plug in the gossip pages. Of course, I had as much intent of talking to Tony Valentine as I did to O.J. Simpson, but that's the beauty of an internal monologue.

"You got ten minutes," he said. "And after that your ass is kicked and your clothes go to the incinerator."

"I accept."

"And I expect some ink from Valentine."

I gave him the most noncommittal thumbs-up in my arsenal.

Shawn nodded at the bouncer, who unhitched the velvet rope and allowed me passage. He took my suitcase and carried it to the coatroom, where a girl in a tight black top and capris unlocked a door so he could heave it behind the barrier. There were plenty of groans from the people waiting on line as they saw me enter. I hoped if they knew what was going on they'd understand.

But this was New York, so I doubted it.

The Kitten Club was a massive place, with two different levels of action. This was about as far from my scene as I could get without being in the desert. I had no idea where to look first. My eyes were half-blinded by the strobe lights, and it took a healthy equilibrium not to get knocked over by the horde of drunken, dancing revelers. I could barely see five feet in front of me, let alone distinguish the VIP lounge.

To clarify the mess, I approached the bar, waited to get the tender's attention. When he came by, he said, "What'll it be?"

"Where's the VIP lounge?" I asked.

He nodded and turned around. I had no idea what had happened, but then he turned back holding a glass of champagne with something sparkling at the bottom. He held it out to me.

"The VIP champagne," he said. "That'll be a hundred fifty."

"No," I shouted. "The VIP *lounge*."

The bartender, looking quite pissed off, said, "Tables are upstairs." As I turned to go, I saw him fish the gem from the bottom of the glass and drop it into a small pail.

I pushed and shoved my way through a sea of fitted jeans, open-collared shirts revealing chests adorned with thick gold chains, and shimmering bosoms with even spray tans. At the back of the dance floor I found a short staircase that led to another level. Sliding through a couple making out on the railing, I managed to find the VIP area, a lounge of about a dozen round tables, each with between half a dozen and a dozen people circling them. Each table had several bottles of alcohol sitting in buckets of ice, with various mixers—cranberry juice, orange juice and tonic water—ready to go. According to Amanda, each bottle ran about a grand, and nobody bought just one bottle.

Then I heard a laugh. A distinctive laugh. Amanda's laugh.

I fast-walked past the tables until I finally found the one I was looking for. Sitting in a circle were Devin and Darcy Lapore, several suited men with gelled hair and manicures, and Amanda Davies.

Amanda was laughing hysterically at something, then she looked up and noticed me. I didn't believe that smile could spread any wider, but it did.

"Henry!" she shrieked, jumping out of her seat, knocking over an empty glass and toppling one of the guys onto the floor. She threw her arms around me, squeezed tight, and I gave her one right back. Her breath smelled like vodka, her body like sweet perfume. Her hair dripped onto my shirt and I held her tight, for reasons vastly different than hers.

"Hey, baby," I said, struggling to disentangle myself.

Suddenly Amanda looked confused. "Wait," she said. "What're you *doo*ing here?"

"I don't have time to explain right now," I said, taking her hand. "But you need to come with me."

A sultry smile spread across her lips. I didn't see her drunk all that often, so part of me couldn't help but be slightly amused. "So," she said. "You're taking me home?"

"Not exactly," I said, pulling her away. I apologized to Darcy and Devin, who seemed too preoccupied with how each other's lips tasted to notice.

"If we're not going home," she slurred, "where *are* we going?"

"A hotel," I said.

"Ooh baby!" Amanda said, suddenly grabbing a chunk of my ass and squeezing. She likely meant to be flirtatious, but the girl had some serious nails and I was reasonably certain she broke the skin. Hopefully stitches wouldn't be required, because that'd be one awkward explanation for the doctor. "Have you been working out?"

"Not recently, I haven't had time, but…that's not the point. We need to go."

Amanda finally relented, and we made our way down the steps and toward the exit. For the first time it seemed to dawn on Amanda that something was wrong. I couldn't walk too fast due to the fact that she was in heels and had no hand-eye coordination to speak of, so to other clubgoers I looked like the no-fun boyfriend dragging his fun-as-hell girlfriend away because he didn't approve of her shenanigans.

I had to give Amanda credit, though. She looked stunning. Outclassed every girl at the club. I'd have to remember to tell her tomorrow, when she would remember.

We got to the tunnel leading to the outside, and the girl inside the coatroom remembered me. Guess not too many guys dropped off their luggage before entering.

"Can I get my bag?" I asked.

"Five dollars," she said, smacking gum between her lips.

"You just saw me with Shawn, I—"

"Five dollars," she repeated, bored by the whole thing. I didn't want or have time to argue, and pulled a crumpled ten from my pocket. She counted change, then swung the door open and let me take the suitcase.

As I lugged it into the hall, Amanda said, "Where *are* we going?"

"A hotel, baby," I said.

"I thought you were kidding," she said, a joyous glow in her eye. "I have the best boyfriend in the whole *world*."

She threw her arms around me again, and I nearly stumbled over a small girl trying to make her way back into the club. She called me a name that I'd most definitely never been called by a girl before.

Gripping the bag with one hand and Amanda with another, we stumble/bumped our way outside. A row of cabs was waiting five deep down the block, knowing every minute brought another inebriated person out who needed a ride home (hopefully to another borough).

It was a delicate balancing act carrying Amanda and the suitcase outside since they were both essentially dead weight. The next cab in the line pulled up, and thankfully the driver came outside to help me with my, er, belongings. He hoisted the bag into the trunk while Amanda and I slid into the back. As soon as he closed the door and said, "Where to?" I realized I had no idea where we were going.

The list of New York hotels I knew offhand was quite slim, and one of those, the Plaza, hadn't reopened yet.

Before I knew what I was doing, I said, "Times Square. The W Hotel, please."

"Henry," Amanda cooed, her cheeks flushing red her hand delicately tracing the curve of my calf. "I had no idea…"

"Me, neither," I mumbled as the cab sped away. Amanda spent the whole cab ride either staring outside, the world swimming by her drunken haze, or awkwardly trying to grope me. Ordinarily I might have felt frisky enough to try a little something in the backseat while the cabdriver wasn't looking, but Amanda was as subtle as a hyena and I had too much on my mind to truly focus.

Who was that guy outside my apartment? Clearly somebody knew I was following leads, but nothing had been printed in the newspaper, which limited the list of culprits significantly. I wondered, could it have been Scotty Callahan? Sure seemed like it. The notion that this guy, an admitted company man, would have spilled his guts and walked away seemed awfully unlikely. But there were others. Rose Keller. She was a friend of Stephen's, perhaps better than I knew. Stephen was more than I'd previously thought, so it occurred to me that Rose might have been as well.

I lowered the window, breathing deeply as I inhaled the warm air. Now Amanda was leaning back against her seat, eyes closed. I wondered if she was sleeping, dreaming peacefully.

Fifteen minutes later the cab pulled up in front of the W Hotel. I ran my credit card through the cab's machine, gave him a twenty percent tip and helped Amanda out. We walked into the lobby quite a sight, Amanda wearing a slinky dress and clinging to my arm, me looking like I'd just rolled out of a bed in a sewer and carrying a single suitcase. The building itself was beautiful and massive. I'd read somewhere that it housed a staggering fifty-seven floors, but in the dark of night it looked like even more, a mammoth structure in the heart of Times Square. The lobby was awash in subtle blue and gray tones, and a waterfall ran down one of the walls.

There were two receptionists on duty, two young women who looked remarkably similar. They both had dark hair and skin, red fingernails and bright smiles that seemed almost attuned to one another. As we walked up they both said, "Good evening, sir."

Their name tags read Rae and Gabrielle. You could have switched the tags and I wouldn't have known the difference.

"I'd like a room, please," I said.

The one with the Rae tag began to punch some keys on her computer while Gabrielle stared at me with that same, unwavering smile. Suddenly I felt Amanda's breath on my cheek, and then a big kiss followed suit. A split second later I felt her tongue on my jawbone, winding its way toward my earlobe.

Gabrielle was still grinning, but now it was the kind of grin you gave to your neighbor who got his morning newspaper while wearing nothing but tighty-whities.

Rae looked up and said, "We have two rooms available, one with two twin beds and another with one queen."

"I'll take the queen," I said, trying to push Amanda away while I feel my face turn bright red. Rae noticed what was going on, and her bright smile quickly turned like bad milk.

Gabrielle looked at Amanda, then looked at me, then looked at my suitcase. Her eyes went back and forth between the three while I stood there confused. Then I realized what she was thinking. Attractive girl wearing revealing clothes. Dorky guy wearing the same clothes he'd probably worn the last three days. A suitcase.

No doubt Rae and Gabrielle thought Amanda was a hooker, and would end up chopped to bits and stuffed into the suitcase by the end of the night. I noticed neither of them had made any movements to confirm my room or make a key.

"You okay, *honey?*" I asked, stressing the last word

in an attempt to let Rae and Gabrielle know that we did, in fact, know each other.

"I'm just peachy, Henry." I smiled. *See, she knows my name!*

"So…about that room…"

"I'll need a credit-card imprint," Rae said. I slipped her my AMEX, and she ran it through, never taking her eyes off of us.

"Hen-*ree,*" Amanda whined. "I'm *ti*-red."

"Just a minute, baby," I said.

Gabrielle seemed to be softening up, but Rae was eyeing me with squinty eyes, letting me know she could have hotel security at our room if she got the slightest hint that an ax might make an appearance.

"How many nights will you be staying?"

"I'm not sure," I said. "Can we just keep it open?"

"Sure," Rae said, taking two plastic cards and running them through the machine to magnetize them. She slid them into a paper sheath, wrote a number on it and handed it to us along with my credit card. "Room 2722 on the twenty-seventh floor. Please call if you require any assistance."

"Please," Gabrielle added. "Any assistance."

"Anything at all, for you or your friend," Rae added.

"One thing," I said. "I don't want anyone to know I'm here. So can you put me down under a different name, just in case anyone calls?"

The sisters looked at each other with a worried glare.

"Sure…" Gabrielle said. "What name would you like to put on the room?"

"Put down…Leonard Denton," I said.

"All set Mr.…Denton."

"Thanks. Come on," I said to Amanda. "Let's get you some sleep."

I felt their glare in my back as we headed to the elevators. The ride was silent and smooth, and I barely felt like we were moving, let alone going nearly thirty stories. At some point, right around floor twenty-five, I felt my eardrums pop. Once the elevator opened, we made our way down the hall to room 2722, where I managed the task of propping both Amanda and the suitcase against the wall as I opened the door. Once open, I threw the bag inside and helped Amanda in.

She collapsed on the bed, and I sat down next to her. For the first time all night, I realized just how tired I was. My nerves were still on edge, and tomorrow would be a long day. I needed to find out who that man was, who sent him, and just how deep in my brother was.

But in the meantime, Amanda had somehow wriggled out of her dress, and was wearing nothing but a silk bra and underwear, her eyes suggesting that sleepiness had taken a hiatus for the time being.

Tomorrow would be a long day. As I climbed into Amanda's waiting arms, I hoped the night would be long enough to stay with me.

27

I woke up the next morning with my boxer shorts dangling off my shoulder, the taste of secondhand vodka in my mouth and a strange pain in my right knee. Then the previous night came back to me, and I smiled.

Turning over, I saw Amanda lying next to me. She was wearing my old Oregon Ducks sweatshirt. It was at least three sizes too big for her, and I'd seen her spend many nights sitting on the couch reading a book, the sweatshirt pulled over her tucked-in knees.

My body ached as I threw my legs over the side of the bed and surveyed the room. It was stunning. Satin sheets, state-of-the-art stereo, a bar countertop on the porcelain bath, a flat-screen television wider than our bed at home.

Then I noticed the sunlight pouring into the room from what seemed like every angle. Standing up, my breath was taken away by the beautiful view outside and the massive wraparound balcony just outside our room. I opened the door, stepped outside and felt alive. The cool, crisp air washed over me as my eyes adjusted to the light. The sight of New York from twenty-seven stories up. It truly was a magnificent city, and I smiled when I thought of the last time Amanda and I had hidden out in a hotel room under a fake name. It was a sleep-n-save somewhere outside of Springfield, Illinois. Even though I hadn't lost my natural ability to get in way over my head, at least we were starting to hide out in classier hotels.

Reentering the room, I found my jeans crumpled into a ball on the floor, found the room-rate card. When I looked at it, I nearly had a heart attack. There had to be other hotels in this city that wouldn't wipe me out within days.

Amanda stirred. I got up and went into the bathroom, not wanting to wake her just yet. I ran a hot shower, stayed in a little longer than I needed to, thinking about the previous day.

It was no secret that I would want to get to the bottom of Stephen Gaines's death, and while yesterday I thought about the possibility of Rose Keller or Scotty Callahan being involved, the options were likely far greater.

The *New York Dispatch* had certainly mentioned my father's arrest, as did my own paper, and surely a few other locals as well. Anyone who knew me and my reputation would correctly assume that I would do anything to clear my family's name. It was possible I was being followed, that somebody had seen me talk to Sheryl Harrison, to Rose Keller, to Scotty. It was even possible that my discovery of Beth-Ann Downing's body had alerted someone to my interest. Whoever killed Stephen wanted it to be seen as one single murder. A lone death, unconnected to anything else.

I knew better. And someone else knew *that*.

When I stepped out of the shower, a towel wrapped loosely around my waist, Amanda was sitting up in bed, her knees tucked up to her chin, her arms wrapped around them. She smiled at me. Her eyes were blood-shot.

"Hungover?" I asked.

"Just a little."

"Hang on." I went to the minibar, did a little trolling and found a packet of Advil. I ripped it open, poured her a glass of water and watched her down the pills.

"Thanks, Henry," she said.

"How you feeling?"

"Like a raccoon run over by a truck. Don't ever let me go drinking with Darcy again."

"I think I told you that the last time you went drinking with her."

"Well, next time come with us, so you can monitor my alcohol intake."

"If memory serves me right, the reason you didn't invite me last night was because you didn't want me to monitor your alcohol intake."

"And you listened to me?" she asked with a smile. I sat back down next to her. She scooted over, rested her head against my shoulder. I could smell her hair, hear her breathing. Then she sat back up and looked at me. "Now, tell me why we're here."

Sighing, I faced her and told her everything that had happened. About my meeting with Scott Callahan. Finding the man waiting for me at the apartment last night. The fear that if they knew where I was, that if somebody had been following me, they could have been doing the same for her. Enough young women had been killed in New York coming home from bars over the last few years, the confluence of paranoia made it imperative we get to safety.

"How long do you think we need to stay here?" she said.

"I honestly don't know. Until I know who killed Stephen, and know that person isn't a threat to us anymore. With any luck I can do that before my credit card starts getting declined."

"And what am I supposed to do? Just stay here? I don't think so, Henry."

"Today's Friday," I said. "Call in sick. If Darcy shows up, she'll surely vouch for you. Then we have the weekend. And I need to get my father out before the grand jury convenes. But right now I just need to keep you safe. Once things calm down we can talk about what to do next."

"You need to keep me safe?" Amanda said with a laugh. "You realize that since I met you I've had my life jeopardized approximately a hundred and ninety-six times. I won't be surprised if we both get turned down for a life-insurance policy. Safe to say if I never picked you up on the side of the road, Henry, I wouldn't have to worry about my safety quite as much."

I opened my mouth, ready to question why, if that was the case, she was still with me, but smartly stopped before a word came out. I learned a long time ago that she was still here by choice. No other reason. She'd had plenty of opportunities to leave and had not, and every moment I wasted contemplating why only divided myself from the reality of our relationship. She was here to stay. And knowing myself, knowing that I'd learned from past mistakes, as long as it was in her hands, she wasn't going anywhere.

So instead of bucking for a compliment and starting an argument, I just leaned over and kissed her. Her lips were soft, and I could tell she was smiling.

"I've been meaning to ask you," Amanda said. "Where is your mother in all of this?"

I sat back, rubbed my forehead. "To be honest, I don't know. Probably nowhere. I remember the last few years before I left for college, she and my father barely spoke. It wasn't like she was angry with him, it was as though she'd just withdrawn. To her, he was more like a piece of furniture than a husband. He was there whether you liked it or not. It was your choice to put him there. But like a table or desk, you could ignore it."

"Why didn't she leave him?"

"I don't know. I wish she had. She turned inward. You saw those knitting needles at the police station— they became kind of her solace. She was a kind woman, never hurt anybody. So whenever he went on one of his rampages, she would take it like more of a man than he ever was, then go back to her needles."

"That's awful."

"She deserved another chance at love, at life. It was almost like at some point she became shell-shocked, just her nerves and her wits fried by everything he'd done. I remember one night when I was about eight. I spent that summer working at a corner deli, restocking shelves a few hours a day for a dollar an hour."

Amanda laughed. "Even for an eight-year-old that's pretty far below minimum wage."

"It wasn't the money. They couldn't afford to send me to camp, and I didn't want to be around the house any more than I absolutely had to. One night I came home around seven, usually when we had dinner. It was one of the few times he was getting a regular paycheck. He got home from work around seven-thirty most days, and he would walk in and head right for the dinner table, sit down and start eating. It didn't matter if we were there to join him. To him, that's what he worked the day for. To be alone. This day, though, he came home early. We both arrived home about seven, and the meat loaf was still in the oven. One thing about her, my mom made the best meat loaf in the world. Onions, red peppers, just delicious."

I continued. "He went to the table, sat down and noticed there was no food out. No drinks set. He yelled her name—Marilyn—and waited. She came out, stared at him, simply said, 'It'll be about twenty minutes.' It turned out he found out that day they were cutting back his shifts, and he'd lose about twenty percent of his salary. I didn't know this. Neither did she.

"He took a glass, threw it at the wall. It shattered into a thousand pieces. My mother just stood there, her mouth open, more confused than scared. Then he took a plate, did the same thing. It exploded. Then he took another plate, then another, then every piece on the table and threw it at the wall. I remember screaming, telling him to stop, worried he would hit her or me. Instead, he kept throwing until piles of broken glass were laid over our floor like a carpet. He was breathing heavy. My mother just stood in the doorway, mouth open. Then she turned around, went back to the stove and checked the temperature on the food. I called 911, but the cop they sent over ten minutes later was in a bowling league with my dad. Since nobody was hurt and my mother wouldn't press charges, it all went away. After that my father went upstairs, and twenty minutes later the food was on the table and he was eating. Nobody picked the glass up for a week. That's when I knew there was something wrong, that she wasn't like most of my friends' mothers. And it was eighteen years of my life before I could leave. I actually tried to take her with me, to convince her she could start a new life somewhere. You know what she said to me?"

Amanda shook her head.

"She said, 'Why would I leave everything I have here?' I had to leave before living there sucked the life out of me like it did her."

"Mya," Amanda said. "Me. That's why you always come back."

"I don't know," I said. My eyes felt heavy, my body too tired for the morning. "I just never imagined at any point in my life that I would lift a finger to help that man. And now here we are."

"Doing what you're doing, helping him," she said, "is why you're not him."

We sat there, the bright day outside hiding something dark that was waiting for me. I stood up. Went to the now-infamous suitcase and found a clean shirt. My cell phone was on the floor. I picked it up, noticed I had a message. It was from Wallace Langston. My heart sped up as I listened, a surge within me as a ray of hope appeared.

"Henry, it's Wallace. I have those files you wanted.

Let me know how you want to get them. Call me. Hope you're okay."

I immediately called him back, Wallace's office picking up on the first ring. His secretary connected me. It was great to hear the editor in chief's voice.

"Henry, how are you?" he said. "I was beginning to worry."

"About me? Why?"

"If you've given me one reason not to worry about your safety in the time we've known each other, I'm not aware of it."

"I'll try harder."

"So I have Jack's files," he said. "Of course, there could be more at his home, but this is everything he kept at the office pertaining to *Through the Darkness*. They'll be here waiting for you. They're in my office for the time being."

"Wallace, you're a lifesaver. With any luck this will shed some light on this Fury thing and help get my dad out. And when it's all over, I think there might be a hell of a story."

"I was hoping you might say that," Wallace said, "And frankly, if there wasn't, we'd need to have a serious chat about all this 'personal time' you've been taking. So in case I'm not here, I'll make sure you have access to my office."

"You know," I said, "is there any chance you could have them messengered over?"

"Why?" Wallace asked.

"Something happened last night, let's just say I need to stay out of sight for a little while."

"What the hell did you do, Henry?" I could sense the frustration in his voice.

"Nothing. Really. It should all blow over soon."

"Spoken like someone who has no idea what he's in for."

"Please, Wallace," I said.

"Fine," he sighed. "I think I have your address somewhere in my Rolodex here…"

"Actually, I need them sent to a different address."

"Okay, where to?"

"It's on the notepad here, one sec."

"On the notepad?" Wallace asked. "Where the hell are you, a bar?"

"Not exactly. But on that note, there's one more thing…if this does lead to a story, I might need to talk to you about extending my expense account for a few days. Oh, and I'm staying under the name Leonard Denton."

"Henry," Wallace said, "what the hell have you gotten yourself into?"

I had an hour before the files were to arrive, so I went downstairs and found a deli where I bought a bagel with cream cheese and a bran muffin with two large coffees for breakfast. I could almost feel Wallace's hair turn a deeper shade of gray when I told him where we were staying, but there was a chance if a story came out of all of this that the *Gazette* would pick up the tab. Since I might have to resort to selling locks of my hair if the charges remained on my credit card, I hoped for my sake and theirs that one would emerge.

When I got back to the room, Amanda had showered and was wearing a pair of jeans and a tank top. She was sitting out on the balcony, the breeze whipping through her hair, a glass of water on the edge of the lounge chair.

She turned her head to look at me, smiled.

"This is kind of nice," she said. "Maybe we should move in here."

"I'll go buy some lottery tickets."

"Sit down," she said. "Stay a while."

We ate on the balcony, the skyscrapers of Times Square surrounding us. When the coffee was done, I went inside and brewed another pot from the instant machine and we had seconds. It might have been the greatest breakfast I ever had.

When we finished, the phone rang from inside. I picked it up. It was the front desk. A package had arrived for me.

I went downstairs and signed for the package, a large, bulky padded folder with Wallace's messy handwriting. A minor miracle it didn't end up somewhere in Antigua.

I brought the package upstairs, cleaned off the bed-spread and laid out all the papers in front of me. There were reams of pages, half a dozen thick notebooks filled to the brim. This is what Jack had worked with while writing one of the seminal books of his generation on crime. Just looking at these old pages brought a smile to my face and courage to my heart.

And with those in mind, I began to read.

Amanda stayed in the living room, watching something on television at a low volume. I was perched on the bed amidst a mess of files, trying my best to keep them in order. From the smell of the pages I could sense that nobody had gone through them in some time. No need to, until now. I knew that wherever he was, Jack would approve.

The amount of research and notes Jack took was staggering. *Through the Darkness* was forty-two chapters long, and these pages only touched on twelve of them. Jack had transcriptions of interviews with dozens of people, from street dealers to middlemen, to cops and politicians, to local residents who'd witnessed their streets regress from thriving neighborhoods into third world countries.

He'd looked at this story from every angle. And I would have killed to be able to discuss it with him.

Some of the statistics Jack had uncovered were staggering, and in the years since the book was published they could have only grown more bleak.

According to the U.S. Department of Justice, over four *million* people in the United States had used crack cocaine at some point in their life, including nearly five percent of all high-school students. The drug was used primarily by men over the age of twenty-five. The typical user was African-American, aged twenty-eight, with an income at or below the poverty line.

The main reason, Jack had written, that crack cocaine had become so prevalent was due to its relative cheapness to manufacture, as well as the immediate high it produced. An eight ball, or an eighth of an ounce of rock, cost about thirty dollars depending on where it was purchased.

According to Jack's interviews, a surprising number of people would actually cook the mixture themselves rather than buy it ready-made, simply due to monetary concerns. It was cheaper to be your own chemist than go to the store. It was carried and sold in everything from glass vials to cellophane to tinfoil, even the rolls people generally used for coins. It was most predominant in larger cities with more densely populated urban areas, such as Los Angeles, New York, Baltimore and Chicago.

It was also surprising to note that in interviews with nearly twenty dealers, Jack was unable to find one person who actually used the drug.

Flipping through the pages, I came upon an interview with Butch Willingham that Jack had apparently conducted just weeks before Willingham was killed. Willingham denied ever using the drug, and in fact said that anyone who did was frowned upon. Jack had pressed in the interview:

> BW: People who smoke don't do their jobs. They sit around all day acting stupid. They ain't out there making money. They ain't out there selling product. This a business, man. Isn't one of the first rules of business to always get rid of the bottom ten percent?
>
> JO: I've heard that before:
>
> BW: See, in our line of work, that's more like twenty-five percent. Figure ten percent get stoned, take themselves out of the game. Another ten percent get busted.
>
> JO: And the other five percent?
>
> BW: They gots ta be made gone. I been around the country, man. Lived in L.A. and Baltimore before coming to NYC. Got family and friends everywhere. Cities change but things ain't that different. Don't matter where you are or where you work. If you sell, you gotta sell right.

JO: Butch, you said if someone doesn't sell right, they have to be "made gone." What do you mean by that?

BW: I mean, if you run a business, and someone's screwing up the bottom line, what do you do with them?

JO: Somehow I don't think you're talking about early retirement, a pension plan.

BW: You might call it an early retirement.

JO: So if someone needs to be "taken out," where does that come from?

BW: Come again?

JO: Who decides that bottom five percent? Who makes the final call which people, pardon the expression, live or die?

BW: Don't know, man. Ain't up to me, that's for sure.

JO: But surely you don't work for yourself. There are other people higher than you, I guess you might call them the board or something along those lines.

BW: Always report to the crew leader (Note: Willingham refused to identify his crew leader's name, but it was confirmed by several subjects to be a man named Marvin Barnett, age thirty-one), and I know he don't take home every penny that come into his hand.

JO: So where does the rest go?

BW: I don't know that. Don't know about no "board" neither. Heard rumors about one dude who runs the whole show, but not like anyone's ever seen him, so it's probably bullshit.

JO: So where do you see yourself in five years? The main man?

BW: Hell no, man. The main man got too many problems. There's a reason it's called the crown of thorns. You only sit at the top for so long before someone decides he don't like your way of doing business. Guys in my spot, as long as we keep our head down and keep selling, we be all right. Might not make as much money as the big man, but I'll be alive a lot longer.

I read the interview again. It wasn't much, but even then Willingham seemed to think there was some higher power, some authority figure running the show. The strange thing is that Butch seemed adamant about not doing drugs, about respecting the hierarchy of which he was a part. I wondered if there was a chance Willingham was killed over the book, but the book came out long after Butch was killed.

In addition, most of the numerous references to dealers were protected by fake names, monikers used to protect them in case their employers sought retribution along the lines that Butch had received. From Jack's perspective, he probably figured he didn't need to protect Butch Willingham's name since the man was already dead.

I found it to be a little too much of a coincidence that just weeks after this interview, the man was found dead with the words *The Fury* scrawled in his own blood. It didn't seem like Butch would have overstepped his bounds, but I couldn't be sure. Dealing wasn't exactly the most legitimate enterprise, so it was entirely possible he was blowing smoke up Jack's ass just to make himself sound like a good soldier.

Regardless, something had happened in those weeks between the interview and Butch's death. He'd done or seen something that required him being "made gone."

Looking back through the interview, I noticed this line of questioning:

JO: How do you come to grips knowing that the product you sell will be used by children?
BW: That ain't on me. I got a son, and I raise that boy right. Clarence gonna be fifteen next month. He knows if I ever see him lift a pipe or a needle, he's gonna feel a pain a lot worse than what those drugs can do to him. Grown-ups make their own decisions. I ain't got no sympathy for a grown man who uses. But a child, that's on the parent. If you can't raise your boy or girl right, and they end up sucking on a pipe, well, then, that's on the parents. There's a manhole in my street. City ain't never bothered to fix it. But I know it's there and step around that sucker. Someone else falls in? It's their own damn fault for being stupid.

Butch Willingham had a son. Clarence. It was a long shot, but there was a chance.

Using my cell phone, I went to 411.com and plugged in the name Clarence Willingham. Two matches came back; one living in Crown Heights, the other by Morningside Park on 107th Street.

I called the first number. A man picked up.

"Yeah?"

"Hi…is this Clarence Willingham?"

"Um, no," the man said, sounding irritated. "This *was* Clarence Willingham."

"Excuse me?"

"My name is Clarence Savoy now. Just got married last month."

"You…married…oh, I get it. Was your father Butch Willingham?"

"Butch?" the man said with a high-pitched laugh. "Try Albert. But close." Then Clarence Savoy hung up.

I tried the second number. It rang half a dozen times but didn't go to voice mail. I let it keep ringing. After three more rings, a man picked up. He sounded tired, like I'd just woken him from a nap.

"Who's this?"

"Is this Clarence Willingham?"

"Yeah, who's this?"

"Clarence, was your father named Butch?"

"Yeah, the hell's this about?"

"My name is Henry Parker. I'm a reporter. I was wondering if I could ask you a few questions."

I told Clarence about his father and Jack's book. I needed to know if he knew anything else about his father's murder or business practices. Clarence was eight years old when his father died. There's a chance he remembered something.

"I don't talk about this stuff over the phone," Clarence said.

"Well, my story is running tomorrow," I lied. "If you see me in person, we can talk about you giving me information as an unnamed source. If you don't cooperate, I can't promise anything."

I heard a rustling noise in the background. Then a female voice said, "Who is it?"

I must have interrupted Clarence. Too bad for him.

He shushed whoever was there and said, "Listen, man, I'll tell you whatever I know about my dad, but this is opening some seriously old wounds."

"Great. I'll be there in half an hour. What's your address?"

He gave me his address, which I jotted down before hanging up.

I checked my watch. It was almost noon. I stopped at a Staples store and bought a new tape recorder, some pens and paper. These were the tools I brought along when conducting interviews, when talking to sources. I hadn't used them much recently because this investigation had been more personal than professional. I thought everything revolved around my father's arrest. Only now could I see how wrong I'd been.

28

I kissed Amanda goodbye, made sure I was presentable and headed uptown to meet Clarence Willingham.

I rode the 2 train to 116th and Lenox Avenue. It was a hot day outside, the breeze that had felt so cool on our balcony gone.

Morningside Park was actually part of a cliff that separated Manhattan from Morningside Heights. It was also the location of a massive protest in 1968, when students of Columbia University staged a sit-in in and around the proposed construction of a gymnasium on the park grounds. With separate east and west entrances, many assumed this was to segregate the gym between black and white. University spokesmen denied the claims, but abandoned the plans after students barricaded themselves inside numerous university buildings.

After a group of students opposed to the protests blockaded the occupied buildings, police came in to end the struggle. Over one hundred and fifty students were injured during the forced removal, and over seven hundred were arrested. Because of the terrible public relations, specifically stemming from the student-on-student violence, Columbia scrapped its plans and built an underground gym instead. Ironically the blueprints for the gym were then sold to Princeton University, which appropriated them for their own use.

The address Clarence gave me was for a five-story brownstone within walking distance of the park. A pretty nice neighborhood. The Columbia campus stood directly on the opposite side of Morningside Park, and though Clarence did live far from student housing, the university owned such huge swaths of real estate in upper Manhattan that the neighboring streets were clean and graffiti free, devoid of clutter and garbage. It must have looked great in a brochure.

Before turning onto Clarence's block, I called Amanda's cell phone. She picked up, answering with a hard-to-distinguish, *"Heh-wo?"*

"Amanda?" I said. "Everything okay?"

"Eating," she said, removing whatever had been in her mouth. "Chocolate-covered strawberry. I swear, we need to move in here."

"Where did you buy that?"

"I didn't buy it. They were in a small tin by the television. I think they're complimentary."

"Amanda," I said, shaking my head, "nothing in hotels is complimentary. Check the box."

"Hold on." I heard her ruffling with something, then whisper *oh hell* under her breath.

"What happened?"

"Um…you know that bonus I got for Christmas?"

"Yeah?"

"Well, it's going to have to go toward paying off these strawberries."

"It's okay," I said. "Just enjoy them. Watch something crappy on television, I'll be back later."

"Okay, *fine,* I'll finish them. Be careful, babe. See you soon. Love you."

"I love you, too."

When I arrived at Clarence's building I rang the buzzer. I expected him to simply unlock the door, but within a minute I saw a man coming down the stairs toward me. He was wearing a bathrobe, loosely tied, with white briefs and blue slippers. A paunchy stomach hung over the elastic band of the briefs. It was a comical look, and it was safe to say he was coming to greet me rather than go for a stroll.

He opened the door, and I extended my hand.

"Henry Parker, nice to meet you, Clar…"

Clarence was ignoring me. My hand sat there unshook, a lonely hitchhiker. Clarence wasn't even looking at me, he was too busy looking down the street, both sides, behind me, as though expecting a boogeyman or a ninja to jump out and kill him. His eyes flickered back and forth, widening and then closing. He squeezed them shut hard, then opened them again. Perhaps this allowed him to see better, or give him some extrasensory perception.

When he seemed content that nobody was waiting to jump out at him, he said, "You come alone?"

"Of course I did."

"You sure about that?"

"Um…yeah. Pretty sure."

"You a cop?"

I snorted out a laugh. "Are you serious? I said I was a reporter."

"Cops lie. I don't believe that BS about cops having to declare themselves. If someone's recording this, I'm calling entrapment on your ass."

I turned out all my pockets. Showed him I was carrying nothing.

His brow furrowed. "That's not an answer."

"No. I'm not a cop, I'm a reporter." I showed him my business card.

"What'choo got in there?" he said, pointing to my bag.

"Tape recorder, notepad."

"You can't bring that to my place."

"What do you mean?"

"Nobody records or writes down what I say. You can't deal with that, you can leave."

I didn't have much choice, so I said, "What do you want me to do with my stuff then?"

"Bernita down the hall will watch it."

"Bernita?"

"You can trust her. She got a plasma TV. Anytime you have something you need stored safely, Bernita's your woman."

I wasn't quite sure how that was supposed to convince me to leave my equipment with her. I guess I didn't have much of a choice but to trust Clarence's sterling recommendation of Bernita's safe-deposit skills.

"Okay, whatever you say."

"All right. Come on."

Clarence led me into the hallway, past a row of rusty mailboxes and up the first flight of stairs. The building smelled of mold, and the paint was chipping on the staircase railing. Clarence took a left and knocked on the first door. A scraggly woman wearing a pink bathrobe and smoking an unfiltered cigarette opened it. I wondered if this was actually some sort of spa.

"Bernita," he said. "This is Henry. He's gonna be leaving his bag with you for a while."

Bernita's apartment beyond her looked rather massive, with a hallway splintering off to several different rooms. The floors were scrubbed clean, and a single dining table sat in the middle, uncluttered with the exception of a pair of crystal candlesticks. It seemed like quite a lot of space. Bernita wasn't wearing a wedding ring. The fact that she had at least three or four rooms for what looked like herself made me all the more conscious of my own dwelling.

"How long?" she said.

Clarence looked at me. "How long you need?"

"Hour. Two, tops."

Clarence said, "Forty-five minutes."

"Whatever," she replied. Then she looked at me, her upper lip curled back. "Henry. Ain't never met a young boy named Henry."

Bernita closed the door before I could reply.

With my belongings safely—hopefully—squared away, Clarence led me to the fourth floor. He lived in apartment 4J. When we got to the door, Clarence stuck his hand into his bathrobe pocket, pulling out a key ring with at least thirty keys on it. I marveled at the man's security methods. Then he went to work unlocking the half a dozen dead bolts on his front door.

Once Fort Knox was fully unlocked, he opened the door and beckoned me inside.

For the life of me I couldn't figure out why he went to such ridiculous lengths, because Clarence's apartment was an absolute pigsty.

Garbage littered the floor like he was trying to save room in the city landfills. Empty Chinese food and pizza boxes were stacked in one corner. Beer cans were strewn about, creating an aluminum carpet. I could identify at least a half-dozen different brands, as well as a few bottles of various liquors: José Cuervo, Courvoiser, Hennessy. Clearly, Clarence Willingham was not picky when it came to his booze.

"Take a seat," he said, gesturing to a beanbag chair crisscrossed by duct tape like a low-budget surgical patient. I sat down, immediately feeling the beans shifting under me. The last beanbag chair I'd sat in was during college, and I'm pretty sure a box of wine was involved. "Can I get you a drink? Beer? Soda? Absinthe?"

I was tempted to ask for the absinthe out of curiosity, but decided I wasn't that thirsty. "Thanks, I had lunch before I came."

"Suit yourself, man." Clarence reached under a desk and pulled out a small wooden box. He opened it, and took out what appeared to be a piece of rolling paper and a bag of pot. He looked as me, pleased. "This is some pure hydro. Fifty bucks a gram. You can snag an ounce in Washington Square Park for about six hundred. Sometimes you go up by the George Washington Bridge, around 179th Street, you find some real fiends who'll sell it for cheaper, but it won't be as good. And you'd be surprised at how many of the kids from Columbia deal right in Morningside Park."

"Thanks for the info," I said, "but I gave up smoking in college. I eat enough Cheetos these days as it is."

"Suit yourself, reporter man."

Clarence sprinkled some of the weed onto the paper. Then he spent a minute picking through it, removing any clumps or twigs. Once the mixture was in a slight cone shape—wide to narrow—he began to roll. Clarence stared at the joint with an almost trancelike intensity. He began in the middle, using his thumbs to roll it evenly, gradually moving his fingers to the ends of the paper. Once it was a cylinder, he licked the top edge of the paper and folded it over. When that was completed, he took a small piece of thicker paper and rolled it tightly into a spiral. He inserted that into one end of the joint. Clarence twisted the end without the roach so nothing would fall out.

Taking the joint between his thumb and index finger, Clarence held it to his lips, sparked a lighter and took a deep drag. He drew it deep into his lungs, his eyes closing as the end of the joint glowed. Finally he removed it from his lips and puffed out a dark cloud that hung over his room for a minute before disappearing.

When all that was done, he opened his eyes, looked at me, held out the joint. "Best weed you'll smoke in this city."

"No, thanks," I said. "I'm working."

"Whatever. So you said you wanted to talk about my pops. What about him?"

"Your dad was Butch Willingham."

"S'right." Clarence took another drag. I noticed a small corner of his upper lip was turned up. Either he wasn't entirely fond of speaking about his father, or hadn't in a long time.

"Was he a good father?"

Clarence held out the joint. I don't think he meant it that way, but I saw that as somewhat of an answer.

"No better or worse, s'pose."

"How do you mean that?"

"I know a lot of kids my age who had more'n I did. Know a lot that had less. My dad, he didn't have much of an education. No college, no high school. Dropped out at fourteen, spent the rest of his life slinging rock. That's all the man knew. As far as I knew he was good at it."

"How so?"

"Kept me well fed. My moms died when I was a kid and I never had no brothers or sisters, so it was all up to him. He made sure I went to school, beat my ass if I didn't get good grades. I know a lot of dads who bought the rock my dad sold and just sunk into a hellhole because of it. My dad never smoked, never drank. To him this was his livelihood, like someone who goes to a plant, punches a clock. He didn't take his work home with him."

"I find that a little hard to believe. I mean…" I motioned to the joint. Clarence laughed.

"Yeah, I used to do harder stuff. Crack. A little heroin here and there. The weed's a cooling-down drug. I'll get off it at some point." He took another long, deep, drawn-out puff, then smiled lazily. "Just not yet."

"The sins of the father," I said under my breath.

"What's that?"

"Nothing. So do you remember when your father was killed?"

"Remember?" Clarence said, coughing into his fist. "I was the one that found him."

"You're kidding," I said.

"Nope. Thursday nights I had me a pickup game of basketball in the park with some other kids. I was about six-two by high school, and could handle it like a dream. I thought if I kept growing I could be another Magic Johnson, the kind of big guy who had the skills of a point guard. Then one Thursday I came home. Picked up one of those ice-cream cones in a wrapper, you know with chocolate around the cone and nuts in the vanilla? Carried it home with me, went upstairs, first thing I see is blood on the carpet. I couldn't see my dad, that's how big the puddle was. He was lying in the living room, the puddle had spread into the hallway. I go in there, and he's facedown, arms above his head like he was trying to fly and fell from the sky."

"You saw the words?" I said.

"Yeah. Just barely, but they were in the carpet. Lucky for us we had an off-white carpet, otherwise I might have missed it. The Fury. That's what my dad wrote while he was dying on our floor."

"I can't even imagine," I said.

"No," Clarence said, putting the joint into an ashtray. "You can't. The cops told me they used a silencer. It took a few years until I knew what that meant."

"My brother was killed the same way," I said. Nobody spoke for a moment. Then I said, "So once you came out and saw him, you called the cops?"

"No. First I tried to wake him up," Clarence said. He spoke slowly, the words rusty like they hadn't been spoken in a long time. His voice was soft yet gritty, and it chilled me to the bone. "I turned him over. The back of his head was almost gone. I remember seeing bone and brain on the floor, but I was a kid. I figured there was always a way to put someone back together. I turned him over, saw that glassy look in his eyes, the same look you see on the mannequins in department stores. And I held my father's head in my hands and tried to get my daddy to wake up. Finally a neighbor heard me crying and called the cops. She actually reported it as a domestic disturbance, thinking my dad was beating me. Then when they came in and saw him…man, that's a picture that'll never go away."

I was almost afraid to ask, but I said, "What happened then?"

"The cops came and took me away. I stood outside and watched a whole mess of them go into our building, wearing gloves, carrying all sorts of equipment to bag and tag my dad. I'd seen bodies before. Even if my dad was straight, that's a dirty game, and some of his friends didn't play the same way. It's not the same when it's your kind. Whether you love 'em or not, when it's your own flesh and blood lying there, something just dries up inside of you. Drains the life out of you."

Inside, I knew how Clarence felt. Only to a much smaller degree.

"Then I got sent to foster care. Lived with a nice old family until I turned eighteen. Moved out, went to school and never seen them since."

"You graduate?" I asked.

"Cum laude," Clarence said. "I don't like to keep up appearances, but this is my crash pad. My real place of business is in Gramercy."

"What kind of work do you do?" I asked.

"Graphic design," he said.

"That's funny," I said. "Do you know a woman named Rose Keller?"

"Sounds familiar, why?"

"Friend of my brother's. Also works as a graphic designer."

"Hmm…" Clarence tapped a finger against his lower lip. "Think I might have smoked with her once or twice. Or maybe more." He smiled.

"She's kicked her habits. I guess creative people do creative things to their mind."

"I never lose the sharpness. It doesn't affect my work."

Then Clarence rattled off the names of several multibillion-dollar companies. He took a business card from a pile on his desk and handed it to me. It had his name, address, e-mail and Web site URL. The tagline read *Your dream can be a reality*. "I have a portfolio of all my clients. You check out their Web sites, that's all me. Half a dozen Fortune 500 companies."

"Not bad at all."

The joint had burned out. Clarence didn't seem to notice.

"That all you need, Parker?" Clarence asked. "I appreciate thinking about the good times and all, but my day is wasting."

"One more thing," I said. "The note your father wrote on the floor. The Fury. Do you remember your father ever talking about anyone who went by that name?"

"Nah," Clarence said, waving his hand. "My dad never brought his work home with him."

"He was killed because of his work," I said. "I'd say that's taking it home with you."

Clarence didn't take to that comment very kindly, and

stood up. "He never mentioned anyone by that name. But I know what you're getting at. I've read the books. I know what some people think. But a hustle's a hustle. There's no greater power. No Keyser Söze sitting up in a tower somewhere twisting the wills of men. It's a big racket, is all it is. People play to make money. The cards are shuffled every so often, and my dad was one of those cards. Sucks for him and for me, but that's the way it goes. So don't go spreading any rumors, 'cause they ain't true."

I wanted to tell Clarence that for untrue rumors, he was quite adamant about making sure I knew he thought nothing of them.

"Thanks for giving me some of your time," I said. "And I'm sorry for your loss."

"About twenty years too late, but I appreciate the sentiment."

Clarence led me to the door. The joint was a sad, forgotten nub in the ashtray. I turned around to shake his hand, when something caught my eye.

There was a futon resting in the far corner. Red cushion. Lots of stains from cigarettes, liquor, or both. Something underneath the sofa was twinkling, shining in the low light.

I stepped around Clarence to get a closer look.

"What're you doing?" he asked.

I felt a tightness in my chest as I walked to the futon. Dropping down to one knee, I peered underneath to see. Something told me I already knew what it was.

I felt a strong hand, Clarence's hand, grip my shoulder and squeeze. Pain coursed through the joint as he found the bone and dug in.

"Listen, man, you've had your fun. Leave or I'm gonna call the cops."

Ignoring him, I reached under the futon and grabbed the item. Standing back up, his hand still like a vise, I opened it to see what lay in my palm.

I felt the grip loosen as we both stared. My heart was hammering. I couldn't believe it.

Turning to face Clarence Willingham, I held out a small diamond earring in my hand. The companion to the earring I found up at Blue Mountain Lake by Beth-Ann Downing's body.

"Where is Helen Gaines?" I asked.

29

"I don't know what you're talking about," Clarence said, but the tremor in his voice belied that statement. I looked around. This apartment was too small. There was nowhere for her to hide. She had to be somewhere else.

But if Helen Gaines was hiding, if she'd left Blue Mountain Lake because somebody was trying to kill her, she wasn't out and about in New York City, sightseeing and having her caricature drawn in Times Square. If she'd come to Butch Willingham's son for help, chances are he knew where she was at this moment. She had to be somewhere close. In his office, perhaps. Or somewhere nobody would expect. The office might be out. Where...

I could hear Clarence screaming at me, trying to push me out of his apartment. My body didn't respond. She couldn't be at his office. She'd be somewhere nobody would know about. Somewhere...

Then I remembered my bag. Bernita. Clarence's words. *Anytime you have something you need stored safely, Bernita's your woman.*

I bolted out of Clarence's apartment, the diamond earring still in my hand. The footsteps behind me said that Clarence was right on my heels. And I didn't think he was going to argue with me anymore.

The stairs disappeared under me two at a time, and I used the railing on each landing to swing onto the next set, trying desperately to keep ahead of Clarence. I didn't know how we'd fare in a fight, but I was sure that if we made enough noise one of the tenants surely would call the cops. And I didn't have time for that. I needed to know. Needed to see.

Safely stored.

As I hit the first-floor landing, I felt Clarence's fist grab a chunk of my shirt. I pulled away, but not before it ripped a sizable hole in the collar. I turned around, saw Clarence behind me and shoved him as hard as I could.

It wasn't meant to hurt him, merely to buy me some time, and to that extent it worked. Clarence fell back about eight feet, tripping over the foot of the stairwell and falling to the ground. Cursing like a maniac, I was sprinting down the corridor before he could get himself up.

I found Bernita's door. Knocked twice fast. I said, "Bernita, it's Henry. You have my bag."

I saw Clarence on his feet, running toward me. I only had seconds.

Then the door opened in front of me, and Bernita was there in her pink bathrobe, the cigarette still in her mouth. She was holding my bag in one hand, outstretched, expecting me to take it then leave. When she saw the rip in my shirt and Clarence barreling down the hall, her eyes grew wide. She immediately tried to slam the door shut. Instead, I wriggled past her into the apartment, the door slamming shut where I'd just been standing.

"Get the fuck out of my house!" she screamed, slapping at me with both her hands, the cigarette still miraculously dangling from her lip.

Then I heard a small, frightened voice from the farthest room down the corridor.

"Bernita, is everything okay?"

I stared at Bernita for a second, then sprinted down the hall. It was the last door on the right. Without hesitating, I barged in, the door swinging open and smacking against the wall where it hit a doorstop and swung back at me. I stopped it with my foot, then stood there.

I heard two people breathing behind me. Bernita and Clarence. But I didn't care about them; all I cared about was the woman sitting on the bed mere feet from me.

Her hands were on her knees. Back ramrod straight. Her eyes were wide, terrified, as though she'd been expecting this moment for a long time and knew she could only avoid it for so long. Then that terrified look turned to anger, then confusion.

"Who…who are you?" she asked.

"Ms. Gaines," I said. "My name is Henry Parker. I'm James Parker's other son."

30

The apartment was silent for what seemed like ages. Helen Gaines sat there on the bed, unbelieving, her mouth in a silent *O*. I couldn't tell what she was thinking, if she knew who I was, or if I'd even existed. Since she'd left Bend before I was even born, there was a chance she didn't know about me. Didn't know that James Parker had another son. Or that Stephen Gaines had a brother.

But there was a glimmer of recognition there as she searched for a reaction. Perhaps Stephen had mentioned me the night he died. Maybe Helen knew there was another son.

Clarence Willingham's hand was on my back, but there was no force to it. As if he himself wanted to know just what was going on. When he'd first opened the door to his apartment building, I assumed Clarence's paranoia was due to the high, not wanting to get caught. The dead bolts on his door, they were protecting a man whose father had been gunned down mercilessly. He grew up in fear, and now he was protecting Helen Gaines. But why? How did they even know each other?

And how did Helen end up here, of all places, after fleeing Blue Mountain Lake?

Bernita had stopped screaming. Perhaps because they were both curious. Or perhaps because they didn't want to get anyone else involved. Because they were still protecting Helen.

"You're Henry," she said. "Oh my…I've wanted to meet you for so long."

That answered my question.

"I only just found out you existed a few days ago," I said. "Why didn't you ever try to reach me?"

"I didn't know how," she said, but her voice betrayed that thought. She never really tried. The idea of my existence was grander than the reality of it.

I walked over to Helen. Extended my hand. She did not offer hers, and for a moment I was embarrassed, but then she stood up, took a breath and gathered me in her arms. It was a strange sensation, and one I wasn't sure was deserved or appropriate, but soon I felt my arms wrapping around this small, frail woman who'd been a part of my family's life long before I ever arrived.

Her pulse was racing. A slightly sour smell came off of her.

When Helen Gaines pried herself away from me, she stepped back, sat down on the bed with a sigh. The woman's pupils were dilated, and I had to take a moment to realize just how small, just how thin she was. I remember the photo my father had shown me. The vivacious young woman with the unruly brown hair, the bright green eyes. The eyes were still green, but they were slightly dulled. Too much life had passed by them. Not enough love to keep them shining.

The veins in her wrists were thick, ropy. Blue streaks roamed underneath her skin. The brown of her hair had nearly all been wiped away, replaced with a stringy gray.

Then I heard a smacking sound and saw that she was licking her lips. Dry mouth. A symptom of crack addiction.

She was Stephen Gaines's mother all right.

"Wait," I said. Suddenly I was the one confused. I'd been so caught up in discovering the earring and finding Helen that the biggest question hadn't even occurred to me to ask.

"How in the hell do you two know each other?" I said to Helen, then turned to Clarence.

Clarence bowed his head. Then he stepped by me, went and sat down on the bed next to Helen. She placed her hand on top of Clarence's head. He smiled weakly, tilted it slightly.

"Butch Willingham," Helen said, "saved my life. When I came to this city I had nothing. I started using, but I was out of control. I bought from Butch, but he never sold me enough to kill me, which is what I wanted. One day, Butch found me passed out in a gutter. Facedown. Drowning in filth. He took me in. Nursed me back to health. He was my lover. My protector. He was the husband your father never was. The father Stephen never had."

"And when my dad died," Clarence said, "Ms. Gaines always looked after me. The city wouldn't allow her to adopt me because of her…issues…but she visited every day. She was the mom I lost when I was a kid."

"So when Beth-Ann was killed," I said, extrapolating what I'd learned, "you called Clarence."

"He was my only friend left," Helen said. Her eyes were sunken. She began to weep softly, her small body trembling. Clarence wiped her tears away with his finger, took her frail hand and kissed the back. Helen smiled, nestled her head against his neck.

"She was *here* when I called," I said. "That's who I heard in the background."

"I wouldn't let her stay at my pad. Too many people have my business card. Bernita here doesn't even have e-mail."

"I found the earring," I said to Helen.

"Earring," she said, stumbling over her words. "Oh my, from the cabin!"

"That's right."

"I didn't even know I had the other one with me. It must have fallen."

"Onto Clarence's carpet," I replied. "So he shuttled you downstairs to hide while I talked to him."

"Didn't have time for anything else," Clarence replied.

"You went to all this trouble," I said.

"I'd do anything to protect this woman," Clarence said. "Anything." Then he stared at me, his eyes gone from tender to fiery in an instant. "Anything."

I knew he was talking to me. That if I even thought about exposing Helen, about putting her in harm's way, Clarence Willingham would have no problem making sure nobody heard what I had to say.

"So you hid her here," I said.

Bernita chimed in, saying, "Man did pay me."

"I trust Bernita," Clarence said. "Helen wasn't so sure at first."

"I didn't—still don't—know who to trust," Helen said.

"I couldn't keep her with me," Clarence said. "I have clients coming over to my office, and there's no way she could have stayed upstairs. Besides, who would think to look here?"

"I would. I did," I said.

"Yeah, well, most people ain't you, Parker." I wasn't sure whether he meant that as an insult or a compliment.

"We need to talk about Stephen," I said. "Helen, I need to know what happened. The police have arrested my father for Stephen's murder. They know he came into the city to see you. They know you tried to blackmail him. I need to know why. It wasn't for rehab for Stephen. I need to know what that money was for, and what happened that night."

Helen Gaines's hand went to Clarence's and held it tight. He put his arm around her, comforted her as she began to cry, this time harder. She wailed, her hand covering her mouth to stifle the sobs.

"Oh…my baby," she said. "My baby is gone…"

"Helen," I said. But all I could do was wait it out. It hadn't even been a week since Stephen was murdered, and though Helen Gaines seemed far from mentally stable, there were some things that pierced the heart no matter how calloused it had grown.

She cried for several minutes. Clarence held her head, stroked her hair. His eyes were closed, too, and on his face I could see the pain of a man whose surrogate mother was going through hell in every way, shape and form. Clarence had admitted abusing drugs in his younger years, but recently had begun to wean himself off of them. No doubt having a dealer as a father exacerbated any curiosity he had. And even though Butch was a supposedly "clean" dealer, being exposed to that kind of trade could stir a desire that wouldn't have existed otherwise. The temptation was there. His father put it there, and Helen Gaines had become a victim of it as well.

Maybe Helen and Clarence had actually bonded over this. Perhaps it was even Helen who, after Butch was gone, tempted Clarence. But looking at them now, young man and older woman, they needed each other more than anything in the world.

"Helen," I said, "I need to know why you got in touch with my father. After all those years, why did you suddenly need the money?"

Helen removed her head from Clarence's shoulder. She wiped her eyes, only succeeding in smearing the mascara she had on. Clarence took a tissue from his pocket, handed it to her. She thanked him, cleaned herself up.

"The money wasn't for me," she said. "It was never for me. It was for Stephen."

"Rehab?" I asked.

"No. That ship sailed a long time ago. We tried— both of us, actually. But it's easy to say you want to stop, it's another thing to do it. It'd be like rewiring your brain. When you have two people so close, both addicted, you can either band together and use each other for strength…or you can slip into the comfort of nothingness. We chose the latter."

"So you know your son was using, and that he probably started because of you."

Helen nodded. "I was young and stupid when I came

here. Do you know what it's like to be nineteen years old with a baby? To have to leave the only place you've ever known and go somewhere where you don't know anybody? To raise a child in a different world? I couldn't handle it. So I escaped. But Stephen could have made so much more of himself."

"Stephen wasn't just some street dealer," I said. "He was much higher."

Helen blinked. "I knew he wasn't standing out on corners. He had nice suits. Lots of them. He would wear them during the day, even though I knew where he was going. I always found it strange that someone in that…line of work would get dressed up so nicely. We never had money for anything else."

I thought about the building in midtown. All those suited young men entering to get their daily packages. A horde of young, urban professionals. Only the definition had turned a one-eighty.

"How long had he been selling?" I asked.

Helen looked at the ceiling. Wiped her eyes again. Clarence was staring at her as well, his eyes soft. I wondered if he'd ever heard these stories.

"Screw this," Bernita suddenly announced. "I'm getting a beer and watching *Judge Judy*." Her pink bathrobe turned with a flutter, and she left the room.

"She's a great cook," Helen said. "Made chicken à l'orange last night."

"I have about ten pounds of leftovers in my fridge at home," Clarence said with a laugh. "I know what you're saying."

"How long?" I repeated.

"Almost ten years. He dropped out of CCNY after

his sophomore year. I worked about a hundred different jobs over the years, but even with that and the money Stephen made, with his student loans, there was no way we could ever really make ends meet. Not in this city. That's actually where I met Beth. We were both secretaries at a public-relations firm. They fired us both within the month when we came to work high. So Stephen dropped out. Partly because of the money, partly to take care of me. He said the only experience he needed was in the real world. And I was too stupid to stop him. And besides, he was making more money doing that than I ever did working real jobs. And none of it was taxed."

"So he was working for ten years, making good money, obviously moving up the ladder," I said. "Again, why did he need the money?"

"We went through it fast," Helen said. "Stephen started using more, and I was a mess. We never saved much. One day, about a month ago, Stephen came home from work. I remember him coming in the door with this look on his face, and I just froze. He was so scared…oh God, his eyes were wide and his face was pale and I thought he might have overdosed. He collapsed on our sofa and asked for a glass of water. When I brought it to him, he just sat there with the glass in his hand. Not drinking, just staring at the wall. Then my boy started to cry."

"Why?" I asked. "What happened?"

"He didn't tell me," Helen said. "All he said was, 'We need to leave. We need to get far, far away from this city. When I asked him what the matter was, he just said, 'You're safer if you don't know. We'd both be safer if I didn't know either.' I looked into his eyes. They were bloodshot. Not from drugs, but from crying. He'd never spoken like that before in his life. I'd never seen him so scared, so terrified. So I told him we'd find a way."

I said, "My father told me he found a notepad in your apartment. It read 'Europe' and 'Mexico.' That's where you were thinking of going. Right?"

Helen nodded. "We didn't know where to go. What city or country. We wondered if Europe was too far, or if Mexico was far enough. Stephen just wanted to go far, far away. We barely had enough money to cover the rent."

"And that's why you called my father," I said. "For money to leave the country."

"It was a one-time thing," Helen said. "I figured after all those years, after what he'd done to me and our baby—that's right, *our* baby—the least he could do was help us start a new life."

I couldn't really argue with that. My father owed them far more than he could ever make up for.

"So you threatened to sue him," I said.

"I didn't know any other way. The old James Parker I knew would rather burn his money than give it away."

"You couldn't say something a little more noble, like you needed it for a kidney transplant or something? Maybe that would have tugged at his heartstrings a little more than the rehab story."

"I don't know how well you know your father," Helen said sardonically, "but he's not exactly the sentimental type."

I couldn't argue with that either.

"So he came into the city to see you, then what?"

"How much did he tell you?" she asked.

"He told me you pulled a gun on him," I said. "Is that true?"

Helen nodded. "Yes. But it was Stephen's gun. He kept it for protection. He taught me how to use it, just in case. I was scared, of your father and for Stephen. I got carried away."

"Where was Stephen during all of this?" I said.

"I'm not sure," Helen said. "He told me he was going to try and talk to someone. He said there was one person who might be able to do something if he knew the whole story."

"Oh God," I said. "He was with me. He was at the *Gazette* waiting for me." I felt sick. I put that from my mind, tried to focus.

"My father said he took the gun from you. Is that true?"

"It is," Helen said.

"Would you be willing to testify to that? The police say my father's fingerprints were found on the gun. If you testify that they got there another way—other than him actually firing it—it will help his case."

"I don't know if I want to help his case," Helen said. "As long as he's locked up, the cops aren't hunting the person who really killed my son."

"So you know it wasn't my father," I said. Helen said nothing. She turned away. Didn't even look at me. I was taken aback by this indifference. Stunned, I said, "Don't you care about your son's killer getting what he deserves?" I said.

Helen's face turned to stone. She said, "It must be nice to live in a world where everyone who deserves justice gets it. My son was taken from me. I tried to save him…help him save himself. And now he's gone. And let me tell you what I want now, Henry… I want to live. And if living means letting this end, letting the people out there think that someone is taking the fall, I can't say that's an ending I dislike."

"You must know, though," I said. "You have to know who killed your son."

"I don't know for certain," Helen said. "After James and I had our…talk…he left for the airport. He put the gun back down. We both knew I wasn't going to use it. And I knew that was the last time I would ever see your father."

"Then what did you do?" I asked.

"Then I went out. I needed a drink. Needed to smoke. James didn't have that much money, only a few thousand dollars. I didn't know what was going to happen with Stephen. He was so scared, so afraid."

"So your choice then was to go out rather than see him."

"That's right. I did. I had to calm my nerves. I just needed something to get me by. And I thought if I could relax, I could figure out just how we were going to get out of the city. I must have been gone for, I don't know, two hours or so. When I came back to the apartment, I walked in and saw him…Stephen…facedown on the floor. Blood everywhere. And I just started screaming."

"And you felt you were in danger."

"I knew I was," Helen said. "Whoever killed him did it because they thought he knew something he wasn't supposed to. And if he knew, then chances were I would too. I left that night, before the cops ever came. And I remember the street, the quiet, the neighbors who didn't even know what had just gone on. I went right to Beth-Ann's apartment, and we went up to the lake. I had no idea they would find us there."

"So you didn't see who killed Stephen," I said.

"No. Just the people on the street. Neighbors, people I'd seen around before…" Helen trailed off, looked at Clarence.

"What is it, Mom?" he said.

"One man," Helen said. "There was one man standing on the street, staring at me as I left the apartment. He was just there, standing by a lamppost, and I could have sworn he was crying. And honest to God, I think that boy looked at me and said…"

"Said what?" I asked.

"Said he was sorry. And all I could think to do was run."

"I don't understand," I said. "Why didn't you call anyone? The cops? Someone?"

"Stephen told me a long time ago not to trust anyone in this city. He said the people he knew, the people he worked for, if they thought you might hurt them they would hurt you first, and hurt you worse than you could ever do to them. When he came home that night, scared out of his mind, he told me our only option was to run. That if we told anybody, we would be in trouble. That's all he said. Trouble. But the thing is—" Helen stopped, looked at the floor.

"What is it?"

"The night he died," she said, "Stephen told me there might be one way out. He said he knew one person who might be able to help us. He knew about your father, about his family, and I told him there was a good chance James Parker wouldn't give us a dime and we wouldn't be able to leave the country. So finally he told me there was one last option. There was someone he knew wasn't on the take, wouldn't hurt us. Someone who could give them more trouble than they ever imagined. He went out that night. Never told me who he was going to see. And then, a few hours later, he was dead."

It felt like a piece of coal was burning in the pit of my stomach. I knew Stephen had been talking about me. For some reason, he considered me his last hope. And then he died. Because I didn't trust him.

"You said the night Stephen died, you saw someone outside the apartment. A young man crying. Who was he?" I asked.

"I don't know. It was dark out," Helen said, her voice sorrowful, apologetic. "And my mind, I was so confused, so scared. I didn't see his face. All I remember is noticing something on his neck…a birthmark. Such a young man, younger than Stephen even…"

I nearly fell to the floor. The room went blurry on me. Clarence got up, came to my side, helped me stand.

"You okay?" he said.

I nodded, but felt anything but okay. I knew who that man was. And now I knew who killed Stephen.

And I knew where he lived.

31

"I have to go," I said, standing up. Right under my nose the whole time. My brother's killer. I didn't have time to talk to Helen. To worry about how disturbing it was that a mother would prefer to protect her own hide than find justice for her son's killer.

I couldn't think about how this might affect Helen. She could be helped. She could be protected. And if her eyes hadn't deceived her that night, I knew who had killed Stephen Gaines.

"Tell me you'll be here," I said to Helen, looking at Clarence. "I swear on my life I know people who can protect you. And if I'm right, you won't have to worry anymore, because the man who killed Stephen will be behind bars the rest of his life. There's nobody else who can hurt you."

"You don't know that," Helen whispered. "Stephen was much stronger than I ever was. And look what happened to him."

There was no boogeyman. No higher power. It was the law of the jungle. Kill or be killed. Stephen found himself on the shit end of that equation. And it was time for me to even the score.

"Please be here," I said. "If I'm right, you'll need to testify."

"If you're wrong," she said, "neither of us will be around long enough for it to matter."

I said nothing. I thanked Clarence for his help. Then, crossing over to Helen Gaines, I put my hand on her shoulder. The bones protruded, sharp angles. There was no muscle, no strength there. She was a skeleton with skin. A woman whose soul seemed to have left her long ago.

Helen Gaines smiled weakly at me. I didn't know if she would still be here later. There were only so many lives I could affect. My duty was to the truth, to uncover it at all costs.

"Watch after her," I said to Clarence. His nod told me he would.

I left Bernita's apartment, exiting the building. The sun was hanging bright and hot over the city. Every second seemed to take an hour. Every moment he breathed thinking he'd gotten away with murder was one that made my blood boil.

Before I left, I took out my cell phone and my wallet, then removed the thick stack of business cards that had turned brown from the leather. Shuffling through them, I picked out the one I needed. Then I called the cell phone number listed.

"Detective Makhoulian," came the answer.

"Detective," I said, "it's Henry Parker. I know who killed Stephen Gaines."

I gave him the address and told him when to be there.

Only, I would be there ten minutes earlier. We needed some time alone.

I headed toward the subway, my mind completely clear except for the anticipation of what was about to come. The judicial system would have its turn. But first I needed mine.

The train was hot, crowded and sticky. It only served to get my blood up. Once I got out downtown, the walk was short. My legs carried me faster than I knew they could. In my mind I could see images of the people I knew. Had known. And had never known.

My father.

My mother.

Jack.

And Stephen Gaines. The brother I never had.

I arrived on the block with half an hour to spare. I checked my watch every thirty seconds, trying to contain the rage building inside of me. Everything had led up to this.

I paced up and down, breathing steady, controlled. It wasn't easy. The last time I remembered feeling like this, helpless yet ready to explode, was several years ago when my then girlfriend Mya was attacked and nearly raped. That night I paced the street, a fifth of vodka in a paper bag, praying I would somehow find the man who was cowardly enough to attack a woman half his size. Though Amanda and I had been through some trying ordeals, to the point where I wondered if we would live to see the next day, we were both strong-willed people. We could overcome it. We knew that. Stephen wasn't strong enough to overcome his demons. He'd been seduced by the vial, the needle, and once they were in they were in for good.

And suddenly I turned around and there he was. Wearing a brilliant suit, slightly disheveled after a long day's work. A briefcase slung over his shoulder. His shoulders were slumped as he walked, his eyes cast down to the street. As he got closer I could see the birthmark on his neck. The same one Helen Gaines saw the night he killed my brother.

He didn't see me waiting for him. That was probably for the best.

"Scott Callahan," I said.

Scotty's eyes snapped up to meet mine. At first he was confused, then a small smile crossed his lips when he recognized me. Then that smile disappeared when he realized I was not there for a social visit. Nothing like it.

"Henry?" he said, trying to understand what I was doing there.

I walked toward him. Picking up my pace with every step.

"Cops are on their way," I said, voice even, teeth gritted. Scott kept on walking, tentative, until we were just a few feet from each other. "But they won't be here for a little while. So we have some time to chat."

Scotty's face went an ashen gray. "The cops?" he said. "Wha…I don't understand. You promised me you'd keep my name out of this. Goddamn it, you *promised* me!"

"I promised I wouldn't turn you in for dealing. I was looking for something more. But I never said a word about keeping your name clean from murder, you piece of shit."

"Murder? What the hell…" Scotty was breathing

hard. I saw his eyes flicker to the building next to us, where he lived. He was carrying nothing but his brief-case and his wallet. There was nowhere to go. No place to hide.

And then, from the opposite end of the street, we both heard the faint shrill of police sirens. Scotty whirled around. The cops weren't within sight yet. He was sweating, nervous. Then all of a sudden Scotty came around and punched me in the stomach.

It wasn't a hard blow, but I was unprepared. Rather than buckling and trying to absorb the hit, it landed square in my gut, knocking the wind from me. I fell to a knee, gasping for air. Scotty began to run. So I did the only thing I could. I grabbed his ankle as he ran past.

Scotty's leg went out from under him, and he landed with a thud on the pavement. His briefcase went flying, fluttering pathetically in the wind. Forgetting about my own lack of air, I leaped up and pounced on him. I dug my knee into the small of his back, then rolled him over and reared back to deliver my own blow. Scotty brought his elbows up to protect his face, and my punch hit nothing but bone. The pain was terrible, but it dissipated in an instant. I connected with a solid right to Scotty's ear, knocking his face sideways. A scream escaped his mouth.

I threw another punch, but Scotty was able to block it, twisting sideways. I still hadn't recovered from his punch, so I was thrown off balance and fell off him. I managed to keep my hand on his shoulder, pulling him back down as he tried to get up.

Scotty was crawling for something; I couldn't see what. My face was still close to the ground, and I could smell the concrete. Then I heard a clang as something toppled over, and that was followed by a whoosh of air as he swung what appeared to be the lid of a garbage can at my head.

I managed to roll away, catching a glancing piece of the aluminum on my jaw. It stunned me and I fell back. Scotty stood up, limping, clutching his knee. The sirens were growing louder. Not long ago the police had been after me, and I'd managed to escape. At least for a while. Scotty had lived here for years, knew every inch of the city. He had friends who would protect him. If Helen Gaines, a frail junkie, could find a safe house, no doubt a dealer with innumerable contacts could as well. I couldn't let him get away.

As Scotty began to run, I got to my feet, dived forward and tackled him from behind. His legs gave out, and Scotty screamed again as his knee slammed down on the ground. By this point I could see several pedestrians watching us, hands over their mouths in shock and terror. A few were on their cell phones, no doubt calling 911.

A little late, but I appreciated the gesture.

Scotty was still writhing, and I managed to turn him over, placing my knees in the crook of his elbows. Just like I had to the guy who tried to jump me at the apartment. Scotty's head was bleeding from where I'd punched him. There was a ragged hole in his pants by his right knee. There was a nasty cut that was bleeding pretty heavily. I could feel the slow, hot trickle of blood running down my neck, where he'd clipped me with the lid.

I raised my fist, ready to exhaust all the rage and fury

of the last few days. To get payback for my brother's murder, for my father's incarceration.

This man, this killer, this hired dealer. The world would be better off without him.

Yet as I stared at my own fist, poised and ready to strike the helpless murderer, suddenly my hand went slack. My fingers uncurled. I couldn't do it. Justice wasn't about taking an eye for an eye. I was above that. I had to be.

So I sat there, knees on his arms, the man below me in terrible pain, tears streaming down his face.

"Please," Scotty blubbered, "let me go. You don't know what you're doing…"

"I know exactly what I'm doing," I said. "I'm giving you the chance you never gave Stephen. I'm going to let you live."

The sirens grew closer. I could see the red and blue flashing off the windows on the street. The air was hot, swirling around us as I waited, my breathing heavy, angry.

"Get the hell off of him."

I didn't recognize the voice. The sirens screamed all around us. I hadn't heard a car pull up. It wasn't a cop talking. The voice did sound familiar, though.…

Turning my head, from the corner of my eye I saw Kyle Evans standing two feet from our sprawled bodies. He was holding a gun in his hand. It was pointed right at my head.

I heard more screams, and anyone who had been on the street watching had run off when the gun was pulled. It was just the three of us.

I took my knees off Scotty, who scooted backward. He clutched his knee, biting his lip.

I stood up. Air was coming back to my lungs, but I was still doubled over slightly.

"He's a killer," I said, the words coming out in bursts. "He's—"

And then I saw it. And whatever breath had found its way back into my lungs vanished.

Kyle was holding a black pistol. And attached to the end of it was a thin metal tube. And I remembered what Leon Binks had said to me the night I identified Stephen Gaines's body in the medical examiner's office.

"The killer was using a silenced weapon. Now, very few guns have those kinds of professional silencers you see in movies, that screw on like a lightbulb. Usually they're homemade, a length of aluminum tubing filled with steel wool or fiberglass."

"It was you," I said. "You killed Stephen."

Kyle went over to where Scott Callahan was lying on the ground. He was still holding his knee, but smiled when he saw his friend approach. Kyle knelt down, put his hand on his friend's shoulder. Scotty tried to prop himself up, but he was too weak. I stood there, my body rigid with anger and dread.

Kyle looked back at me. Then he said, "You gotta do what you gotta do to survive."

Then he placed the gun under Scott Callahan's chin and pulled the trigger.

32

"What the fuck!" I shouted. The gun blast was more of a meek *pfft*, like compressed air escaping from a puncture. Gore sprayed out the top of Scott Callahan's head. His body twitched once, then fell to the ground and lay still.

My hands wouldn't work. I stared slack-jawed at Kyle. He was still on the ground, the gun loose in his hand. He looked at his friend, a sorrow etching across his face for an instant. Then his eyes turned cold and his gaze came to me.

"You have no idea," Kyle said, "how surprised I was to get to Stephen's house and find a gun already there. I had this one all ready. Instead, all I needed was the capper." He pointed to the silencer.

"You used my brother's own gun to kill him," I said. "But he wasn't the last one to use it."

"No, I really should have bought a lotto ticket that night. When I heard that Stephen's *dad* got popped for it? I nearly pissed myself laughing. See, that night I wore gloves, figured it would slow the cops down, but I had no idea about your dad's shenanigans. I was there to take out Stephen, but I kind of took out the whole family. As long as they had someone else pinned for the murder, we were in the clear."

"We?" I said.

"Scotty was supposed to do it. He knew Stephen better than I did. They were pals, man."

I thought back to our conversation in the deli. Scotty pretending to barely know my brother. That's how they got so close to him.

"When your dad got popped, we were in the clear. We even took the casings just in case. Turns out we didn't even need to. Now, though, Scotty here's gotta take the fall. Can't have anyone thinking the killer's still out there."

"You son of a bitch."

"On a normal day, I'd get pissed at you for talking about my mom like that, but I'll let it slide. Besides, when I meant nobody could know, I meant it." Kyle turned the gun to me. He had me less than five feet away, dead to rights. There was no tremor in his hand. By the time I even thought about running, he could pull the trigger.

"Why?" I said. "Why did he have to die?"

"You said it yourself," Kyle replied. "The man just had to. When you're the top dog in anything, you're gonna get bitten."

"But Stephen was so young."

"There's no one guy," Kyle said. "It's like Ronald McDonald. Every now and then someone new steps up to the plate. Call it a *coup d'etat,* call it whatever you want, but every company needs a regime change. Some new blood at the top. Now it's my turn."

Curt Sheffield had told me that five people connected to 718 Enterprises had been killed recently. Add to that number my brother and now Scott Callahan. Helen Gaines told me that Stephen had wanted to leave the country, that he feared something terrible. Clearly he'd gotten wind that there were rivals who wanted to take him out. So, was Stephen systematically wiping out his competition? Is that why Kyle killed him—just to beat him to the punch?

If what Kyle said was true, and Stephen and Scotty had been friends, Stephen trusted them both. That's how Scotty and Kyle talked their way into my brother's apartment. They were couriers for him, yet he didn't fear them. My brother had been betrayed by his own friends.

When Stephen came to the *Gazette* that night, he'd wanted to come clean. He knew the chances of getting enough money to hide were slim. So my guess was that he was going to spill on the whole operation. He didn't fully trust the cops to protect him, but he figured if it made the papers first he couldn't be killed without the public being aware of it. His only hope was to cause a big enough story that he would be forgotten. That he could disappear in the maelstrom.

But he was killed before he could ever come clean. And his story was about to die as well.

Kyle then took the gun and placed it in Scotty's dead hand. He wrapped his own finger around Scotty's in the trigger guard and aimed it at me.

Just then a car sped onto the block. It was a black Crown Victoria. Kyle's attention turned from me to the car. The door opened. And out got Detective Sevi Makhoulian.

"Freeze, police!" the officer yelled. Kyle couldn't turn away from Makhoulian. A strange look crossed his face, and I swear the gun began to lower. He was going to give up.

And then three successive explosions turned the air into a thunderstorm, and Kyle Evans's body was flung backward onto the street. He landed next to Scotty, his friend, Kyle's eyes and mouth open.

I turned to Makhoulian, hands covering my ringing ears. He was saying something to me, but I couldn't hear the words.

He walked closer, gun at his side, the flashing lights now on our block. I felt the detective's large hand on my elbow. He was mouthing, *Henry, are you all right?*

I knew instinctively that my voice wouldn't work, so I nodded. Then I turned back to see the dead littering the street.

33

One week later

LaGuardia Airport was surprisingly empty. We bought a couple of coffees at a java stand in the food court. I waited while he came back from the newsstand, carrying a bag with a paperback book and a copy of the *Gazette*.

My father was thinner than I'd ever seen him. His eyes were sunken and his skin wrinkled. Gray hair taking up most of whatever was left. My father no longer looked angry; he just looked old.

Prior to a few weeks ago, I hadn't seen James Parker in years. My family was a memory, one I'd longed to forget. If you leave a person, your memory retains your last image of them. My last image of my father was an angry middle-aged man. Now he sat here, one step from broken, waiting for a flight back home.

"Mom's picking you up in Portland?" I said.

"That's what she said," my father answered, as though not believing her.

"If she says she'll be there she'll be there." He

nodded, thinking more about it and agreeing with me. I popped the top off my coffee and took a sip. Strong and sweet. "At least you've got a great story for your bowling league."

"I missed three league tournaments," he said, resentment in his voice. "I'm sure they replaced me by now."

"Didn't you once tell me you had a 187 average? I'm sure they'll want that back in the rotation."

"One-eighty-seven, huh?" he said, thinking. "That seems a tad high. Maybe one-forty."

"Still not too shabby." He shrugged his shoulder, then took the lid off his coffee and took a long gulp. When he set the cup back down, there was a scowl on his lips. "You know, prison food gets a bad rap. The eggs and joe down there weren't half-bad."

"If you really want, I'm sure you could figure out a way to go back."

"S'alright. Hopefully my TiVo recorded all the *Law & Order* episodes I missed."

"At least your priorities are straight again." He nodded, missing the joke.

"You told me you saw Helen," my father said, looking back at me. He actually looked concerned. Even sad.

"She's in rehab," I said. "The state is paying for it. Clarence Willingham is quite a guy. She has some good people looking out for her."

"I never got to tell her I was sorry," he said.

"I have her address," I said. "Write her a letter. She'd appreciate that."

"Maybe I will." The way he said it let me know that no such thing would ever be done.

"So they got the guys who did it. Who killed Stephen."

"They're both dead. The real killer, Kyle Evans, tried to frame his friend. Then the cops killed him."

"Good riddance," he said. "It's all tied up with a pretty pink bow. I never want to set foot in this city again."

"I still don't fully get it," I said. "If Stephen was really as high up as Kyle and Scott said he was, did he really need to leave the country to get away from them? And if they were able to get close enough, obviously Stephen didn't think they were a threat. Which makes me wonder just who Stephen was afraid of."

"No disrespect to the dead," my father said, "but I don't think any of those boys were in their right mind."

"And the cop, Makhoulian. I'm glad he worked so fast to get you out. I just didn't think he needed to kill Kyle. He looked like he was giving up."

"You're saying the guy who killed your brother should have lived?"

"One death doesn't always merit another. We have a justice system."

"Which would have probably screwed up somehow and either let that boy walk on a technicality, put him in some cushy detention facility because some quack doctor on somebody's payroll said he has woman issues. Or he'd be out in enough time to kill somebody else's son. I don't know what's going on in this city, Henry, but being among criminals day in and day out is no way to live."

"Maybe I'll move back home with you and Mom," I joked. That made him laugh. He checked his boarding pass.

"I should head to the gate. They'll probably give my ticket to some freak if I'm not there on time."

His flight didn't board for another hour, but the Parker family bonding hour had run its course. We both stood up. My dad stepped forward, then wrapped his arms around me, the most tentative hug I could imagine. I returned it. Just a little stronger.

"Thank you for your help," he said. The feeling was genuine. He wasn't going to apologize for the years before that, and I wasn't going to ask him to.

"Take care of yourself," I said. "And please take care of Mom. Do me one favor?"

He frowned. "What?"

"Mom was knitting something when I saw her in Bend. If it's not too much trouble, I'd like to have it."

"I'll tell her," he said.

"And if you change your mind and decide to take a vacation in NYC, at least give me a call."

"I will. And give my best to your girlfriend. She seems like a catch."

"One in a million," I said. "Without her you'd still be in jail."

"Guess I owe her a thank-you then. Pass it on for me, will ya?"

"I will. And Dad?"

"Yeah, Henry."

"I'm sorry too. About Stephen. I wish I'd had a chance to know him. Maybe we could have saved him."

His eyes closed as he took a deep breath. When he opened them, he sighed and said, "Take care, Henry. It's good to see I raised you right."

Then he was gone.

34

We were almost done packing. After several years in that apartment, the time had come to say goodbye before the floor gave out or a black hole opened up that sucked us into some alternate universe. A man can only face so many attempted assaults on his doorstep before rethinking his living situation. And since I'd already been thinking about more space, when Amanda agreed with me it made sense. My lease was up in a few weeks. It was as good a time as any to start over.

We were submerged amongst folded cardboard boxes, masking tape, clothes, books, papers and everything else you forget about and probably have no need for. My books took up the most room. I packed all of my first-edition Jack O'Donnell tomes in a padded box, reinforced with enough masking tape to hold up the Brooklyn Bridge. My clothes were another story. There were two small boxes marked Henry's Clothes. They weighed about as much as a pizza.

"You know," Amanda said, "you could have saved on the moving van and just rented a bike. You could have fit all your stuff into one of those E.T. baskets."

"I'm not a shopper, what do you want from me?"

"Not a shopper?" she said, putting down her Sharpie. "Even being able to use the word *shopper* implies that you have, in fact, shopped in your life. I'm guessing most of these clothes survived from college, or else the local Salvation Army dropoff is pretty bare. When we get settled, first thing we're doing is taking you on a proper shopping spree. You could use a new suit. And new pants, new shirts, and don't get me started on your underwear."

"Is this what we'll be like five years from now?" I said, smiling. I went up to Amanda, wrapped my arms around her. She snuggled in, resting her head on my shoulder. "On each other's cases about clothing and stuff?"

"I'm playing with you, you big baby." She tilted her head up until I was staring into those beautiful eyes. "Besides, I just want the best for you. You're great at your job. I just want people to know that just by looking at you."

"You know that just by looking at me."

"Hopefully, most people won't need to wake up next to you in the morning in order to know you're the best young reporter in the city."

"Best young reporter?"

"Don't get ahead of yourself. Give it time, Henry."

I gave her a quick kiss, then went back to packing. Though there were enough bad memories here to make me want to run away from this block screaming like a banshee, I'd miss it ever so slightly. Like that crazy first girlfriend who showed up at your apartment drunk at 4:00 a.m. and burned all your CDs when you broke up, there would be a small (well-guarded) place for it in my heart.

I wished there would be room for Stephen Gaines in my heart, but I couldn't force what was never there. I don't know how many people have pasts that exist without their knowledge. There was more to Stephen's life than what I'd uncovered. He'd lived for thirty years, abandoned by his family, given up by his father. The man who killed him had faced the most severe retribution possible. Yet a lingering doubt still remained, as I could see him on that street corner, tortured by something. Not Scotty Callahan. Not Kyle Evans.

Having dealt in vice for ten years, Stephen had seen more evil than most men did their whole lives. To do what he did took resolve, the knowledge that you were bringing poison into the world, that you couldn't be scared of the consequences. Every day could have brought jail or death. Yet he kept on living that life. And finally the odds caught up with him.

So what scares a man who isn't afraid of losing his freedom or his life?

My cell phone rang. It was the moving van. They were here to pick up our furniture, though we'd be lucky if it made it to their warehouse without disintegrating. I answered, and a hoarse voice told me the van would be there within fifteen minutes. I turned to Amanda, said, "Moving company's almost here. Should we, like, start bringing stuff down?"

She looked at me like I'd just admitted to wearing women's underwear. "Henry. They're a moving company. We pay them to move us. That's their job."

"I know, I just feel a little silly watching people carry all my stuff."

"This is New York. If you can pay four bucks for a

coffee and not feel bad, paying someone to carry and store your crap shouldn't even register on the guilty-o-meter. So enjoy it, babe. It's not too often people are going to do your heavy lifting for you."

Suddenly the buzzer rang. "That was quick," I said. "They told me fifteen minutes."

I went over to the window, expecting to see the truck and some burly, impatient men. Instead, I saw just one man standing on the street. He was wearing brown pants and a blue shirt that was untucked and flapping in the wind. He turned up to look at me, palms facing upward as if to say, *Are you gonna let me in or what?*

"No way," I said. Amanda came over to join me at the window. She looked out.

"Who is that?" she asked.

"It's Jack," I replied.

"I thought he was…"

"In rehab. Me, too. I guess he's out."

"Well, you should go…"

I was out the door and running down the stairs before she could finish her sentence.

The steps couldn't be passed fast enough. I hadn't seen Jack in months, since his name was dragged through the mud and he disappeared to presumably battle his internal demons. He'd left no forwarding address, no note. And now he was here, at my doorstep. I had so many questions to ask I hoped he didn't have plans for the next year.

When I arrived on the first floor, I sprinted through the lobby and burst through the front door. Jack O'Donnell was standing on the sidewalk, hands in his pockets. Then he took them out, checked his watch.

"Forty-three seconds from buzzer to outside. Not quite Olympic caliber, but not too shabby for a guy who sits in front of a computer most of the day." I didn't know what to say. So I just went up to Jack and threw my arms around him. He stumbled backward, saying, "Easy now, Henry."

When I untangled myself, I took my first real look at Jack in months. His gray hair was neatly combed, if slightly disheveled due to the weather. His face had none of the red ruddiness I was used to, and his cheeks seemed fuller. Jack's beard was neatly trimmed, cut razor sharp along his jawline, and he looked like he'd put on a few pounds.

"You look good," I said, patting him on the shoulder. "Scratch that, this is the best I've seen you look since we meet. Where have you been?"

"Away," Jack said. "We can discuss the wheres and whys later. Just think of what I went through as dialysis of the soul."

"I'm getting a disturbing image of you passing Ghandi through your urethra." Jack laughed, a quick *ha*.

"It's good to see you, kid. Been a long time. I spoke to Wallace before. He filled me in on what you've been up to, you busy little bee."

"You already talked to Wallace?"

"Hell, yes, my young friend, I spent all of last night in the office, getting reacquainted with my computer. Making sure nobody stole my Rolodex. And asking him for permission to chase one particular story."

"Oh yeah? What's that?"

"Well," Jack said, "while I was on my little sabbatical, I got the *Gazette* delivered to me every day. Generally it was the same old stuff. World's going to hell in a handbasket, the dollar can barely buy so much as a loaf of bread, foreign investors are buying the Statue of Liberty. And Paulina Cole still has a job. All things that make you want to hide under your bed and cry. Then I read one story last week, and that's when I knew I was ready to step back into the light."

"What story was that?" I asked.

"Stephen Gaines's murder," Jack said. His face was now solemn. The grin gone.

"I didn't write that."

"I know you didn't. Wallace told me he wouldn't let you since Gaines was your half brother. But there was one line in that story I knew came from you. Wallace told me how close you were, how you were right there when the Callahan and Evans boys bought the farm."

"What line are you talking about?"

"Twenty years ago," Jack continued, "I wrote a book called *Through the Darkness*. In that book, I mentioned a man named Butch Willingham who scrawled the words *The Fury* in his own blood before dying. Wallace told me that you spoke to Willingham's son. All of this brought back my memories from that time. Willingham, that's a name I hadn't even *thought* of since my hair was still brown. See, I believed then, and I still believe now, that the Fury does exist. I don't know who he is or how he's stayed around for over two decades, but if anything, all these drug deaths have proved that what worked twenty years ago works today. Butch Willingham was one of many dealers killed during that period for reasons I couldn't uncover, and I got surprisingly little help with from the authorities."

"I'm shocked," I said with a grin.

"I think these murders," Jack said, "Gaines, Evans, Callahan, the kid Guardado—are all history repeating itself."

"I don't understand," I said. "You want to, what, write a story linking the murders?"

"Better," Jack said, that smile coming back, sending a chill down my spine. "I want to find the Fury. Once and for all. There's a reason behind all these murders. I don't think Kyle Evans acted of his own accord. And I sure as hell don't think your brother was behind it all. I want you to help me find out the truth."

"You really think he exists," I said, a statement. Not a question.

"Do you think it ended with Scott Callahan and Kyle Evans?" he retorted.

"No." I said it definitively. Perhaps I'd thought it all along, but hearing Jack, a man whose instincts had served him well for nearly seventy years, say it gave me courage to speak it out loud. I didn't believe Scott and Kyle were acting of their own volition. I didn't believe Stephen Gaines was the Noriega of that operation. "I want to know what 718 Enterprises is. Plus I get the feeling my brother wasn't as high up as Kyle thought he was. There was someone else pulling the strings. I'm sure of it."

"Then we start tomorrow," Jack said. "I want you at the office at eight-thirty. Every minute you're late, you owe me ten bucks. That goes as long as we're working on this. And bring me a triple espresso. As long as I'm not drinking anymore I can do my best to make up for it with other stimulants."

"I'll be there at eight-fifteen," I said. Just then a large moving van turned onto the street and pulled up in front of our building. The driver climbed out, looking at a manifest, and eyed us both.

"One of you Henry Parker?" he said.

"That'd be me."

The driver nodded, went around to the back to start unloading their gear.

"Looks like you've got a long night ahead of you. Don't be late tomorrow."

"I won't."

"I know." Jack turned to leave.

"Hey, Jack?" I said.

"Yeah, kid?"

"It's good to have you back."

He smirked at me, said, "I'm not back yet. There's a whole lot of story out there and we haven't even started yet."

I watched Jack leave, then went back inside and took the elevator to my apartment. Amanda let me in.

"So, that was Jack? How is he?"

"He's great," I said, my mind already starting to think about all the threads that needed pulling. Then I saw all the boxes waiting for us to pack up, thought about the movers that would be up here at any moment. Looking at Amanda, I said, "It's gonna be a long night."

Epilogue

The car pulled up to the chicken-wire fence and slowed to a stop. The driver lowered the window and waited for the guard to approach. When he came over, the driver nodded at him, and received nothing in return but a stone stare. One hand on the car's hood, the other on his side, pushing out his hip just enough so the driver could see the semiautomatic strapped to his side.

The driver did not flinch at this. In fact, he'd seen the same man carrying the same gun numerous times. They knew each other by now, and the display was merely a reminder. Not a threat, just a friendly tap on the shoulder to let the driver know it was still there.

After a minute, the guard pressed a button on a remote and the gate began to creak open. When it was wide enough for the car to pass through, the driver sped off, gravel spewing out from under the tires.

The gravel soon turned into a dirt road, surrounded on either side by fencing, and topped by razor wire. Several trees stood on either side of the fence, numerous branches caught in the wire. If removed, the wood would be shredded instantaneously.

The road went on about two miles before widening into a small field. Standing in the middle of the field was a brown warehouse, two stories high and surrounded on either side by trees and, beyond that, more razor-wire–topped fencing. Three cars sat in the entrance in front of the warehouse, half a dozen large men trolling about. And unlike the guard out front, these men weren't shy about hiding their guns.

The driver pulled up behind the last car. Like moths to a flame, all six men walked toward this new arrival. The driver shifted into Park, turned the car off and stepped outside.

The six armed men nodded to him. He returned the gesture. One of them, a tall, lean Caucasian man with white hair and a chiseled face, strode up to the driver's side. He'd heard rumors that this white-haired man had been on the ground in Panama in December 1989, as a member of the Green Berets. The driver didn't quite know how he'd ended up here, but he had one hell of a hunch.

"Malloy," the driver said to the man.

"Detective," Malloy said back.

Malloy led the driver up to the warehouse's entrance. He went up to a small control panel that appeared rusted and bent. He inserted a small key into the side of the panel. A tinny whirring noise emanated from the box, and the panel receded, revealing a keypad and an electronic monitor.

Malloy pressed both of his thumbs on the pad. A green light flickered on. Malloy then entered a ten-digit code on the pad. When that was complete, he opened the door and ushered the driver inside.

Inside the warehouse was a corridor that led to two doors. The driver had seen this part of the warehouse many times, but had never entered the door to his left. He knew what went on behind it, but had not witnessed it with his own eyes. Better he didn't. Better it stayed in his mind as long as possible.

Malloy led the driver to the door on the right side. He opened it, led the driver up a flight of stairs. At the top floor, Malloy inserted a key card into a slot on a metal door. The driver could hear a mechanism unlock, and the door swung open.

The driver entered. He turned back to watch the door close. Malloy stood on the other side. He would wait for the driver. He always did.

The driver turned back around. He was in a room about twenty feet long, fifteen feet wide, with high ceilings. Track lighting adorned the ceiling, casting white beams that harshly illuminated the room.

At the far end of the room was a small desk. It was uncluttered, save for a reading lamp, a desk blotter and assorted pens and pencils. Behind the desk was a woman of about forty-five. She was of Latin descent, dark skin and green eyes, silky black hair that flowed down to the small of her back. She wore a sleeveless black top. Each arm was muscular, solid, lithe. Though the woman's face was beginning to show lines of age, her body tone and the quickness of her gestures were those of a woman half her age.

She watched him approach with a serenity on her face, no sense of strife or impatience. He had only met her twice before, but each time felt unnerved, like there was something roiling beneath that calm exterior, something that if unleashed could tear him apart. Because of that he never got closer than a few feet. Though they'd met twice, he'd heard stories. The kind of stories that, even if embellished (which over time they surely were), must have had a ring of truth somewhere. He was taking enough risks as it was. He wanted no part of anything else, any part of the minimum ten men who were currently in the ground because of her.

The woman looked up as the driver approached. She stood up and said, "Detective Makhoulian. It's been far, far too long. Please, sit down." She gestured for him to sit at the table. There was a smile on her face that made him feel queasy.

He nodded, approached and took a seat, making sure to subtly push the chair back so it was not within reach. He said, "With all due respect, I prefer it that way. If I'm here it means there's a problem."

"Well, that really depends," the woman said. "If I know all I need to know, then there is no problem. The boys. Callahan and Evans, they're both dead, correct?"

"That's right."

"Then this murder of Stephen Gaines ends with them. I'm led to believe there are no further investigations into the deaths of any of those three men."

"As of right now, no. The department officially declared Evans's death a clean shoot. He had a gun, and there are numerous witnesses who concur that he killed Callahan in cold blood. The newspapers are playing it as a heroic cop putting himself in harm's way. The families would be stupid to press charges. Their children have already dragged their names through the mud, and any protesting on their part would only deepen the wounds. My guess is the families will mourn quietly and be out of the city within the year."

"That would make my holiday," the woman said. "Now, you mentioned the newspapers. This reporter who was on the scene. Parker. I don't like his reputation, and he is one of your 'numerous witnesses.' The last thing we need is for him to suddenly think he saw something he didn't see. Do you think he will be a problem?"

Sevi Makhoulian unfolded his hands, placed them palms down on the table. From the angle he was standing at Detective Sevi Makhoulian could see the three numbers tattooed across the woman's toned right shoulder.

7.1.8.

"I don't think so. Parker and I have spoken numerous times over the last few weeks. Parker's only concern was finding his brother's killer. He did that, in Evans. As far as Parker is concerned, the case is closed. I do have sources within the industry that will tell me if that changes."

"You don't sound convinced," she said. Her eyes narrowed. Makhoulian found his palms sweating. He wiped them on his pants, hoping she didn't notice.

"Parker has a reputation as a young bulldog. He was involved in the death of Michael DiForio a few years back."

"That's right!" she said, now beaming. "DiForio thought Parker had stolen from him. He even went so far as to hire Shelton Barnes."

"That's right."

"And look how that turned out." She smiled. Makhoulian did too. "Bodies like Callahan, Gaines and Evans can disappear without many tears. The families bury them, the city moves on. They were insulated. Parker has friends. I never authorized the hit on Parker at his apartment. That was Evans acting alone when he realized Parker was getting too close. We *do not move* unless we are forced."

"I understand that. If I hear anything…"

"You will let Corporal Malloy know before you take another breath."

The woman stood up, revealing her full height, full frame. She was a shade under six feet tall. She extended a grip, which the detective took. She clasped Makhoulian's hand, fingers digging in until the detective winced. Her eyes were locked on Makoulian's, the pupils wide, burning. For an instant, Sevi Makhoulian feared for his life. Then the grip loosened. The woman turned around and sat back behind her desk. As he stood up to leave, Sevi Makhoulian noticed one more thing sitting upon the nearly empty desk. A small black rock, no larger than a pebble. It had a rough surface, the color of coal.

With nothing else of note, Makhoulian knew it was not there by mistake.

"Is that it?" the detective asked, pointing to the small stone.

"I expect to be able to begin shipments within six months," the woman continued, ignoring the question. "Right now I'm taking your word that we can resume without any further interruptions, issues or problems. If I feel for one moment that you're holding back from me, or information is coming faster than you can relay it, I will detach your head from your body with the tips of my fingernails and find someone useful. Do you understand me, *Detective?*"

"I do," Detective Makhoulian said, looking at that small black rock. "And I give you my word when I say that they have no idea."

* * * * *

Coming in December 2009,
The next Henry Parker novel:
THE DARKNESS
by Jason Pinter

Acknowledgments

You don't write one book, let alone four, without some incredible support, advice and a heaping helping of good old-fashioned luck. Many people have been in my corner from day one of this journey, while many I've been fortunate enough to meet along the way. If I actually thanked everyone who had any positive impact on my first four books, this page would run longer than a Charlton Heston movie. So here's the condensed list, the people who've had the biggest impact (and the people who groveled the most).

A sincere, knees-on-the-ground, *we're not worthy* thank-you to Joe Veltre, my agent, and Linda McFall, my editor. Joe and Linda have had tremendous input on every book, have made me a better writer and a better author, and their passion and guidance resonates on every page. If you're able to find my books, read them and enjoy them, they deserve the credit.

My thanks to the MIRA team is unending. I owe a debt of gratitude to Margaret O'Neill Marbury, Donna Hayes, Dianne Moggy, Heather Foy, Michelle Renaud, Andi Richman, Craig Swinwood, Don Lucey, Adam

Wilson, Emily Ohanjanians, Ana Luxton, Maureen Stead, Jayne Hoogenberk, Ken Foy, Katherine Orr, Loriana Sacilotto and Stacy Widdrington. Having seen the publishing beast from inside the belly, I can appreciate these folks even more.

Just recently I've begun working with the MIRA U.K. arm as well, and it's wonderful to see that my publisher's expertise and enthusiasm literally cross oceans. Thank you to Catherine Burke, Belinda Mountain, Oliver Rhodes, Selma Leung, Darren Shoffren and Ian Roberts for introducing my work to a whole new continent of readers.

I've been fortunate to work with some great publicists both here and abroad. Susan Schwartzman, Sophie Ransom and Grainne Kileen have helped spread the word with incredible tenacity. You make my job a whole lot easier.

Thanks to Paddy McDonald and Paddy Breathnach, who saw something in my work that made them believe that it could translate to another medium. I hope you're right.

Jonathan Hayes, a talented author in his own right, was a tremendous help on the forensics side. If I ever want to commit a homicide and get away with it, Jonathan's the guy I'd call to help me cover my tracks.

I've known Joel Hirschtritt and his family for years, and I was finally able to take advantage of that for the benefit of one of my books. Thanks to Joel for his legal help, and also to Nancy, Jon, Stef, Ali and Marissa for lending him to me for a little while.

A special thank-you to Philip Schnelwar, who untangled many of the legal loopholes Henry and Co. had to jump through in this book. Philip was more than gracious with his time, and if for some reason I ever end up in hot water, it's Phil I'll call to right the ship.

Sergeant Steve Rodriguez of the NYPD and Officer Michael Gill of the Bend Police Department informed me of procedure on opposite sides of the country. I appreciate their help, and admire them for their service.

Both of my families—Mom, Dad and Ali, and Jane, Jeff and Sabrina—have been as supportive as could be expected from anyone not on your payroll. Thank you for everything, including flagging down strangers to attend my signings. You might have scared a few people away, but I appreciate it nonetheless.

Susan, who has been my partner, my rock and my heart for years. You gave me the courage to pursue my dreams, and I can't wait to spend the rest of my life reciprocating.

Thank you to the booksellers and librarians who've hosted events and invited me to speak to their communities. It's been a real pleasure, and I hope you'll see more of me in the coming years.

And, most important, to the readers. When it comes to carving out a career as a novelist, your words of enthusiasm, kindness and support are just as important as mine on the page. Thank you for all of it.

$1.⁰⁰ OFF

MIRA®

From the bestselling author
of *The Mark*

JASON PINTER

comes the newest novel in the
acclaimed Henry Parker series.

THE DARKNESS

*Available November 24, 2009,
wherever books are sold!*

$7.99 U.S./$9.99 CAN.

- ✂ - - - - - -

$1.⁰⁰ OFF the purchase price of *THE DARKNESS*
by Jason Pinter.

Offer valid from November 24, 2009, to December 31, 2009.
Redeemable at participating retail outlets. Limit one coupon per purchase.
Valid in the U.S.A. and Canada only.

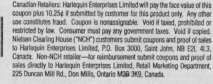

52608793

65373 00076 2   (8100)0 11625

MJP2671CPN

**Look for the first three novels in
the acclaimed Henry Parker series
from bestselling author**

JASON PINTER

Available now!

MIRA

REQUEST YOUR FREE BOOKS!

2 FREE NOVELS FROM THE ROMANCE/SUSPENSE COLLECTION PLUS 2 FREE GIFTS!

YES! Please send me 2 FREE novels from the Romance/Suspense Collection and my 2 FREE gifts (gifts are worth about $10). After receiving them, if I don't wish to receive any more books, I can return the shipping statement marked "cancel." If I don't cancel, I will receive 4 brand-new novels every month and be billed just $5.74 per book in the U.S. or $6.24 per book in Canada. That's a savings of at least 28% off the cover price. It's quite a bargain! Shipping and handling is just 50¢ per book.* I understand that accepting the 2 free books and gifts places me under no obligation to buy anything. I can always return a shipment and cancel at any time. Even if I never buy another book from the Reader Service, the two free books and gifts are mine to keep forever.

185 MDN EYNQ   385 MDN EYN2

Name	(PLEASE PRINT)	
Address		Apt. #
City	State/Prov.	Zip/Postal Code

Signature (if under 18, a parent or guardian must sign)

Mail to **The Reader Service:**
IN U.S.A.: P.O. Box 1867, Buffalo, NY 14240-1867
IN CANADA: P.O. Box 609, Fort Erie, Ontario L2A 5X3

Not valid to current subscribers of the Romance Collection,
the Suspense Collection or the Romance/Suspense Collection.

Want to try two free books from another line?
Call 1-800-873-8635 or visit www.morefreebooks.com.

* Terms and prices subject to change without notice. Prices do not include applicable taxes. Sales tax applicable in N.Y. Canadian residents will be charged applicable provincial taxes and GST. Offer not valid in Quebec. This offer is limited to one order per household. All orders subject to approval. Credit or debit balances in a customer's account(s) may be offset by any other outstanding balance owed by or to the customer. Please allow 4 to 6 weeks for delivery. Offer available while quantities last.

Your Privacy: Harlequin is committed to protecting your privacy. Our Privacy Policy is available online at www.eHarlequin.com or upon request from the Reader Service. From time to time we make our lists of customers available to reputable third parties who may have a product or service of interest to you. If you would prefer we not share your name and address, please check here. ☐

BOB

JASON PINTER

32572	THE STOLEN	___ $7.99 U.S.	___ $7.99 CAN.
32489	THE MARK	___ $7.99 U.S.	___ $9.50 CAN.
32463	THE GUILTY	___ $7.99 U.S.	___ $9.50 CAN.

(limited quantities available)

TOTAL AMOUNT	$ _____
POSTAGE & HANDLING	$ _____
($1.00 for 1 book, 50¢ for each additional)	
APPLICABLE TAXES*	$ _____
TOTAL PAYABLE	$ _____

(check or money order—please do not send cash)

To order, complete this form and send it, along with a check or money order for the total above, payable to MIRA Books, to: **In the U.S.:** 3010 Walden Avenue, P.O. Box 9077, Buffalo, NY 14269-9077; **In Canada:** P.O. Box 636, Fort Erie, Ontario, L2A 5X3.

Name: _____
Address: _____ City: _____
State/Prov.: _____ Zip/Postal Code: _____
Account Number (if applicable): _____

075 CSAS

*New York residents remit applicable sales taxes.
*Canadian residents remit applicable GST and provincial taxes.

MIRA®

www.MIRABooks.com

MJP1009BL